DATE DUE

THE CUT THROAT

THE CUT THROAT

Simon Michael

St. Martin's Press
New York

THE CUT THROAT. Copyright © 1989 by Simon Michael. All rights reserved.
Printed in the United States of America. No part of this book may be used or
reproduced in any manner whatsoever without written permission except
in the case of brief quotations embodied in critical articles or reviews. For
information, address St. Martin's Press, 175 Fifth Avenue, New York, N.Y.
10010.

Library of Congress Cataloging-in-Publication Data

Michael, Simon.
        The cut throat / Simon Michael.
                p.   cm.
        ISBN 0-312-04292-2
        I. Title.
        PR6063.I213C85   1990
        813'.54—dc20   89-77683
                                                                        CIP

First published in Great Britain by W.H. Allen & Co.

First U.S. Edition
10 9 8 7 6 5 4 3 2 1

Part One

Chapter One

The telephone rang.

The unshaven man, still in his pyjamas, sprawled in an old stained armchair, one leg dangling over its bald arm. He had kicked off one slipper, and was absently picking at his toe-nails with one hand as the other turned the pages of a tabloid newspaper on his lap. He was in his late forties, and looked ten years older. The television in the corner of the room showed a cartoon. The telephone sat on a coffee table next to the armchair, but he ignored the ringing for some time. Then, with a great effort, he reached down and picked up the handset.

'Yeh?' he said, still reading.

'Del?'

'Who is it?' he asked.

'It's Charlie, Charlie Sands.' Sands's voice was hard, Glaswegian. Del sat up, the paper falling to the floor.

'Are you there, Plumber?'

'Yeh, yeh,' he replied, 'you just took me by surprise, that's all. When did you get out?'

'Last week,' said Sands.

'Yeh? Well, I'm honoured, Charlie, that you should have thought to look me up so soon after your release. Very . . . wasname . . . thoughtful.' He said it

3

humorously, but there was an undercurrent of strain in his voice. He was nervous.

'Cut the crap Del. I need tae see you.'

'Sure. I'm a bit tied up at present, but I'll give you a ring in a few —'

'Tonight.'

Plumber paused. 'Look, Charlie . . . see . . . well, things are different now, since you went inside . . .'

'Och, dinnae fret yoursel' Derek. I'm no' mad at you. I ken it was nae you who shopped me. I just wanna talk, right? Just talk. Tonight at the Frog and Nightgown.'

'I can't tonight, honest. I've got something on. Tomorrow maybe?'

'What about this afternoon?'

'Er . . . I dunno . . . yeh, I suppose so,' said Plumber, without enthusiasm.

'Fine. I'll be there at opening time. Dinnae let me down now.' The line went dead.

Plumber put the handset down slowly. He did not look happy.

The clerks' room was at its usual, frenetic, five o'clock worst. Stanley was holding conversations with two solicitors on different telephones, Sally was fending off questions from two members of Chambers while scanning the Daily Cause List, and Robert, the junior, was sending a fax with one hand while pouring a cup of coffee for the head of Chambers with the other. The last had returned from the Court of Appeal ten minutes before, muttering that Lord Bloody-Justice-Bloody-Birkett was to the law of marine insurance what Bambi was to quantum physics, had ejected a conference already in progress from his room, and had slammed the door. He could still be heard giving a telephonic post-mortem of the day's defeat to the senior partner of the firm of solicitors that had instructed him. Superimposed on all this was the clatter of the computer printer spewing out an apparently endless stream of fee notes to go out in the last post.

4

Charles Howard poked his head into the clerks' room, and wondered if he would be able to make himself heard. He watched with a smile as Sally, pert, cheeky Sally from Romford, two O levels and a nice line in caustic sarcasm, politely told Mr Sebastian Campbell-Smythe, a senior barrister of fifteen years' call, to return to his room and not to disturb her. If he caused her to miss his case in the List, he would not be best pleased, would he? Sally, Charles thought not for the first time, was ideally suited to life as a barristers' clerk. She was quick witted and quick tongued, able, without being rude, to keep in line twenty or so prima donna barristers all her senior in years, supposed social status and learning. At the same time she was attractive enough to flatter the crusty solicitors who sent work to the Chambers, all of whom never failed to inquire after her health when they met members of Chambers in court. Stanley, the senior clerk, had high hopes of her.

Sally turned towards the door and saw Charles. She smiled. She liked Mr Howard. He was alright, one of the members of Chambers who didn't talk down to her.

'I'm going to Gloria's,' he mouthed, making cup-lifting motions with his hands.

'Hang on, sir,' she called as he disappeared. His head reappeared. 'Don't forget you've got a con in half an hour,' she said. She reached over for the diary and looked for his initials. 'The buggery,' she said, as nonchalantly as if the case had been a vicar summonsed for careless driving. 'Case of Petrovicj.'

Charles nodded, waved, and departed. He had already read the case papers, and there was time for a cup of tea and a bite to eat at the café on Fleet Street before his client and the solicitor arrived for the conference.

Pulling his coat around him, and jamming his hat more firmly on his head, Charles stepped out from Chancery Court into the rain, and walked towards the sound of the traffic. He still loved the sensation of dislocation that he experienced every time he stepped from the Dickensian Temple into twentieth-century Fleet Street. The feeling that the Temple was caught, like a pressed flower in a yellowed book, in an accidental fold in time, was always strongest in the winter, when the gas lamps were still lit at four o'clock by a man with what appeared to be a six-foot matchstick.

As Charles opened the café's steamy door, the smell of fried food and cigarettes greeted him. Gloria's offered cheap meals for sixteen hours a day and, until the recent departure of the newspapermen from Fleet Street, had been second home to an interesting amalgam of barristers and journalists. In recent months it had lost most of the latter trade, and had tried, unsuccessfully, to move up-market to catch the growing number of young executives and secretaries working in the area. On this occasion it was almost full, mainly with barristers, many of whom he recognised, but none he knew well. Some were alone, but many were with their solicitors on their way back from the Old Bailey. Charles liked the feel of the place, the easy conversation, the jokes about cases, clients, judges. It was a welcome change from the rarefied air of 2 Chancery Court, where most of his Chambers colleagues dealt in the bills of lading, the judicial review, and the leasehold enfranchisement of civil work. It was, he thought with a wry grin, exactly the sort of place Henrietta detested. He took his cup of tea and slice of toast and sat in the corner.

When he returned to Chambers twenty minutes later, he could hear an argument in progress before he even opened the door. A tall barrister in pin-striped trousers was shouting at Stanley from the doorway of the clerks' room. He whirled round at Charles as he entered.

'There you are! Now look here, Howard,' he said, using the formality of Charles's surname to show his displeasure, 'this is positively the last time. I'm going to take it up at the next Chambers' meeting.'

Charles looked up at the man. His name was Laurence Corbett. He was at least six inches taller than Charles, blond and handsome. 'What *is* the problem, Laurence?'

asked Charles quietly, deliberately using the man's first name.

'That!' replied Corbett, jabbing his finger in the direction of the waiting room.

'Your con's arrived, sir,' explained Stanley.

'Yes?' asked Charles.

'My fiancée has been sitting waiting for me in that room with that rapist of yours!'

'Yes?' inquired Charles.

'Don't act the fool, Howard. I know for a fact that I and several other members of Chambers have asked you to keep your smutty clientele out of Chambers during normal office hours.'

'Is Mr Petrovicj with Mr Collins?' Charles asked Stanley.

'Yes, sir. Mr Smith's conference is waiting in there too, sir.'

'Well,' continued Charles, turning to Corbett, 'I would have thought it unlikely that your charming betrothed would be ravaged in front of three witnesses, even assuming that my client was interested in her, which I doubt. Irresistible though you no doubt find her, Mr Petrovicj is charged with buggering another male. He's not, if you'll excuse the pun, into women.' Charles smiled.

'That makes no difference at all, Charles —'

'Howard,' corrected Charles.

'—as you well know.'

'I would have thought it made quite a deal of difference, particularly to Mr Petrovicj. However, if you'll let me go and start my con,' said Charles, turning his back on Corbett, 'I'll be able to remove the evil influence from the room.'

Charles opened the door to leave, and then paused. 'By the way, Laurence, I know you don't do much criminal work, but I would have thought that even you knew that a man's innocent until proven guilty. Mr Petrovicj isn't a bugger, or even a rapist for that matter, till the jury says he is.'

* * *

7

'Over here, Del!'

Charlie Sands waited for Plumber at a table in the corner of the bar, two empty spirit glasses before him. Plumber made his way over and sat down opposite the other man. Sands looked straight at him, his hard blue eyes narrowed.

'My God, you've got soft,' he said quietly. Plumber smiled and shrugged. 'You must ha' put on two stones since I last saw you.'

'I suppose so. I'm older,' said Plumber. 'How have you been?'

'Och, no' bad, all things considered.'

'Had a bit of trouble?' asked Plumber, nodding towards Sands's face.

'What, this?' replied Sands, fingering a long scar on his left cheekbone. 'You know what they say: you should'a seen the other guy. He was in the hospital wing for a month. Well,' he said, after a pause, 'are you gonna buy me a drink or not?'

'Sure, sure Charlie. What'll you have?'

'I'll have another large whisky, thank you very much.'

Plumber bought the drinks and returned to the table.

'So, what have *you* been doing for the last four years?' asked Sands.

'Nothing. That's what I was trying to tell you on the blower. I ain't done a single job since that one. I reckoned it was a warning, what with what happened an' all that, and I gave it up.'

'So?'

'So nothing. I've been doing a bit of decorating when I could get the work, drawing wasname, dole, you know.'

'How's Mary?'

'Dunno. She left two years ago. Haven't heard a word since. My eldest, Maureen, she had a postcard from . . . wasname . . . Ireland once, about a year ago. That's it.'

'You must be happy,' said Sands with heavy irony.

'I get by,' replied Plumber disconsolately. 'Anyway,

8

Charlie,' he said, knocking back his drink, 'I've got a lot on this evening, and I really—'

'Patience,' said Sands, putting his hand firmly on Plumber's arm, 'is a great virtue.' Plumber sat back in his seat reluctantly. Sands took a small sip of his whisky, looked about him, and lowered his voice as he spoke. 'There are two things I want from you, Derek, and the first is the whereabouts of a certain Robbie Millar.'

Plumber looked surprised. 'Didn't you hear?'

'Hear what? Do you no' remember where I've been for the last four years?'

'Yeh, well . . . he's dead.'

'What?'

'Yeh. Heart attack. He was in the launderette doing his smalls or whatever, and keeled over. Dead as a . . . wasname.'

Sands banged his glass down on the table in fury, spilling most of the contents. 'Bastard!'

'Well, I can understand your feelings, Charlie, but the bloke's dead, so what does it matter?'

'Dead? He's not half as dead as he would ha' been if I'd got hold of him! That fat slob always was lucky.' There was a long pause while Sands assimilated the information.

'What was the other thing, Charlie?' asked Plumber.

'Eh?'

'The second thing you wanted from me.'

'Och, right. What d'you say to £100,000 for two hours' work?'

'No, sorry, Charlie,' said Plumber getting quickly to his feet, 'I knew it was gonna be something like that, and I'm just not interested. Like I said on the blower—'

Sands reached up and grabbed Plumber's wrist in a vice-like grip.

'You sit down!' he hissed dangerously, pulling the other man back to his seat. 'You owe me, Plumber.'

'I didn't grass you—'

'I know you didnae grass me, Derek,' he replied, putting a nasty emphasis on his companion's name, 'but

9

I did four years inside, whereas you spent that time on your fat arse, free as a bird. Do you no' think they asked me who the driver was, eh?'

Plumber looked down at his shoes.

'They did, let me tell you, they did, and I remained silent, my mouth clamped firmly shut, thinking, why should ma wee friend Derek suffer like this? That would be most unfair, I said to mysel', as I'm sure it wasnae *he* who grassed me up, was it, eh?'

'Oh, honest, Charlie, I swear it wasn't!' cried Plumber, genuinely frightened.

'Of course it wasnae, Derek my boy, or else we'd no' be sitting here having a wee drink, would we now? You know I'm not joking, don't you, Derek?' He retained his hold on the other man's wrist.

Plumber knew. Sands had been tried, and acquitted, some years before, for the murder of a hapless East End cabbie who had had the misfortune to witness one of Sands's more successful enterprises, and who had been persuaded to give a statement to the police.

'The point I'm making is that you owe me, Derek, for four years of silence.'

Plumber looked away unhappily.

'After all, it's not as though I'm asking for something unpleasant. I'm gonna make you a rich man. You could retire, buy yoursel' a wee place in . . . where was it your Maureen lived? Bournemouth?'

'Hove.'

'There you are then.'

'I'm really not sure—'

'Oh, but I am sure. I'm sure that this one's a winner. I'm sure no one else's on to it, 'cos the bloke inside whose idea it was, got involved in a most unfortunate fight just as he was about tae get parole–'

'I don't believe—' started Plumber, but Charlie held up a warning finger to let himself finish.

'—and most of all, Derek, my friend, I'm sure that Detective Sergeant Donegan would love to hear who *did* drive the getaway car four years and eight days ago on a certain robbery—'

'You wouldn't!'

'Aye, I would. This job's perfect. We could both retire forever afterwards. And I need you to be able to pull it off. You'd better believe me, Derek: there's nothing I wouldnae do to persuade you.'

Plumber stared hard at him. 'I'll get us another drink,' he said wearily. Sands released him.

'Thank you, Mr Howard,' said the alleged bugger as they shook hands.

'That's perfectly alright, Mr Petrovicj. I'll show you the way out, as I should think my clerk's gone by now.'

Charles showed him to the door and pointed down the stairs. 'Are you going to the tube?'

Petrovicj nodded. 'Yes. I got quite lost on the way up.'

'I know, it's quite a maze in the Temple if you don't know it. Go down the stairs and turn right. Turn right under the arch, go across the courtyard, and down the steps in the far right corner. Follow your nose, and you'll come out on the Embankment.'

'Thanks again, Mr Howard. See you in court.'

Charles returned to his room where Mr Collins, his instructing solicitor, waited.

'Well, what do you think, Charles?'

Collins and Son had been instructing Charles loyally since he had been in pupillage, and Charles did not mind Collins junior, who had been at the same college as he, albeit a few years later, using his christian name.

'I don't know, Ralph. It's certainly helped, seeing him in conference. I think he'll make a good witness. He has a reasonable chance of acquittal, but it depends on what we can make of the complainant in cross-examination. You know the risks. Cross-examining children can so easily backfire.'

'Yes, I know. Changing the subject for a second, have you had a chance to read the Aaronberg papers I sent down?'

11

'I'm afraid I haven't yet: things have been a bit hectic for the last week.'

'There's no hurry, but Dad and I would appreciate it if you could give them your special attention. The client's *mespuchah*,' said Collins, lapsing into Yiddish.

Collins senior had been born Raphael Cohen, but, like Charles (né Charles Horowitz), he had realised that too Jewish a surname could be a disadvantage in the law. Charles never referred to his Jewish background and would have preferred others to forget it too, but somehow, despite the camouflage of the false surnames, Collins & Son had recognised the young barrister's roots, and had sent him work when he was struggling to establish himself. It wasn't a matter of an 'old boy network', as some of Charles's colleagues liked to think; had he been no good, Charles would never have received a second brief, but as long as he was as good as the next man (or better), there was nothing wrong, as old Mr Collins used to say, in instructing a nice Jewish boy, even if he pretended he wasn't. A man's got to live, right?

'Family?' asked Charles, slightly embarrassed at not being sure of the exact meaning of the word, and slightly angry at the assumption that he would know.

'In-laws,' replied Collins. 'Not that close, but close enough that Mum's giving us a hard time.'

'What's the charge?'

'VAT fraud. He's in garments, Mile End.'

'I'll look at it tonight if I can.'

'No rush. It was only committed from the Magistrates' Court two weeks ago; next week will do.'

'OK,' said Charles, rising. 'I'll see you on Tuesday in any event at Isleworth Crown Court.' The two men shook hands, and Charles showed the solicitor out.

The Frog and Nightgown was getting quite crowded as the evening trade came in.

'Well, Derek, what do you think?' asked Sands, leaning forward and raising his voice just enough to be heard over the jukebox.

12

'It sounds alright, Charlie, assuming you've done your homework–'

'I've done ma homework, Derek, believe me. I've spent the last week checkin' it out—'

'—but I'm worried about the shooters. We never needed them before, and I don't see why we do now.'

'You've never done a job like this before. I'm telling you, we need them. Like I said, they're no' real anyway, just good imitations; just enough to put the fear of God into the bastards.'

'I still don't know,' said Plumber, shaking his head. 'You're talking a lot of time if we're caught.'

'But we won't be caught, not if you do everything exactly as I told you.'

Plumber didn't answer at first. 'But I'm just a driver, right? Can't you get someone else to cross the pavement?'

'It does nae need three people; it needs two. You 'n' me. Why split it three ways when there's no need?'

'Alright, but I'm not happy with it.'

'You'll be plenty happy with a hundred grand. Come on, smile, you miserable bugger. You're gonna be very, very rich.'

Charles wrestled with the key in the lock of his front door, unable to get the thing to turn. His grip on the blue cloth bag containing his robes, and the huge briefcase, both in his left hand, began to slip, and the set of papers clamped between his head and shoulder slid to the floor. He threw everything to the porch floor in exasperation, reached again for the keyhole, and the door was opened to him. A pretty girl of about twenty stood on the threshold, her hair tied back. She had some sheets over her arm, as if she had been caught in the middle of making up a bed.

'Yes?' she asked. 'Oh, it's you, Charles,' she said, opening the door to him. Her pretence of not knowing Charles raised his ire one degree further. She was the au pair, Fiona, brought into the household against Charles's wishes four weeks previously. Her older sister had been at school with Henrietta, and Henrietta had been prevailed upon to give her a temporary job while she looked around London for something more permanent. Once she had arrived, however, Henrietta had warmed to the arrangement, and Charles had cooled to it. With no children and a cleaner who came twice a week, Charles had protested that there was no earthly reason to pay the girl good money to sit around drinking coffee all day, but by now she and Henrietta were the best of friends and Fiona's stay seemed to be becoming indefinite. Her insolence, which delighted Henrietta and grew more offensive daily, was learned at her mistress's shoulder.

Charles scooped up his papers and other burdens, and brushed past her. 'Where is—?' he began, but Fiona had closed the door and disappeared towards the rear of the house. Charles threw his things on the floor, and stomped upstairs. He walked into Henrietta's dressing room. That was another innovation he had not liked. When they had moved into the house a year earlier (a house he had personally thought far too expensive, and ostentatiously large for the two of them) it had at least had the advantage of two spare bedrooms. Henrietta, however, had decided that she required a 'dressing room' which, in fact, became her own bedroom with a bathroom *en suite*. At least once a week her 'bad head', or the demands of his late-night working, meant that she slept there.

'Oh, there you are. You're late.' Henrietta was standing at her dressing table, trying to fasten a necklace. 'Here, do this for me, will you?' she said.

She was in evening dress, her chestnut hair piled on top of her head. As she approached Charles and handed him the necklace, Charles could smell the perfume he had bought her for Christmas with the proceeds of the indecency plea he had done at Knightsbridge Crown Court. It was strange how almost everything they owned, at least all those things not the gifts of her family, he could refer to the payment for a particular case. It amused him, and irritated Henrietta, to identify their belongings by reference to the crime that had paid for them. Thus, last year's holiday had been the fraud case at the Old Bailey; Henrietta's dress, the one she was wearing, was the drunken driving of a substantial company director, and so on. The proceeds of crime: who said it didn't pay?

'You smell good,' he said.

'Thank you.'

He finished fastening her necklace, and kissed her on the nape of her neck. She moved away without responding.

'You, on the other hand, look dreadful,' she said, looking at him in the mirror of her dressing table, and inserting her ear-rings. 'Late con?' she asked.

'Yes. The buggery I told you about. It's one of the Collins's cases.'

'Oh, the barrow boy,' she said, with infinite contempt. 'I bet half the Temple covets your practice, Charles.' She disappeared into the bathroom.

'Look,' he replied, calling after her, 'I've had a hard day, and this is not the time to discuss—for the hundredth time—why I do crime and not civil work.'

'Your social conscience, no doubt,' called Henrietta from the bathroom.

' "Had a hard day dear? Sit down and have a drink, and I'll massage your shoulders," ' mimicked Charles, with heavy irony. ' "Supper will only be a few minutes." '

'Fuck off, Charles,' said Henrietta, emerging from the bathroom and beginning to search through her wardrobe. The words somehow carried added venom when spoken so beautifully, and by such a beautiful woman. Charles sat on her bed, and watched her bare back and slim hips, hating her and wanting her. She found what she was looking for: a fur coat, a gift from her father on her last birthday.

'Etta,' he said more softly, using what had once been his pet name for her, 'will you please stop bustling about long enough to tell me where we're supposed to be going?'

15

'*We* aren't going anywhere. *I'm* going to Peter Ripley's do with Daddy, as you very well know.'

'What?'

'Charles, for God's sake, don't pretend you didn't know about it. I asked you over a month ago if you wanted to come, and you made it plain in your usual charming way that you wouldn't—and I quote—"dream of voluntarily spending an evening with that load of pompous farts"—close quote. So I made an excuse to Daddy as usual, and agreed to go with him. Mummy's away till next week. Now do you remember?'

Charles nodded. He did not remember the exact words he had used to decline the invitation, but the gist was familiar. This particular 'do' was the dinner to mark the end of Mr Justice Ripley's last tour on circuit before he retired. A number of judges and barristers who practised on the circuit had been invited, and Charles's father-in-law, the erstwhile head of his Chambers, and now a judge on the same circuit, was giving a speech. In the absence of Martha, Henrietta's mother, who was visiting her sick sister, Charles and Henrietta had rather unexpectedly received an invitation.

Charles had often attempted to explain to Henrietta why he hated these dinners, but she refused to understand. It wasn't that he didn't know which fork to use, or how to address a waiter. The judges, the benchers, their wives, the High Sheriff—they all shared a common background. They had gone to the same schools, same universities, played cricket in the same teams, attended the same balls, knew the same people. Charles could 'busk it'—be convivial, pretend to know what, or who, they were talking about—but it was an act. The Jewish sons of Jewish furriers from Minsk, by way of Mile End, did not mix well with the sons and grandsons of the British Empire. He might have cast off his Jewishness while at university, but he knew he would never be one of them. On the few occasions he had attended these dinners he had come home hating himself. He had not yet analysed why, but he knew enough now to avoid them.

16

Henrietta must have read his mind. 'How you expect to move on at the Bar, when you refuse even to make an effort, is beyond me.'

'Not again, Etta. Not now. I don't believe the only way to get silk is to fawn on a lot of upper class, county snobs. And if it is, I'll live without it.'

'Frying again tonight,' commented Henrietta acidly, referring to the chip she alleged Charles carried on his shoulder. 'If you mention your East End origins once more, Charles, I'll puke. Your father may have grown up in Bow or wherever it was, but it's hardly the Warsaw ghetto. The only person who's conscious of your religion is you.'

'What? Do you suppose for one minute that I'd have got into Chambers had I not committed the dreadful *faux pas* of marrying you? Half the members of Chambers can't stand me.'

'Quite right. But that's nothing to do with your religion. That's because of your charming personality and winning ways. And then every time you upset someone, it's their fault because they're anti-Semitic. It's a perfect self-defence mechanism, and I hope you and it will be very happy together.'

Charles stood up wearily, pulling off his tie. 'Can we please leave this one for now, Henrietta? I've had a particularly difficult day.'

'Yes, we can leave it for now, Charles, because I'm off. I believe Fiona has made something for you both for supper, but if not I suggest you go to the pub.' She swept past him, checked, and returned to plant a kiss on his cheek. She was about to move off again, but Charles grabbed her forearms. He looked hard at her, shaking his head slightly, a puzzled and pained expression on his face. Henrietta looked reluctantly up to his eyes, and held their gaze for a second. Then the armour of her anger cracked, she bit her lip, and looked away, but not resisting his hold on her.

'I don't know, Charlie,' she said softly, in answer to his unspoken question. 'I wish I did.' He pulled her gently towards him, wanting to put his arms round her, but she resisted, shrugging her shoulders and shaking her head. She ran from the room. Charles listened to the rustle of her dress and the sound of her feet flying down the stairs, and then the slam of the front door. He did not hear her crying as she drove away.

Chapter Two

'Three . . . two . . . one . . . GO!' screamed Sands.

Plumber's foot stamped on the accelerator and the two of them were pressed back into their seats as the BMW surged forward down the narrow path.

'Faster!' bellowed Sands.

'I can't control it any faster than this,' shouted Plumber. 'It's the surface.' The vehicle bounced and shuddered as it hit another pot-hole and Plumber braked hard. The wheels locked, but he controlled the skid, the car sliding to a halt in a cloud of dust and pebbles, knocking a dustbin flying. He rammed it into reverse, and they shot backwards for a few feet, and then, with the tyres screaming, he turned sharp right. Garden gates, wooden sheds and dustbins flew past them in a blur. They emerged after a few seconds into a garage area behind a block of flats, shot across its face, and out on to the road. Plumber slowed the car to a normal speed.

'Derek, this will never do.'

'Look, Charlie, you got me in on this 'cos I'm a driver. I'm telling you, there isn't a fucking police driver in Britain that can take that alley quicker. We've only got about six inches' clearance on each side in any event—why do you think I took off the wing mirrors? Any faster, and when we hit a wasname we'll go straight into the side. How long was it, anyway?'

Sands checked his watch. 'Thirty-five seconds.'

'What are you complaining about? You asked for thirty. That ain't bad for the first go.'

'Aye, first and last go. We daren't risk another. One will be put down to kids on a joy-ride. More than one equals practice, and I don't want the local constabulary wondering what for.'

'That's fine with me. I'll get five seconds off on the day anyway. Always do, it's the nerves. Nice car – where did you get it?'

'Outside Deptford station.'

'Ain't that a bit close to home?'

'Look, it was the right car, and it was left unlocked. It was asking to be nicked.'

'But it's only a hundred yards from your front door!'

'I know, but then half a dozen cars go from my street in one night! One more BMW won't be noticed.'

'I still don't like it, Charlie. The Old Bill aren't fools. Even with false plates, they'll work out where it was nicked, and then start wondering who lives nearby.'

'Nah. You worry too much, Derek,' said Sands, dismissively.

Plumber shrugged. 'Where to now, then?'

Sands looked at his watch again. 'Wembley Station.'

'Why?'

'We're gonna see a man about a dog. A gun dog, you might say.' Sands's thin face screwed up in a grin of appreciation at his joke. His pale blue eyes almost disappeared behind slitted lids, and the scar was pulled taut across his cheek.

'What, already?' asked Plumber, looking concerned. 'I don't like it, Charlie. The longer you keep those things, the more risk you're in. You want to pick them up on the day of the job and dump them straight after.'

'I know.'

'Well, then?'

'We're picking them up tonight, 'cos the job's tomorrow.'

'Tomorrow? You're joking! Why so soon?'

"Cos it's to our advantage, Derek. There's a new Tesco's opened up ten days ago, and they've no' paid their milk bill for all that time. There'll be at least fifteen grand more'n usual tomorrow.'

Plumber thought about that. Then: 'How is it you know all about this, Charlie? You got a wasname? Inside man?'

'Never you mind your wee head about that. Your share won't be affected. Straight over the roundabout.'

'I know where Wembley Station is.'

They continued in silence. Plumber stopped outside the underground station, and Sands got out.

'Wait here,' he said. 'I'll only be a sec.' He walked off away from the station towards a small parade of shops, and went into a launderette. Two minutes later he emerged carrying a brown paper supermarket bag. He strode quickly towards the car, opened the rear door, put the bag on the floor behind his seat, and got in the front passenger seat.

'Home, James,' he said. 'We need an early night.'

It was sometimes said of Simon Ellison by his masters at school that he had been rather too conspicuously blessed. He was tall and fair, with a *Boy's Own* hero's rugged good looks, and he was a brilliant sportsman—cricket, rugby, athletics—it didn't matter what sport, he led the school team. He was, however, rather less clever than he thought he was, and he was certainly not as bright as his two older brothers. Nonetheless, he went to Buckingham where he scraped a third, again excelling on the sports field rather than in the examination hall. He had hoped that one of his father's friends might be able to get him something in the City, but somehow that never materialised. Instead, he had resurrected the former family tradition, and had joined the Guards, where he spent four happy years. He had then been injured in a riding accident. His left leg was damaged in such a way that even the six or seven operations that were performed could not restore it. His excellence in sports and his army career were ended.

He had decided to go to the Bar. Two years of cramming for exams, and he was called by the Inner Temple at the relatively late age of 29. Once in Chambers, his family connections, relaxed style and abundance of charm combined together to ensure a satisfactory practice, but he was still not the man he had been. He hid his disability with a fervour bordering on hysteria and forbade his family to speak of it. He even captained the Chambers' cricket eleven on its annual outing against a clerks' eleven, although he would be in agony for days after playing. Something inside him had changed too. The one thing at which he had always known he was best had been taken from him a and he was still angry – a blind, bitter anger that he could not resolve. 'The one thing about Scruffy', his mother would say of him, 'is his temper. Ever since he left the Guards, he has had a deuce of a temper.' And as Stanley, the senior clerk at 2 Chancery Court, was appreciating, 'Scruffy' Ellison was in a deuce of a temper at that moment.

'Just look at that!' commanded Ellison, throwing down the court diary on the desk before Stanley.

'What about it, sir?' asked Stanley. He had been summoned to Ellison's room and told to sit down, at one of the busiest times of the day, and he was anxious not to prolong the interview. The telephones would be ringing constantly back in the clerks' room, and although Sally and Robert were competent, he would be needed to fix fees and sort out the diary.

'What am I doing tomorrow?' demanded Ellison.

'Well, nothing at the moment, sir. It's been a bit quiet the last few–'

'But what *was* I doing?' Ellison pointed to an entry against his initials which had been scored through. It had read 'R. v. Mousof'.

21

'That was a case for Richters—' began the clerk.

'Not "was" a case, Stanley. It *is* a case. It's just that I'm not doing it any more. What's that?' He pointed to the initials 'C.H.' further down the page. His finger traced a line across the page. The words 'R. v. Mousof' had been inserted against Charles's name. 'That suggests that Mr Howard is now doing the case.'

'Yes, that's right.'

'And I want to know why.'

'When the brief came in I assumed it was for you, as Richters are your clients. But then they telephoned and asked to speak to Mr Howard about it, and I checked. His name was on it. So I altered the entry in the diary.'

'Do you realise what this case is? It will probably be the best-paid case Mr Howard does all year! Mousof is stinking rich. He'll pay thousands on the brief, and the case will last a week. It's worth a fortune!'

'I'm sorry, sir. I did check with the solicitors to make sure there hadn't been a mistake, but Mr Howard acted for them on the double-hander two weeks back while you were in Wales and they were very happy with him. He does have more experience than you at crime,' Stanley suggested gently. It was not a wise comment.

'Of course he fucking does! He does all mine!'

'I don't know what I can do about it, sir, when the solicitors actually ask for someone by name.'

'I'm going to tell you exactly what you can do about it, Stanley. You're bloody well going to ring Richters again and see if you can switch the brief back to me.'

Disputes of this nature over work were not uncommon in any set of Chambers, and it was the clerk's job to ensure that ill-feeling was kept to a minimum. On one hand, all the members were part of a team, able to offer solicitors a range of experience and expertise on a particular subject, from the Head of Chambers to the junior tenant. On the other hand, each set of Chambers was a microcosm of the Bar at large: every member was in competition with every other, and the rules of the marketplace applied. Touting for work was absolutely prohibited, but one could not prevent solicitors from expressing a preference for a particular barrister if he did a better job than his room-mate. Ellison mainly did licensing work for the large casinos, but that increasingly threw up criminal cases, and if he was not available, Charles Howard was the obvious choice. Stanley had realised over the years that Mr Ellison was rather more sensitive about his 'returns' than most, and he required gentle handling. So Stanley ignored his aggressive tone, and replied as reasonably as he could.

'I can't do that, sir, and you know it. If you consider that Mr Howard has done anything improper to obtain the brief you had better speak to Sir Geoffrey about it,' he said, referring to the Head of Chambers. 'But honestly, sir, as far as I know Mr Howard had no hand at all in obtaining the instructions.'

Stanley had never before found himself in the position of defending Mr Howard. Howard's practice did not fit in with those of the rest of Stanley's 'guv'nors' and, frankly, he was happier clerking civil work where he knew what he was doing. He had nothing against Howard personally, but he wished he'd go to some set where they did nothing but crime, and then both he and Howard would feel easier. But on this occasion Howard had just done a good job, and had been rewarded for it by the delivery of this brief.

'Now I really must get back,' he said to Ellison as he stood to leave. He held out his hand for the diary, but Ellison did not move. Stanley picked the book up from the desk, and left the room.

Chapter Three

Both sides of the suburban road were lined with semi-detached houses. They had been built before the First World War, at a time when few had family cars, and thus most of the houses had no garages. Two-car families, and the splitting of family homes into flats, meant that there was insufficient room for all the cars in the street, and both pavements were lined from end to end with cars, frost glistening on their roofs. A careful observer would have noticed an exception; one car, a blue BMW almost at the end of the road, had no frost on its roof. Indeed, the steam on its windows indicated that it was occupied, and had been occupied for some time. On the other side of the road, almost directly opposite the BMW, was a block of flats, the only break in the line of identical houses. Beside the flats was a small service road which led, in the first instance, to a row of garages behind the block, for the use of residents. Behind the garages, however, the service road turned left and continued parallel to, and along the back of, the houses. It emerged on the main road, next to the Express Dairies, London North depot, the rear entrance of which, secured by two eight-foot high iron gates, opened on to the service road.

The depot did not deal in milk: it dealt in money. Every large supermarket in the area was supplied daily with cartons of milk. The bigger supermarkets demanded such quantities that a lorry was required to make their deliveries. And once a week security guards, divided into four teams each responsible for a different area, would make a tour of the supermarkets in their area, and collect what the dairy was owed. These were hand-picked men. Not for Express Dairies the retired policemen, bouncers and assorted thuggery often employed as security guards. They selected and employed only the best. Their men were intelligent, well-trained, and hard. They had never been successfully robbed in the seven years since the present system had been introduced.

Charlie Sands opened his eyes and looked at the clock on the dashboard: 5.52 a.m. He closed his eyes again. Plumber sat next to him, looking worried. Once again he felt in his anorak pocket. The gun was heavy, bigger than he had imagined. He had examined both his and Sands's guns carefully the night before, and would have been unable to distinguish them from real ones. Sands had told him that the barrels had been blocked originally, but that they had been drilled out to make them look real from the point of view of someone staring down the barrel. Plumber looked, and felt, deeply uneasy.

He checked his other pocket, also not for the first time. He could feel the cold metal of the handcuffs, four pairs, and the pliant, skin-like feel of the plastic mask. He, too, looked at the clock.

'Okay. Time to move,' said Sands, opening the passenger door, and stepping on to the pavement. He looked up and down the road. It was deserted.

'Shut the door,' pleaded Plumber. 'It's friggin' freezing.'

Sands closed the door quietly and walked to the vehicle in front, an inconspicuous white Ford van. He opened the door, and sat inside. His breath came in white clouds, and within seconds the inside of the windows were covered with condensation. He reached forward to wipe them clear, and then stopped. There were footsteps approaching from the far end of the road. He slipped down in his seat and held his breath. A young man wearing a duffel coat and a long green scarf appeared, walking towards the two occupied cars. He stepped off the pavement three cars up from where Sands sat, and crossed to the far side of the road. He approached the service road. He was out of Sands's vision, but Sands heard the sound of his footsteps change from sharp 'clicks' to the crunch of gravel as he reached the service road.

Plumber turned the key, and the BMW engine coughed into life. His hand delved into his left pocket, and drew out the plastic mask. He put it to his face and pulled the elastic over his head. He looked in his rear-view mirror. A caricature of Margaret Thatcher with black eye holes smiled back at him. He looked forward to the van, and saw Ronald Reagan—Sands—looking back at him and pointing at the service road. Plumber signalled his readiness, and Sands turned back. Sands reached down underneath his seat and pulled out the brown paper bag. He fumbled inside with one hand, and drew out a short, heavy gun with a wooden stock. It had two barrels, sawn off about eight inches from the stock. He slipped it inside his jacket, took out the imitation revolver and put it beside him on the seat, turned to wave again at Plumber, and pulled away from the pavement. Plumber moved off behind the van. He turned into the service road. The van passed the flats and bounced across the bumpy forecourt of the garages. Plumber could see the man in the duffel coat ahead, approaching the bend in the service road. The van caught up with him as he rounded the corner. The man turned and looked at Sands as he approached, and started. Sands accelerated, the rear wheels spun in a whirl of pebbles, and the van drove straight at him. He scrambled backwards until his back was against the wall. Sands braked hard and leapt out. He grabbed the man's hair with one hand, and shoved the revolver under his chin.

'No' a peep outta you, sonny, or you're dead meat!' he snarled.

The man turned as green as his scarf, and twisted his head as far back as it would go. Plumber drew up behind the van in the BMW.

'Now, where are your keys?' asked Sands.

'In . . . in my coat . . . left pocket,' stammered Duffel Coat. Sands reached in and took them out. He handed them to the man.

'Open up!' he ordered, whirling him round and shoving him at the gates, a few feet away down the road. He did as he was told. Sands pushed him through the gates, and propelled him across a yard towards the door to the building.

'You're gonna unlock that door for us, and then you're gonna turn off the alarm, right?' There was no response. 'Right?' shouted Sands, giving him a further hefty shove in his back, and sending him sprawling on to his face. Sands reached down and grabbed the hood of the duffel coat, and dragged the man to his feet. He had grazes on his face and chin, and there were tears in his eyes. He looked terrified.

'Yes, OK, OK, OK! I'll do whatever you say, but please don't shoot me.'

'I'll no' shoot you. But if you mess with me, laddie, I'll blow your fuckin' head off, and that's a promise.'

They had reached the door to the building, and Duffel Coat started to unlock it.

'How many locks?' demanded Sands.

'Two — plus the combination.'

'Do them!'

Plumber drove the BMW into the yard, and parked it by the wall in one of the parking bays. He got out and raced back into the service road. He dived into the van and drove it past the yard entrance and further down the road. He parked it in a bay next to some dustbins and ran back just in time to follow Sands into the building. Duffel Coat was crouched just inside the door, turning a key in the alarm. Sands yanked him to his feet.

'Is it off?'

'Yes.'

'If you've left tha' on, and the police arrive, do you understand what'll happen?' The other nodded, and then shook his head. 'Imagine this,' explained Sands. 'The police are outside, and they've got their cars, and their guns, and their blue lights. I'm inside, and all I've got is you. How am I to get out? Answer: I use your wee body as a shield, right? If they shoot at me, they hit you first. If they dinnae shoot me, I take you with me, and then *I* shoot you. I would therefore sincerely advise you to make sure the alarm's off.'

'It's off, I promise.'

'Good.' Sands pointed to the door, and Plumber

slammed it shut. 'Now, today's your turn on the door, right?'

'Yes.'

'And you sit in this wee cabin—' Sands pointed to a cubicle by the door '—and look at your video screens, and you open the door when the staff arrive.'

'Yes.'

'Get tae work then.'

He sat at his desk, looking up at the gun still pointed at him.

'Do you always sit in your coat?' asked Plumber. The man shook his head.

'Take it off then,' ordered Sands. He did as he was told.

Sands indicated to Plumber and pointed away from the cubicle and into the building. Plumber nodded and turned round. He was in a corridor that ran straight back from the door. He hesitated a second, and then set off. A few feet down, to his left, the corridor opened out into a bay into which was set a door, and a glass-fronted cashier's desk. Plumber peered through the glass. He could make out desks, filing cabinets and a safe. He continued down the corridor. Another door opened off to the right. He opened it—a broom cupboard; a final door marked 'WC' on the right, and the corridor ended in swing doors. He pushed them open and looked out. Stairs ran upwards to his right. To his left was a lift, and before him, the front door of the building. He turned and made his way back to Sands.

'OK?' asked Sands.

'Yeh.'

Statement of Lorna Weston
Age: 18
Occupation: Cashier's Clerk
Address: 20 Denham Close, Wood Farm Road,
Hendon NW4

This statement consisting of three pages each signed by me is true to the best of my knowledge and belief and I make it knowing that, if it is tendered in evidence, I shall be liable to prosecution if I have wilfully stated in it anything which I know to be false or do not believe to be true. I have read this statement.

At about 7.30 a.m. on Friday 5th March 1982 I arrived at my place of work, Express Dairies, North London depot, where I work as a cashier's clerk. I was a bit late because my father's car would not start and I had to take a bus. I went up to the security door and through the intercom I identified myself, and asked Tim, who was on duty that morning, to be let in. He opened the door for me. As I went through the door, a man wearing a blue donkey jacket and a mask, grabbed me from behind and shouted at me to keep quiet. He held me round my chest with one arm, and with the other hand (I think it was his right hand) he pointed a gun at the side of my head. It looked a heavy gun, with one barrel, but I was too frightened to notice anything else about it. He pushed me into the cash office. The door to the cash office is usually kept locked, but it was open on this occasion. As I entered the room, I could see all my colleagues lying on the floor. They were in pairs, and were handcuffed, with the handcuffs going round the central heating pipe that ran along the skirting. I was told to lie down, and I was handcuffed alone to the leg of Mrs Webster's desk. We were all told to keep quiet, or else they would kill us.

We lay there for about twenty minutes, and then the crew of Round 4 called in on the radio. Tim was operating the radio, and, at the direction of one of the men, he told them it was all clear. Five minutes later the crew knocked on the door, and Tim let them in. The man who had grabbed me was waiting for them in the same way, and he brought them into the cash office and handcuffed them too. One of the men, I think his name is Trevor, would not lie down at first, and the man who had grabbed me hit him on the side of the face with his gun. Two other crews came in, and they were caught in the same way. I cannot remember the order they came in. I

29

only remember the first crew because Trevor was hurt.

The last crew to come in was from Round 3. Round 3 had an extra call that day, as a new supermarket had opened, and Bill Wright, the team leader, asked Tim to arrange for someone to help them in with the boxes. The robbers would not allow him to go out or to send anybody, and he made up an excuse about there being an inspection from Head Office and that no one could be spared. I was able to see the monitor screens from where I was lying, and I could see that Mr Wright came up to the security door alone. He asked to be let in, but once the door was open, he stayed just outside. The robber who had been standing by the door prodded Tim with his gun, and Tim asked Mr Wright what he was playing at, just standing there. Mr Wright must have suspected something, because he called out to his van 'Code Red', which means that the police must be alerted. He ran away from the door, I cannot say in what direction because he went off camera. The two robbers ran out of the door. I do not know if they were running after him, but the next thing I heard was this loud bang. I heard from outside the robber who had done all the talking shouting 'Go! Go! Go!' A second later they both came running in, picked up the cash bags and ran out.

I was released by the fire brigade about an hour later.

My description of the two men is as follows:
(1) The man who did all the talking was about 5ft 8in tall, with a dark complexion. He was quite slim, and had thin, brownish hair. He was wearing a donkey jacket, jeans and trainers. He wore a Ronald Reagan mask and I saw none of his face. He had a Scottish accent.
(2) The other man was about the same height, but he seemed to have a slightly heavier build. He had darker hair. He wore an anorak, track suit bottoms and trainers. He wore a Margaret Thatcher mask. I did not hear him speak. He also carried a gun, but I did not see it well enough to describe it.

I have checked the accounts from the various stores whose money the men stole, and the total taken is £98,530.16.

'Is that you, Plumber?'

'Yeh, it's me. You've got a fuckin' nerve phoning me, Sands.'

'We gotta talk.'

'I've got nothing to say to you. This time I mean it. You seen the papers? That geezer's probably going to die, you fuckin' lunatic!'

'Calm down, Derek, and listen to me—'

'No, I fuckin' won't! How could you do it, you Scots maniac? You swore they would be imitation! And you go and take a real shooter, without telling me, AND USE IT!'

'Listen, Derek, I now you're upset now, but you've gottae mind what I'm saying. We were both there; we're both in it.'

'No we bloody ain't! I never took no gun, and I never shot no one. That's down to you. I'm getting outa London now, and you can do what you bloody like.'

'Don't be a fool, Plumber. We've both got form, and I only got out a few weeks ago. The Bill will be round asking questions. This is no time tae go off on holiday. Stay put, act like normal.'

'And what if they start asking me about shooters? I'm not going down for murder on account of you.'

'You mean you'll grass me?'

For the first time, Plumber's furious flow was halted. He suddenly realised what danger he might be in, and not only from the police.

'I didn't say that,' he prevaricated.

'Now just listen for a sec, Derek,' said Sands, in a soft, almost friendly tone. 'You know and I know that even if you do grass me, regardless of what that might do to our friendship, the Old Bill will never wear it. They'll have you for an accessory at least, and that's assuming they believe you when you say you didnae know I had a real shooter. Whatever you say, you've had it.'

Plumber thought about it, and knew Sands was right. 'Oh my God,' he whispered, his bluster totally evaporated.

'But I have solution,' said Sands with confidence. 'Are you listening, Derek?'

'Yeh,' he replied wearily.

'They'll never work out who we were, right? But just in case they do, remember this. I've been speaking to a brief I know, and this is what he reckons. The police know there must have been three guns, the two imitations seen inside and the shotgun too, right? If we both swear that we had the imitations, and never knew that the third gun was real—'

'How could we not know?' interrupted Plumber. 'One of us had to carry it to shoot the fuckin' thing!'

'We didn't know it was real, 'cos the third man carried it.'

'What third man?'

'The third man who was the look-out.'

'Don't be ridiculous, they'll know—'

'How will they know? That first geezer was shitting himsel' so much, he wouldna ha' known how many there was of us. As for the rest, they never saw anything anyway. Who's to say we didnae have a look-out outside?'

'They'll never believe it,' said Plumber, shaking his head.

'So what if they don't? They've got three guns, and two men, both of whom deny carrying the shotgun. How can they prove which of us it was? How can they be sure one way or the other? This solicitor reckons that if we were tae stick to our stories, no jury could convict us of murder.'

'What about the masks?'

'That's easy. I dinnae think anyone saw me firing the gun in any event. The guard himsel' was running away, and the two in the van were diving for cover. But anyway, if we both say we were wearing the Maggie Thatcher mask they'll never disprove it. We're near enough the same height and build. It'll work.'

'Yeh?' asked Plumber, sceptically.

'Aye. It's cast iron,' assured Sands.

'As cast iron as the job was, eh?'

'What other options are there, Plumber?'

'Do a runner, like I said.'

'That's as good as puttin' up a neon sign saying "Come and get me". Use your loaf, Derek, act like nothing's happened. OK?'

'Yeh, OK,' sighed Plumber, resigned.

'Right. Now don't contact me for a bit, OK? And for God's sake, Derek, don't go splashing your money about. Put it somewhere safe.'

'I know. Bye.'

'Bye.'

Statement of Peter Roderick Mitchell
Age: Over 21
Occupation: SOCO
Address: West Hendon Police Station

This statement consisting of two pages each signed by me is true to the best of my knowledge and belief and I make it knowing that, if it is tendered in evidence, I shall be liable for prosecution if I have wilfully stated in it anything which I know to be false or do not believe to be true. I have read this statement.

I am a Scenes of Crime Officer presently attached to West Hendon Police Station. On 5th March 1982 I had occasion to examine a white Ford Escort van bearing registration plates number XHB 458T. The van was stationary in a service road at the rear of Corringham Road, Wembley. Its side doors were open and embedded in the walls of the road, so that access to and egress from the road was impossible. I examined the tyre patterns left by the vehicle in the road, and concluded that it had been reversed at speed up the road with its doors open, apparently with the aim of blocking the road, the driver making his escape through the rear doors.

I requested assistance from the fire brigade, and the vehicle was moved.

On 9th March 1982, at West Hendon Police Station, together with SOCO Paul Smith I examined the van. Behind the driver's seat I found a brown paper bag, which I produce as Exhibit PRM 1. I sealed the bag in a plastic container and sent it to New Scotland Yard for further examination.

Signed Peter Roderick Mitchell.   Signature witnessed by PC Clarke 517.

Statement of William James Bellis.
Age: Over 21.
Occupation: Fingerprint Officer.
Address: New Scotland Yard, London SW1.

This statement consisting of one page signed by me is true to the best of my knowledge and belief and I make it knowing that, if it is tendered in evidence, I shall be liable to prosecution if I have wilfully stated in it anything which I know to be false or do not believe to be true. I have read this statement.

I have been engaged in the identification of persons by means of fingerprints for the last fifteen years. In that time I have never known impressions taken from different fingers or thumbs to agree in their sequence of characteristics. On 16th March 1982 I received a sealed container which held a large brown paper bag marked PRM 1 from SOCO P R Mitchell. This bag was chemically treated and marks were found on the outside of the bag. These were developed. The bag was passed to the Photographic Department and on 19th March 1982 it was returned to the Fingerprint Department together with photographs and negatives of the developed impressions. On 28th March 1982 I received from the Metropolitan Police computer records a card containing a full set of fingerprints marked Charles Reginald Sands, which I produce as Exhibit WJB 1. I have examined the ridge characteristics of the marks taken from PRM 1, and I can state that they are similar in sufficient respects for me to be in no doubt that they were made by the same person whose fingerprints appear on WJB 1.

Signed William James Bellis.   Signature witnessed by D I Wade .334.

Chapter Four

The cold morning air of Deptford was shattered by the simultaneous sounds of breaking glass and the splintering of wood, as the rear kitchen window and the front door of the terraced house were breached. Footsteps thundered up the stairs, and three men charged into a bedroom. The first leapt towards the mattress that served as a bed and, arms held in front of him, pointed a handgun at the head of the dazed occupant of the bed.

'Get the blanket!' he shouted.

Another man grabbed the end of the blanket and yanked it off the mattress. Sands lay there in his underpants, shivering.

'Mr Charles Sands?' asked the gunman, rather less excitedly.

'Yeh?'

'My name is Detective Sergeant Franklin of the robbery squad, and these are Detective Constable Pearce and Police Constable Khan.' The detective flashed his warrant card at Sands.

'So?' asked Sands, calmly pulling the blanket back round him.

'You are under arrest on suspicion of robbery at the Express Dairies depot, Wembley. You are not obliged to say anything unless you wish to do so, but anything you say will be taken down and given in evidence. Do you understand?'

Sands did not reply. He lay back, careful to leave his hands where they could be seen.

'Note "No Reply",' said the Sergeant to the two young officers with him, 'at . . .' he looked at his watch, '. . . 6.28 a.m.'

'How long have you been in?' asked Sands of Franklin. Franklin ignored him. 'You did that very nicely; very correct, very polite. One of the prettiest arrests I've been party to.'

'Do you want to put some clothes on, sir, or are you coming to the station in your pants? Get him dressed, would you, Bruce?'

Sands sat at one side of a table in the small room, his back to the wall. Opposite him were two officers in plain clothes. One, Detective Sergeant Franklin, had some sheets of paper in front of him, and a pencil. Sands could see that at least some of the papers were witness statements, but he had tried, and failed, to read them from where he sat. The other officer was older, greyer, and sour-looking. He had small black eyes and a sharp pointed nose. He wore a short bristly moustache that seemed only tenuously attached to his top lip. He reminded Sands of a shrew. His name was Detective Inspector Wheatley, and he and Sands knew one another of old. Next to Wheatley on the table was a microphone and a tape recorder fitted with two cassette tapes. He pressed a button on it, and the tapes began to turn.

'My name is Detective Inspector Wheatley. In the interview room with me are Detective Sergeant Franklin and Mr Charlie Sands. The time is 10.55 a.m. on Tuesday 30th March 1982. At the end of this interview you will be handed a form that will tell you what happens to this tape, and how you may obtain a copy of it. I propose questioning you, Mr Sands, about a robbery that occurred at the Express Dairies depot in Wembley on Friday 5th March, but before I do so, I must remind you that you are under caution, and that you do not have to say anything unless you wish to do so, but if you say anything it will be recorded and may be given in evidence. Do you understand?'

'I can tell you now,' answered Sands, looking totally confident, 'that I refuse to answer any questions whatsoever until I have seen my solicitor, and only then in his presence. That's my answer now, and that will be my answer from now on.'

'It has been explained to you that it is felt that the presence of a solicitor might well hinder the recovery of the property stolen in the robbery. I therefore propose to interview you now. Where were you on the morning of 5th March 1982 at about 6.30 a.m?'

'No comment.'

'You are being given your chance to explain your side of the story. If you are innocent, I am sure you will want to tell us where you were at that time.'

'No comment.'

'Have you read about this robbery, or heard about it on the news?'

'No comment.'

'You must know that firearms were used.'

'No comment.'

'You realise also that a man has been very seriously wounded, and that he is still in intensive care?'

'No comment.'

'At present you have only been arrested on suspicion of robbery, but there may well come a time when I shall arrest you for attempted murder. Are you sure that you would not like to take the opportunity of explaining what happened?'

'No comment.'

'Do you know Derek Plumber?'

'No comment.'

'He has done a number of jobs with you in the past, hasn't he?'

'No comment.'

'And he is the only one of your erstwhile colleagues at liberty—or alive, in fact—at present, isn't he?'

'No comment.'

'Very well. I am about to terminate this interview, Charlie, but before I do so, you might like to think about this: I know you were there. I know you took part in this robbery. The BMW was stolen just around the corner from your house. You left a paper bag in the back of the van with your fingerprints on it. I shall allow you at a later stage to read the statement of the Fingerprint Officer if you wish. Derek Plumber has also been arrested, and I have already interviewed him. He admits being on the robbery, but he says another person, a third person, took the shotgun without telling him, and used it without warning. I suspect that that person was you. Do you still wish to make no comment? This is your last chance to put your side of the story. As far as I am concerned, the robbery is open and shut and you're just wasting everyone's time. It is the gun aspect that concerns me.'

'Still no comment.'

'Very well. It is now 10.58 a.m., and I am turning off the tape.' He did so, and made a note of the time on one of the pieces of paper.

Wheatley stood, hitched his trousers up, and collected the papers on the desk. 'Take him back to the cells,' he directed Franklin.

'Yes, guv,' replied the younger man. He took Sands by the wrist. 'Up you get.'

Sands remained where he sat, ignoring Franklin's grip on his wrist. He looked up at Wheatley, and smiled. 'Hang on a sec,' he said.

'What is it?' asked Wheatley.

'I've decided to talk,' said Sands. Wheatley sat down again, and indicated that Franklin should do the same. He turned on the tape once more.

'It is now 10.59 a.m. on the same morning. Before we left the room, Mr Sands indicated to me that he had something further to say. Well?'

'There were three of us, mysel' and two others. I am not prepared to name either of them. All I will tell you is that neither I nor Derek Plumber knew that the other man was going tae carry a real gun.'

'What part in the robbery did you play?'

'I went in with Derek. He drove the BMW, and I drove the van.'

'You went into the depot?'

'Yes.'

'You were one of the two men who used handguns to force the employees to lie down?'

'Imitation guns, yes.'

'What part did the third man play?'

'He was the look-out.'

'Did he enter the building?'

'No.'

Franklin put his hand on his superior's arm and raised his eyebrows. He wanted to ask a question. Wheatley indicated to go ahead.

'What vehicle did he arrive in, this third man?'

For the first time, Sands looked uncomfortable. He had not thought to agree that with Plumber. It would have to be the van or the BMW, but which? If he said one, and Plumber said the other . . .

'I can't . . . I refuse to answer questions about what either of the other two men did. I will answer questions only about what I did.'

'Why, then,' asked Franklin, 'did you volunteer that you and Derek went in?' Sands did not reply. 'Wasn't it because you and he have made up this third man, and that one of you two shot the security guard?'

'I've said everything I'm going tae say. I was part of the robbery but I had nothing tae do wi' the shooting.'

'I shall therefore end this interview here,' said Wheatley. 'I must however inform you that you're now under arrest for the attempted murder of Mr William

Wright. Do you wish to say anything? You are not obliged to say anything unless you wish to do so, but anything you say will be taken down and given in evidence. Do you understand?'

'I understand.'

'Put him back in his cell.'

Sands lay on his bunk, his hands behind his head, and stared at the ceiling. He had no way of telling how long he had been there—his watch and other personal belongings had been taken from him when he had arrived at the police station—but he calculated that it must now be around tea time; his stomach was growling. He had refused the greasy egg and chips offered to him for lunch. He knew Plumber was probably in a cell along the same corridor, but he dared not risk calling out. It wouldn't have been the first time that the police had waited in such situations for a careless word between cells. He just hoped that Plumber had had the sense not to attempt to make up unrehearsed details of the third man's involvement.

The iron gate that barred the end of the corridor clanged, and Sands heard footsteps approaching his cell. Tea? The door opened, and Wheatley stood on the threshold.

'Stand up, Charlie,' he said. 'This is a big moment for you. You've just graduated to the big time. Charles Reginald Sands, I must charge you that on the 30th March 1982, together with Derek Plumber, you did murder William Wright.'

'What?'

'Yes, Charlie. He just died. You are not obliged to say anything, but anything you say will be taken down and given in evidence.'

Chapter Five

Charles Howard rang the bell once, and once only, as the grubby notice pinned to the door required, and waited. There was a long pause, and then in the distance, from the other side of the door, he heard the jangling of heavy keys. The wicket in the door opened and a face peered at him.

'Yes?'

'Counsel, to see . . .' Charles paused, and looked down at his notebook where he had written his clients' names, '. . . Plumber and Sands.'

The gaoler closed the wicket, and Charles heard him fumbling with the keys. The door swung inwards.

'Come in, sir,' said the gaoler. 'They've just arrived.' He closed the door behind Charles, and led him to another, constructed of heavy steel vertical bars. 'I'm afraid both interview rooms are occupied, sir, so you'll have to speak to them in the cell.'

'That's alright, I shan't be long.'

'Down on the left,' pointed the gaoler, 'last door.'

Charles led the way down the narrow corridor. The gaoler opened the cell door. 'Counsel to see you,' he said to the occupants. Plumber and Sands were seated on the bench opposite the door. Plumber stood.

'I'm afraid I'll have to lock you in, sir,' said the gaoler.

'That's alright,' replied Charles. The door closed behind him.

'You know where the bell is, don't you?' called the gaoler.

'I know.'

Charles held out his hand to Plumber, who shook it, and then to Sands, who also shook it but remained seated.

'My name's Charles Howard. Mr Collins has asked me to come down and represent you on the remand.' Charles drew a deep breath, and then wished he hadn't. As his practice had grown, he did Magistrates' Court cases less

41

than he used to, and he had forgotten the smell of the cells. There was none other like it on earth: an extraordinary blend of fried food, sweat, urine, faeces and fear. The last was the most pungent ingredient—bitter, sharp and completely unmistakable. Charles had noted that for some reason, the cells in Crown Courts did not have quite the same smell: perhaps because by the time he had reached the Crown Court, an accused man had worked out his defence, had met his barrister, and was at least prepared for his trial. The prisoners at Magistrates' Courts, on the other hand, had often come straight from their interrogations, in some cases had been taken straight off the streets; they still smelt of the chase, like animals at bay.

This cell smelled particularly bad, and Charles peered into the lavatory bowl set on the floor in the far corner. It was full.

'We've asked them twice tae flush it,' said Sands, seeing Charles's expression. 'They're too busy.'

'I'll give it a try,' said Charles. He pressed the button on the wall, and shouted through the door. 'Gaoler!'

There was a pause, and then a voice called: 'Are you finished, sir?'

'No, but would you please flush this toilet?'

There was no reply. A few seconds later the toilet flushed, operated by the gaoler from outside.

'OK,' continued Charles. 'Mr Collins rang me and gave me very brief details. This is the first time up, right?'

'Yes,' answered Plumber.

'No application for bail?' asked Charles for confirmation.

'Hah!' snorted Sands with a smile.

'I didn't think so,' said Charles. 'It would be a waste of time, at least until we've seen the prosecution statements. When we know the strength of the case, then we can reconsider.'

'So what're you doin' here, then?' asked Sands. 'PR?'

Charles smiled. 'Frankly, yes. Just holding your hands—'

42

'And making sure we dinnae sign up with another solicitor,' interrupted Sands.

Charles grinned, not upset. 'It just so happens that I do have Legal Aid forms here for you to fill in. Of course, you are quite at liberty to nominate any solicitor you like. I understand that Mr Plumber has been with Collins in the past—'

'Yeh, I was, and very happy I was, too,' said Plumber, turning to Sands.

'Och, it's no skin off my nose,' said Sands, stretching out on the bench and putting his hands behind his back.

'Mr Sands, I shall be quite happy to represent Mr Plumber alone, and get the duty solicitor for you, if you like.'

'No. Sign me up—at least for the present. We'll get a silk in, in any event, won't we?'

'You're entitled to a QC on a murder charge, yes, but I'm afraid you may not find one at the Magistrates' Court today.'

'Fair enough,' said Sands. 'Gi' us the form, and show me where tae sign.'

'Just a few questions first,' said Charles, opening the document. 'Is there room for me to sit down for a moment?' Sands swung his legs down, and Charles sat down. 'OK. You first, Mr Sands. From the top: full name of applicant.'

'Hello, Ralph?'

'Hello Charles. Have fun?'

'God, I'd forgotten how revolting Magistrates' Courts are.'

'I thought you'd enjoy it—can't have you getting too big for your boots. What do you think?'

'Have you met them yet?'

'Well, I've known Derek Plumber for years. Dad represented him on his first TDA 25 years ago. I've not met Sands. I just got a call from the nick asking if I'd like a murder, and if so, get down to the Court.'

'Well, Sands is quite a character. Reckons he's a hard bastard.'

'Is he?'

'Quite probably. Anyway, I had a chat with the officer, and he gave me the general position. They've both admitted the robbery, both denied the shooting.'

'They've got a run, then?'

'It gets more interesting. They both claim a third man was with them, and *he* carried the sawn-off shotgun.'

'What's the police view of that?'

'They think it's a con, but I'm not sure they can prove it.'

'Where does that leave our clients, then?'

'If the jury are sure one of them did it, but can't make up their minds which one, they both have to be acquitted.'

'Both?'

'Of course. To convict, they must be satisfied so that they're sure—beyond reasonable doubt. If it could have been either, they can't be sure beyond reasonable doubt which one is guilty. You know: "It's better to let ten guilty men go free than to convict one innocent man", and all that stuff.'

'I see,' said Collins. He digested the information. 'What if it's a joint charge?'

'Ah, that would be different. If they can be proven to have agreed to the carrying of real weapons, and to their use if necessary, I suppose the Crown might prove a joint enterprise in relation to the shooting. But that doesn't look likely in these circumstances. There were, after all, two imitation guns, and from what I can remember of the statements I was shown, our clients were both seen inside the depot with one each. It does tend to support their story of a third man with the real gun.'

'OK. It looks as if this could be quite an interesting case. Any ideas for a leader?'

'A leader? I thought I was doing this one solo,' laughed Charles.

'Sorry, Charles; next time perhaps,' replied Collins. 'We'll need a silk on this,' he said, referring to the silk gown worn by QCs. 'Now, what was the name of that lady you were talking about recently?'

'Barbara Whitlam. She's excellent. Unfortunately, she's now a judge.'

'Oh. Any other ideas?'

'I don't know. Maybe. I'll make a few calls and let you know. For the present, you'll no doubt be glad to know that Legal Aid was granted subject to their means being within the limits.'

'You mean their declarable means, excluding the £98,000,' joked Collins.

'Correct. The case has been adjourned for seven days, although they're not to be produced until the 14th.'

'Will you ask your clerk to put it in the diary? I don't expect you to do it—do you think there will be a pupil available?'

'I should think so. If there's any problem, I'll give you a call.'

Charles ended the conversation, and dialled the internal number for Stanley.

'Stanley? It's Mr Howard. I wonder if you could get me the clerk to Mr Michael Rhodes Thomas. He's somewhere on King's Bench Walk.'

'Do you want to speak to the clerk or to Mr Rhodes Thomas himself, sir?' asked Stanley.

'Well, if he's in, I'll speak to Mr Rhodes Thomas.'

'Certainly, sir.'

The telephone rang again a minute later, and Stanley announced the QC.

'Hello, Michael?'

'Yes, Charlie, how are you?'

'Not bad, thank you. How's the family?' asked Charles.

'Growing more expensive by the day, thank you for asking.'

Charles had worked with Michael Rhodes Thomas QC on a case some eighteen months before. He practised from a different set of Chambers, where they dealt with a wide mixture of common law, including quite a lot of crime. The members of the set were by and large extremely friendly, and Charles had co-defended with a number of them over the years. Rhodes Thomas himself was extremely able, with an affable personality, and a common touch that juries appreciated. Charles felt that their approaches were similar, and on the last occasion Rhodes Thomas had led Charles they had not only been successful but they'd had a lot of fun too.

'I know you're extremely busy—' began Charles.

'Oh, overloaded,' interrupted Rhodes Thomas.

'—but I wondered if I might interest you in a little murder.'

'Yes?' asked the other, interested.

'It won't be up for a while—it's not been committed from the Magistrates' Court yet—but it's a goodie. The Express Dairies robbery.'

'I didn't know they'd charged anyone with that.'

'This morning. I've just seen them—it's a two-hander— called Plumber and Sands.'

'That's not Charlie Sands, is it?'

'It is,' replied Charles, surprised. 'Do you know him?'

'Yes. I represented him on the Shell Mex Payroll job, about six years ago. Got him off, too. Small world, eh?'

'Indeed it is. What do you think?'

'Subject to availability, I'd be delighted, assuming the solicitors are happy.'

'They're alright. They've asked me to suggest some-one.'

'Fair enough. I assume you don't want me before committal?'

'I don't know yet, but I doubt it. I'll get the solicitors to have a word with your clerk if necessary. Otherwise, perhaps we can organise a conference at the prison after committal.'

'Fine. How are you keeping?'

'Me? I'm OK.'

There was a pause before Rhodes Thomas spoke again. 'How's Henrietta?' he asked.

Charles cast his mind back, and remembered that he had introduced Henrietta to Rhodes Thomas one day

46

when they had met him in the Temple. 'She's fine, thank you.'

'Saw her a few weeks ago,' said Rhodes Thomas.

'At Peter Ripley's party?' asked Charles.

'Well, yes, but after that too. At the Corbetts'.' There was another pause. 'I expect you were burning the midnight oil again.'

'Yes. I expect so,' said Charles absently. 'You do mean Laurence and Jenny Corbett?'

'Yes. He's in your Chambers, isn't he?' asked Rhodes Thomas.

'Yes, he is. I just didn't know that Henrietta saw them socially.'

'Oh, I think it's something to do with Jenny's charity work. I got the impression that Henrietta was involved too.'

'That must be it then.' There was another pause.

'Let me know if you fancy a drink after Court one day, Charlie. For a chat, you know?' he said sympathetically.

'Will do, Michael. Thanks.'

Chapter Six

Ralph Collins led the way up the narrow stairs and knocked on the door at the top. The door was unlocked and opened by a prison officer and the three men filed in.

'You've all been here before, haven't you, sirs?' asked the officer. The others nodded their assent. 'If you'd just empty your pockets in the bowls provided and go through the gate one at a time.'

Charles had already taken out his loose change and keys and went through the electronic gate. The officer frisked him briefly, efficiently, and passed his electronic wand over him to detect any concealed metal. Collins and Rhodes Thomas followed suit. The alarm sounded as Collins stepped through the gate.

'May I have a look in your pockets, please, sir?' asked the officer.

Ralph Collins opened his coat and revealed a pen still in his inside pocket.

'That's the offender, I should think,' said the officer, taking it out and, sure enough, on the second time through, the alarm stayed off. Their briefcases were quickly searched, and their possessions returned to them.

'Solicitor and counsel to see Mr Plumber,' said Collins.

'If you'll just give your names to my colleague, sir, I'll send for him.'

The three lawyers identified themselves to another officer seated at a table, and were shown to a small room. A few moments later, Plumber appeared.

'Hello, Mr Collins, Mr Howard,' he said amiably.

'Hello Derek,' replied Collins. 'May I introduce you to Mr Rhodes Thomas? He's the QC who will lead for the defence.'

Plumber put out his hand. 'Pleased to meet you, sir,' he said to Rhodes Thomas.

'Take a seat, Mr Plumber. Am I mistaken, or do we get offered tea at Brixton?'

'You're dead right, sir. He'll be along in a sec,' answered Plumber.

Tea having arrived, Rhodes Thomas took the ribbon off his brief, spread his papers on the table, and began.

'Now, I've got a great deal to ask you, but what I want to know first is, what's happened to Mr Sands?'

'Beg pardon?'

'He's instructed new solicitors, hasn't he?'

48

'That's right, yeh.'

'You two haven't fallen out, have you?'

'No, not at all. He's used Oppenheims a couple of times before, that's all. Why?'

'Mr Howard and I were just a bit concerned. If you're both going to get off the murder charge, you've both got to stick to your guns, if you'll excuse the pun. There's no apparent conflict between your stories, and so we wondered why he wanted to change solicitors.'

'I don't think there's nothing, wasname, suspicious, about it.'

'Good.'

'Do you mind if I ask a question?' asked Plumber.

'Not at all,' replied Rhodes Thomas.

'Do I have to plead guilty to the robbery?'

'Well, as I understand it, Mr Plumber, you've said in your interview to the police, and to Mr Collins here, that you did take part in the robbery. Is that the case?'

Plumber looked embarrassed. He turned round to Collins, but received no assistance. Charles intervened.

'I'm sure you understand, Mr Plumber, once you've told Mr Collins that you did do the robbery, neither he nor myself nor Mr Rhodes Thomas can represent you if you plead not guilty. We are not able to lie to the Court on your behalf. You will have to find other solicitors—and if you tell them that you are guilty, you'll lose them too.'

'Oh,' said Plumber, clearly disappointed.

'There is, however, one exception to that rule,' continued Charles. 'You are entitled to plead not guilty, despite what you've told us, and we are allowed to test the prosecution evidence. We are still prevented from actively suggesting to the Court that you are not guilty, and we certainly cannot call any evidence on your behalf. If, at the end of the prosecution's evidence, there is a case against you, you will have to plead guilty at that stage. That may all sound rather technical to you, but we are bound by rules of conduct.'

'Do you understand all that?' asked Rhodes Thomas.

'I think so. The thing is, see, I was wondering: if I

plead not guilty to the robbery, at least at the outset, the prosecution might drop the murder if I offered to change me mind, and put me hands up to the robbery.'

Rhodes Thomas smiled. 'They might indeed.'

'Do you reckon?'

'Put it this way, Mr Plumber: if the evidence comes out exactly as it appears in the prosecution statements, I do not think a jury could properly find either you or Sands guilty of the murder. I think further that the prosecution will be well aware of that. That *may* make them amenable to an offer. On the other hand, you've made a full, taped confession, and it will be hard to persuade the Crown that there's any risk of your getting off the robbery in any event. They may therefore decide to take their chances, and see if they can get you for both.'

'I'd like to have a bash anyway.'

'Very well. I'm sure Mr Collins here will inform the Court that both charges are to be contested, and I will certainly have an informal word with the prosecution leader to sound him out. But just in case they do proceed with the murder charge, I suggest we have a look at some of the evidence.'

The conference continued for another two hours and three cups of tea. Unknown to the participants, in an adjoining block at Brixton Prison at exactly the same time, Charlie Sands was also receiving a visit. The conversation with his visitor only lasted 45 minutes, but at the end of it Charlie Sands returned to his cell with a smile on his thin face. The visitor, Detective Inspector Ronald Henry Wheatley, departed with a full notebook. He did not break with the habits of a lifetime and smile, but he was no less satisfied.

Part Two

Chapter Seven

Although his practice had taken him there every now and then for the last eight years, Charles still experienced a particular thrill, a special lightness of step, as he entered the Old Bailey. This was the 'sharp end' of criminal practice, the Court where the seasoned practitioners worked, met, and discussed cases, judges and trials. It was the heart of the web of British criminal justice.

Charles had seen Plumber twice more since April, once with his leader and once without. The second of those conferences had been held only the week before and had lasted just twenty minutes, while Charles tried to placate his client. Plumber had been in custody for five months and he was getting jumpy.

Charles placed his briefcase and blue bag on the conveyor belt and watched as they were taken through the X-ray machine. He walked to the other side, collected them, and went to the lifts. There was a barrister waiting for a lift whom Charles recognised.

'Philip Jewell,' he said. 'What brings you here?'

'Oh, murder and mayhem, as usual. You?'

'About the same. You're not involved in "Plumber and Sands", by any chance?'

'Certainly am. I suppose you're for Plumber?'

'Yes. Are you being led?' asked Charles as the lift arrived.

'Robin Lowe was leading me, but he won't be here today.'

'Why not?' asked Charles, puzzled.

The other did not answer, but grinned mysteriously. The lift arrived at the fourth floor, and they entered the barristers' robing room.

'Court Two, isn't it?' asked Jewell.

'Yes.'

'See you down there, then,' said Jewell, approaching one of the lockers near to the door.

Charles walked right to the end of the line of lockers where there were a few for visiting barristers from other circuits. He was, in fact, a member of the South Eastern circuit, but as the only criminal practitioner in Chambers it was not considered necessary for a locker to be reserved. So, purely from habit, Charles used the table next to the locker his pupil-master had used, years before when Charles was still a pupil.

He pondered Jewell's words. If the case were to start, it would be most unusual for the defence not to be represented by its silk. On the other hand, if Sands were simply applying for an adjournment, something Jewell would have done alone, why the mystery? Puzzled, Charles changed his everyday stiff collar for a wing collar, tied on his bands, put on his wig and gown, and collected his papers.

'Hello there. It's Charles Howard, isn't it?'

Charles turned to see another barrister. It was Marcus Stafford, the junior for the Crown. The two of them had spoken on the telephone a few days before about the evidence in the case.

'Yes. Stafford?'

'Yah. Haven't seen my illustrious leader, by any chance?' asked Stafford, referring to Richard Hogg QC, who was prosecuting the case.

'Not yet. And I don't suppose you've seen Mike Rhodes Thomas?'

'No, sorry. I'm going upstairs for a cup of coffee. Want to join me?'

'Yes, thank you.'

The two of them made their way upstairs, collected coffees, and sat down.

'Is this still to be a fight?' asked Stafford.

'That's up to you,' replied Charles. 'As we've already discussed, he'll plead to the robbery if you drop the murder. We both know you can't make it stick against either of them.'

Stafford just smiled and then winked. 'We'll see.'

This sort of friendly sparring was nothing new to Charles—it happened frequently—but there was a confidence about Stafford that made him wonder what was going on. He did not have long to wait before discovering what it was. A short chubby man bustled up to them.

'Morning, Marcus,' he said, and sat next to them.

'Hello, Richard. This is Charles Howard. Charles, Richard Hogg.'

'Ah,' said Hogg, riffling through his papers, 'got something for you.' He handed a document to Charles. It was a statement headed, 'Charles Reginald Sands'. 'I expect you'll want some time to consider that with Michael, and your client of course. I don't suppose the Crown could object to an application for an adjournment if you decide to make it. In any event, I've spoken to the clerk, and told her that we shall need some time before starting.'

Charles's eyes scanned the document. It was a statement dated that day. In it, Sands retracted his earlier statement, and said that only two men had been on the robbery, himself and Plumber. He claimed that Plumber had taken, and used, the shotgun without his knowledge. His reason for his earlier statement was that Plumber had threatened the lives of his family.

'May I take it that Sands is prepared to give evidence to this effect for the prosecution?' asked Charles, trying to appear unconcerned.

'You may,' answered Hogg.

55

'May I also take it that the Crown is proposing to call him as a witness of truth?'

'You may,' repeated Hogg. 'We shall offer no evidence against him on the murder, and I shall apply to the Judge to sentence him for the robbery before he gives evidence against your client.'

'I'd better get some instructions,' said Charles. 'If you'll excuse me . . .'

Charles went down to the second floor where he found Ralph Collins in the public canteen, and the two of them went together to the cells in the basement. Michael Rhodes Thomas was waiting for them outside the main door.

'Well met,' he said as the others arrived.

'Wait till you've seen this,' said Charles heavily, handing him the statement. The older man read it while they waited for the gaoler to arrive. 'Well, we did suspect something of the sort, didn't we Charlie?' He handed the document to Collins.

'Yes. But there's no doubt, it makes Plumber's position much more precarious.'

'Indeed. Well, we may have to reconsider our tactics.'

The door opened. 'Good morning, gentlemen,' said the prison officer. The door was locked behind them, and they followed the officer up a short corridor to another locked door. The air was redolent of frying bacon.

'I swear, the food down here smells better than that in the Bar Mess upstairs,' said Rhodes Thomas.

'Nothing but the best for our guests,' said the gaoler with a grin.

Five minutes later Plumber was shown into the tiny cell already cramped with three lawyers. Without speaking, Rhodes Thomas gave him Sands's statement. Plumber read it, his face ashen, his expression blank.

'Jesus Christ,' he whispered, 'I'm done for.'

'Sit down, Derek,' said Rhodes Thomas. 'Take a few deep breaths, and start telling us the truth.'

Plumber did as he was told. 'There was only the two of us on the job. God, I never wanted to go, I swear it. I'd gone straight for four years, but he threatened to grass me on the last job. It was cast iron, he said, this would be the last job ever, and it would set us up for life.'

'That's exactly what it has done,' said Collins wryly. Rhodes Thomas gave him a sharp look.

'He persuaded me to take a wasname, an imitation shooter. You can look up my record: I've never touched a gun—real or fake—in thirty years of being a villain till this job. I never even knew he had a sawn-off, on my baby's life, I swear it.'

'Very well,' said Rhodes Thomas. 'Why make up a third man?'

'That was his idea. He reckoned if we both stuck to our stories, we'd neither of us be convicted.'

'He was right. But he hasn't stuck to the story. And for some reason the prosecution believe him rather than you. They're proposing to drop the murder charge against him. Why should they believe him, Derek?'

'I don't know. What're we gonna do?'

'That's up to you. They're obviously not going to take an offer on the robbery alone and, on your instructions, you cannot plead guilty to the murder. The case will depend on which of the two of you the jury believes.'

'A cut-throat,' said Charles.

'Yes,' agreed Rhodes Thomas. 'A cut-throat defence: each defendant blaming the other.'

'What does that mean?' asked Plumber.

'In practical terms,' answered Charles, 'a dirty trial. No holds barred. Your credit with the jury is all-important. Subject to what Mr Rhodes Thomas thinks, you'd be advised to plead guilty to the robbery and tell the jury the whole story. It will look dreadful if he admits it, and you do not.'

'I agree,' said Rhodes Thomas. 'The question I need to have answered now is: do we require an adjournment? The Crown won't oppose us asking for one, if there's any point. But I have your instructions on this new statement, and I personally cannot see what purpose would be served by delaying the trial.'

'But what about forensics, or whatever they're called?

Can't they do tests on the shotgun to prove it was him that fired it and not me?'

'Such tests do exist, but they would have been done by now. No evidence has been served on us, so we can assume that they revealed nothing, or we would have known about it.'

'What do you think, Mr Collins?' asked Plumber, turning to the man he'd known the longest.

'I think counsel are right. I see no reason to delay. It will only give Sands the chance to make up more convincing detail.'

'OK, then,' said Plumber, sounding a lot more brave than he looked. 'Let's go for it.'

The lawyers left the cells and went directly to Court Two. The prosecution team and Sands's barrister awaited them.

'Well?' asked Hogg.

'Very, thank you,' answered Rhodes Thomas with a smile.

'Still fighting?' asked Hogg.

'Oh, my dear fellow,' replied Rhodes Thomas, 'I should hate to deprive us all of a few days' work. We're still fighting.'

'Fair enough. I've asked the clerk if she can arrange for us to see the Judge in Chambers just to explain the position.'

'Hasn't the Court of Appeal disapproved of that?' asked Charles.

'Yes, it has,' answered Hogg, 'but there are other matters which you'll understand I cannot mention now, that have to be aired in Chambers.'

A grim-faced, grey-haired woman of about fifty, wearing court robes, approached the barristers.

'His Lordship will see you now, gentlemen, if you're ready.'

'Are we ready?' asked Hogg, turning to Rhodes Thomas.

'We are.'

The five barristers followed the clerk to a door behind the

Judge's bench and out on to a carpeted corridor, the walls of which were hung with paintings. They filed down the corridor for some distance, until they came to a panelled door. The clerk motioned for them to wait, and knocked.

'Come,' said a voice from behind the door.

The clerk entered, half closing the door behind her, and then opened it wide to usher the barristers in.

'Good morning, Judge,' said Hogg.

'Good morning, gentlemen. Do sit down if you can,' said the Judge. His Honour Judge Galbraith QC had been a recent, and popular, appointment to the Bench. He was of the new generation of judges, those who were not so prosecution-minded as the old school. He was non-interventionist too; he let the barristers get on with the case in their own way, with a minimum of judicial interference.

Richard Hogg introduced the other barristers, and explained who they each represented.

'There are a number of matters I'd like to explain with your permission, Judge,' he continued. 'The indictment contains two counts, robbery and murder. As I expect you will have read, the prosecution case on the first is strong, whereas I concede we would have had difficulty on the murder. The position has now changed, in that Sands has offered to give evidence for the Crown.' He handed to the Judge a copy of the statement. 'That is a Notice of Additional Evidence served on the defence this morning.'

He paused to allow the Judge to read it. The Judge turned to Rhodes Thomas. 'Are you asking for an adjournment?'

'No, Judge.'

'That presumably means that you will no longer proceed against Sands,' said the Judge to Hogg. Charles now understood why Sands did not need a QC: he wasn't to be tried at all for the murder.

'If you accept this evidence as the truth,' continued the Judge, 'it means that you accept that he did not know of the shotgun.'

59

'It certainly means that we cannot prove otherwise,' replied Hogg.

'What gives this statement credence in your view?' asked the Judge. 'It might as easily have been Plumber who approached you. It's still a cut-throat.'

Charles smiled. This Judge was no fool.

'That brings me on to the other matter that I wanted to raise, Judge, and it's a matter that would be best not raised in open court. Sands has been of great assistance to the police in relation to other matters. He has provided information that has led to a number of arrests, and I am instructed that charges will follow. He appears to have been entirely frank in relation to those matters, some of which may result in charges against him personally.'

'And of course, you, Mr Jewell, want me to take these "other matters" into account when sentencing him?' asked the Judge.

'Yes, Judge, I do.'

'And I expect you both want him sentenced for the robbery before we start the trial of Mr Plumber?'

'Yes,' said Jewell and Hogg in unison.

The Judge leaned back in his chair and considered what he had been told. 'If the only evidence against Plumber is that of a potential co-defendant, the jury will have to be warned in any event against convicting him on Sands's word alone. There will have to be corroboration, won't there, Mr Hogg?'

'That's right, Judge. The prosecution says that there is evidence capable of being corroboration, subject, of course, to your ruling.'

'I see. What do you have to say about this, Mr Rhodes Thomas?' asked the Judge.

'There's nothing I can say, Judge. The prosecution have taken a view of the evidence. I cannot change that. I shall clearly need to know exactly what information Mr Sands has given to the police, so I can consider if I want to cross-examine on it, and I would like to know what other charges may follow.'

'Yes,' said the Judge. 'I think you must be entitled to

that. I shall need a note signed by a responsible police officer setting out what Sands has told the police, so that it may be put in the file. I shall make no express reference to it in Court. I must say that I am not entirely happy with the turn of events, Mr Hogg, but I cannot prevent you from taking this course. If you decide to offer no evidence against one of two defendants, I cannot stop you.' Hogg did not answer. The Judge turned to Rhodes Thomas. 'Is Plumber proposing to plead guilty to the robbery?'

'Yes, Judge, he is.'

'Well, thank you, gentlemen. How long will you need before we can swear in a jury?'

'I would have thought we'd need ten minutes before we can start,' answered Hogg. 'We should then be in a position to deal with the guilty pleas, and the sentence of Sands. I suppose the jury in waiting could be asked to stand by for midday.'

'Very well,' said the Judge.

Once outside the Judge's Chambers, Rhodes Thomas winked at Charles. 'I am beginning to think we might have some fun with this, Charlie,' he whispered. 'I wonder if Hogg's bitten off a bit more than he can chew.'

They returned to the cells to see Plumber.

'He's turned grass,' said Rhodes Thomas.

'What?' exclaimed Plumber, incredulously.

'He's given the police information regarding other crimes. That's why they believe him.'

'Where does that leave me?' asked Plumber.

'Mr Howard and I have been chatting about it on the way down. We're not optimistic, but we don't think all is lost. It gives us a lever over Sands. What I'd like to do, Mr Plumber, is keep a very low profile for almost the whole of the case. You admit that you took part in the robbery, and you do not deny the witnesses' accounts of the shooting. You simply say that it wasn't you with the gun. The dead man can't say which of you it was, and the other two members of Round 4, Gilsenan and . . .'

'Barrett, or Barnett,' offered Charles.

'Yes, well, they were both unsighted by their van and

61

by Wright himself. In my view it's simply a question of which of the two of you the jury believe.'

'Do you agree, Charles?'

'Yes, I do.'

'Very well,' continued Rhodes Thomas. 'I propose to ask no questions at all of the other prosecution witnesses. I shall save the whole attack for Sands himself.'

Chapter Eight

Sands got nine years. It would have been less but for his bad record, and it would have been more but for the assistance he had given, and had promised to give, to the police. With remission, and discounting parole, he would probably serve about six years. By the time he had been sentenced it was almost 1 o'clock, and the Judge adjourned for lunch.

At 2 o'clock the jury was sworn in, Plumber pleaded guilty to robbery and not guilty to murder. The trial began. By the end of the afternoon, almost half of the Crown's case had been completed, and the defence had not asked a single question. The jury were looking decidedly puzzled. Charles looked across at them every now and then, and could see them looking at the bench where the defence team sat, wondering what was going on. There was no doubt: by the time Mike Rhodes Thomas stood to cross-examine Sands, the full attention of the jury would be on him.

The Judge adjourned at 4.15 p.m., and Charles headed back to Chambers. He hesitated outside Gloria's, tempted to stop for a cup of tea, and saw a group of barristers at one of the tables. He was about to move on, when one of their number saw him, and waved for him to enter. Charles looked at his watch, shrugged, and went in.

Charles arrived back at 2 Chancery Court at 6.30 p.m., suitably warmed with several cups of tea and rounds of toast. He walked into the clerks' room. Unusually, Sally was still there.

'Hello there,' said Charles, as he peered into the pigeon-hole reserved for his briefs and, more importantly, cheques, as they came in. 'What are you doing here so late? We're not paying for overtime, are we?'

'No, sir. I'm going out tonight and my boyfriend's picking me up. So, as I had to wait anyway, Stanley asked me to hang on for Mr Clarke's brief to arrive. It's being sent over by courier. Are you staying, sir?' she asked.

Charles did not answer. A large brief had been awaiting him in the pigeon-hole, and he undid the ribbon on it and looked at the instructions. 'Damn!' he said softly as he read. 'Sorry, Sally, did you ask something?'

'Yes. Are you going to be staying, as I've locked up on the other side.'

The set of Chambers was split into two sets of rooms divided by a central landing, and each 'side' required its own keys.

'Well,' answered Charles, 'I *was* going to go straight home, but they want an indictment drafted by tomorrow *and* an Advice on evidence,' he added, tapping the papers in his hand. 'Why they always leave it to the last minute I shall never understand. The sooner we get a central prosecution service, the happier I shall be.'

He gathered the papers together and left the clerks' room. He opened the door to the corridor, still reading as he walked, and bumped straight into someone coming in the other way. He knew by the smell who it was, without even looking up.

'Evening, Kellett-Brown,' he said, stepping back. Ivor Kellett-Brown was the oldest—and the oddest—member of Chambers. He had come to the Bar late, some time in the mid-sixties, having failed at a number of other careers, and had promptly failed in the Law, too. However, incredible as the members of 2 Chancery Court found it, he appeared to have friends in high places. Mr Justice Bricklow, who had been Head of Chambers in 1966, had brought Kellett-Brown in, and he had stayed ever since. He had no discernible practice but, unlike in most other professions, every now and then a complete duffer managed to survive at the Bar, living off the crumbs from other barristers' tables. As long as he paid his Chambers rent (and no one knew how he managed even that, as his earnings from the Law were certainly insufficient), and he caused no one any trouble, he was permitted to occupy a corner of the pupils' room.

He lived in a single room in Lincoln's Inn with a dozen budgerigars whom he permitted to fly free within the confines of the room. Droppings and feathers covered every available surface, and the floor crunched underfoot with decades of dried filth. Kellett-Brown himself invariably wore threadbare striped trousers, the seat of which was so shiny that the pupils in his room on one occasion all wore sunglasses to protect their eyes from the glare (a joke that was utterly lost on the wearer of the trousers). He owned one jacket, the cuffs of which he trimmed regularly, and over that he wore, like an overcoat, the evidence, visual and odiferous, of his domestic companions.

To add to this unprepossessing appearance, Kellett-Brown had an 'unfortunate manner', as some of the more charitable members of Chambers termed it. As far as Stanley, the senior clerk, was concerned, he was an argumentative bastard who should have been kicked out years ago. He frequently appeared in Chambers in the late afternoon, plainly the worse for drink (the sherry served in Hall at luncheon was subsidised), when Stanley was sorting out the diary for the next day. He would peer over the clerk's shoulder, like a tipsy, disgruntled vulture, reminding Stanley repeatedly that he was available for anything that might be going spare.

Charles wrinkled his nose with distaste. Kellett-Brown

bore his usual pungent air of sherry and decrepitude.

'Sorry, Ivor,' said Charles, attempting to circumvent Kellett-Brown and get to his room.

'I beg your pardon?' said the other with very great dignity, turning slowly to face Charles after he had spoken, and peering at Charles from under heavy lids.

'I said, "Sorry, Ivor". For bumping into you,' explained Charles. He watched as Ivor swayed slightly. 'Forget it,' said Charles with impatience, and brushed past him.

Charles unlocked the far door, and walked down to his room. He threw the papers on to his desk, reached across to the desk-lamp, and settled himself down to read his new brief.

He was unaware of the passing of time, but he had read about a hundred pages when there was a faint tap on his door. It was so quiet that he ignored it at first, but then it was repeated, slightly louder.

'Come in,' he said, putting down his pen. The door opened very slowly, and Sally's head appeared timidly round the door. 'Yes, Sally? What are you doing still here?' He looked at his watch. It was almost 8 o'clock.

Sally looked down at the mass of papers spread about Charles's desk, and the pile of law books on the floor. 'Oh . . . no . . . It really doesn't matter if you're busy, sir . . .' she said in a strange voice. She stepped backwards, and began to close the door behind her. Charles pushed his chair back and followed her. She looked at him over her shoulder like a frightened rabbit. Charles held her gently by the arm, and turned her round. Her eyes were red, and she had been crying. Her eyeliner, which was usually applied (albeit in large quantities) very carefully, was smeared, and her hair was awry.

'What on earth's the matter?' asked Charles gently. Sally was usually so competent and brisk that he was quite startled to see her so upset. She took a deep breath as if to start speaking, but her voice broke and all that emerged was a deep sob. Charles led her back into his room, and sat her down on his chair. He searched his drawer and came up with a packet of tissues and handed one to her.

'Now. Take a deep breath and tell me what happened. Is it your boyfriend?'

'He didn't come . . .' she started.

'Oh, that's nothing to get upset—' She waved her hand to stop him. That wasn't it. Charles waited for her to take another deep breath and let her start again.

'I was waiting for him over there,' she said between gulps of air, pointing to the clerks' room, 'when Mr K . . . K . . . Kellett-Brown came in . . .'

'Yes?' asked Charles, crouching beside her.

'Oh, Mr Howard sir, I don't know . . . what's best . . . I'd better not . . .' Her voice rose sharply with each phrase. She was on the verge of hysteria.

'Just take it easy. One word at a time.'

'I . . . can't . . . I'll get into trouble, Mr Howard.'

'No you won't, I promise you.' He lifted her chin with his hand and looked up into her smudged eyes. 'If something's happened, you must tell me.'

She looked straight at him, and nodded. 'Mr Kellett-Brown came in.' Her voice was calmer, but she spoke very quickly, as if afraid that if she paused, she would be unable to continue. 'I was waiting for Wayne. He . . . Mr K-B . . . he asked me if I didn't think it would be better if I shut the outer door, so no one could come wandering in. Stanley told me about downstairs being burgled, so I thought perhaps I should. Wayne'd always knock anyway.' Now she had started talking the words tumbled out in a cascade. 'So I did, I shut it, and went back to my desk. I was typing a letter, for Mr Smith, when Mr Kellett-Brown called on the phone. Wanted me to bring him in some paper. So I went in there, and he wasn't at his desk. I turns round, and there he is . . . behind the door . . .' She laughed, a peculiar high-pitched giggle, that turned into a cry. 'He had his . . . thing . . . you know? Sticking out his trousers. He kept saying he wouldn't hurt me . . wouldn't hurt me . . . just wanted me to . . . to . . .' She had to stop again.

Charles stood up, and moved towards the door. Sally grabbed at his trousers and held him. 'Please don't go! Don't go, Mr Howard!' she cried.

66

'I'm not going. I just wanted to see if he's still there.'

'He ain't. He left after . . . after . . .'

'After what?' asked Charles, turning back to her. 'Are you saying he raped you?' he asked gently.

She shook her head violently. 'No, he never, but he grabbed at me . . .' She opened her cardigan, and showed Charles her blouse. Two of the buttons in the middle of her chest were torn off. Charles averted his eyes from her breasts.

'I pushed him away, and he fell over. I ran to the loo and locked myself in. I've been there nearly half an hour. I heard the door go, but I was too scared to come out till now.'

'My God, you poor thing,' said Charles. 'Let me get you a drink. I keep a bottle in the desk for—'

'No,' she replied firmly. 'I don't want nothing. I just want to go home.'

'Stay here a minute,' he ordered. 'I shall be a minute at most. Lock the door after me if you're worried.' He crossed to the other side of the building into the clerks' room. The place was empty. Charles picked up Sally's coat and returned to her.

'He has gone,' he reported. Sally was sitting where he had left her, looking forlorn. Charles drew up another chair alongside her.

'Now, what do you want to do?'

'Like I said: I want to go home.'

'No, I mean so far as Kellett-Brown is concerned. You are quite entitled to call the police and have him charged with indecent assault.'

'No!' she replied very firmly. 'No,' she repeated, 'I couldn't do that.'

'I'd come with you,' Charles offered. 'Maybe we should give your mother a call?'

'It's not that,' she said. Her voice became softer, more controlled. 'He's a horrible old man . . . a dirty old—no—' she said, seeing Charles's half-smile, 'I mean he doesn't wash. And he smells, too. But . . . I know what you're going to say, Mr Howard . . . but I feel sorry for him. He's lonely—'

'I don't care how lonely he is! That doesn't give him the right to go flashing, and grabbing at you like that!'

'I know. But I couldn't get him sent to prison—'

'It might not be prison, you know—'

'I don't care,' she said adamantly.

'I think you ought to think about it, Sally. Don't make any snap decisions. You could easily have been raped.'

'No I couldn't. I could punch his lights out any time,' she said vehemently. Charles looked at her with surprise and some admiration. He believed it too. 'I was just a bit frightened,' she went on. 'That's all.'

'So you're happy just to forget it? Smile and say "Good morning" to him tomorrow? Pretend it didn't happen?'

The girl looked at him with wide eyes. She hadn't thought about that.

'I . . . don't know. I'll have to talk to me Mum.' She paused, her brow contracting in thought. 'Ooh, I'm gonna have to give up the job, aren't I?' The tears began to fall thick and fast now. 'I could never face him again. And they're never gonna throw him out, are they?' She looked up at Charles, eyes streaming rivulets of black mascara down her cheeks.

'I don't know. We'll have to see. Anyway, if you're absolutely sure you don't want me to call the police, I agree you should go home. I'll walk you up to Fleet Street, and you can get a cab.'

'I ain't got enough for a cab from here to Romford.'

'That's alright. It can come out of petty cash. It's the least Chambers can do.'

Charles helped her into her coat, handed her her bag and, leaving his papers where they lay, escorted her out of Chambers.

'It might be a good idea not to come in tomorrow, eh?' he said. She nodded in reply. 'I'll tell Stanley you weren't well tonight, and that I sent you home. OK?'

She nodded again, and sniffed. 'Tell him it's me throat. I've been coughing all day, anyway.'

'Fine.'

Charles locked the doors behind him and they set

off. Sally felt for his hand as they walked down the stairs.

'Thanks, Charlie,' she said, looking up at him with a smile, and squeezing his hand. It was the first time she had ever used his first name, and it was, according to the protocol of the Bar, quite wrong. She could never have done it with any other member of Chambers, and they both knew it. Charles was flattered. He smiled back at her. 'I don't know what I'd have done, if you wasn't in,' she continued. He squeezed her hand in reply.

Chapter Nine

Charles left home the next morning at 6.30 a.m. He had to complete the work he had left unfinished before he went to the Old Bailey. He also had business in Lincoln's Inn.

The building where Kellett-Brown had his room was occupied on the ground floor by barristers' chambers. Charles passed the board that announced the names of the barristers practising inside, noting, as he passed, that he did not recognise a single name. He climbed the rickety wooden staircase with care. The second floor housed a firm of solicitors and a book-binding business. The staircase leading to Kellett-Brown's room on the top floor was particularly ill-lit and Charles had to feel his way up step by step. He finally came to a door at the head of the staircase. There appeared to be no bell or knocker, so Charles rapped on the door with his knuckles. There was no sound from within. He repeated his knock, much harder this time, and, after a few seconds, he heard movement.

'What do you want? Do you know what time it is?' came Kellett-Brown's querulous voice.

'It's Charles Howard, from Chambers.'

There was a pause. Then: 'What the bloody hell do you want?'

'Will you open the door, Ivor? This is very important.'

'For God's sake, Howard, go away. I'll be in Chambers this afternoon if you want me.'

Charles could hear Kellett-Brown's footsteps retreating from the front door.

'I suggest you open up now, Ivor. I doubt you'll want me to shout through the door, but if you force me to do so, I shall. It's about Sally.'

The footfalls ceased. Charles could imagine the old man, motionless, only a few feet away from him on the other side of the door, debating whether to open up or not. Eventually, curiosity—or fear—got the better of him, and the footsteps approached again. Charles heard a chain being withdrawn, and a bolt sliding out of its place. The door opened. Kellett-Brown faced him, wearing an old blue dressing gown, skinny pyjamaed legs sticking out underneath.

'You'd better come in,' he said.

Charles walked past him into a smelly darkened room, overcrowded with heavy furniture. There were a number of small birds on perches dotted about the room, apparently asleep. Kellett-Brown closed the door and turned to Charles.

'Well?' He whispered, apparently so as not to disturb his pets.

'I'll come straight to the point,' replied Charles. 'I was in Chambers last night when you assaulted Sally.'

'Assaulted Sally? What on earth are you talking about?'

'You can pretend not to know if you like, Ivor, but if you take that line, you'll have to continue it with the police. I'm not here to mess about. I know what sort of state Sally was in last night after you finished with her, and if necessary I'll give evidence of exactly what I saw.'

'The girl's raving!'

Charles shook his head. 'Very well,' he said quietly. 'You may expect a call from the police.' He took a step towards the door, but Kellett-Brown did not move. 'Do you want to reconsider?' asked Charles. 'I have told no one about it as yet, and if you choose, that's the way it can remain.'

'How do you mean?'

'I mean that I'm sure Sally will not press charges, and last night's events will be forgotten.'

'And what am I supposed to do to prevent these false charges being brought against me? You do realise that this is blackmail? You could be prosecuted yourself for this!'

'I am trying, Ivor, to save your reputation, such as it is, and prevent this whole thing being dragged through the courts. I am also trying to save a young girl's job.'

'I repeat: what's the price?'

'Your resignation from Chambers, effective as from today.'

'Preposterous!' replied Kellett-Brown.

Charles pushed past him and opened the door. 'It's entirely up to you. If, by the time I return to Chambers this afternoon, I have heard nothing, I shall report the matter to the Head of Chambers. What he does then is up to him. Likewise, it will be up to Sally to decide whether or not she wishes to prosecute. In my view, there's absolutely no doubt that she should. Good morning.'

Charles slammed the door after him and descended the staircase. There was a considerable fluttering and squawking behind him.

Once at Chancery Court, Charles continued reading his new brief until 9 a.m., hastily dictated an Advice and an indictment to be typed, and walked down to the Old Bailey. Before leaving he left a note on Stanley's desk saying that Sally had become ill the night before while still at Chambers, and that she would not be in for the day.

In the Old Bailey's Bar Mess he ordered an enormous fried breakfast, and settled down with a cup of coffee to read the newspaper.

At 10.20 a.m. it was announced that His Honour Judge

Galbraith was dealing with a bail application and that all parties in the case of *The Queen versus Plumber* were released until 11.00 a.m. That was in due course extended to 11.30 a.m. and then midday. The case finally resumed at 12.15 p.m. By 4.20 p.m. the evidence for the Crown was completed apart from the evidence of Sands. His Honour adjourned until the morning.

Charles walked directly back to the Temple. As he entered the clerks' room, Stanley beamed at him in a most unusual way.

'Have you been drinking, Stanley?' asked Charles with a smile.

'Not a drop, thank you, sir. Mr Kellett-Brown has resigned from Chambers. Came in at lunchtime, paid a quarter's rent, took his desk, and departed. Ill-health, he said.'

'Well I never,' said Charles. 'He always looked perfectly well to me.'

Charles went to his room, and closed the door. He picked up the telephone and called Sally.

'You can come back tomorrow,' he told her. 'Mr Kellett-Brown has resigned, and he has already gone.'

'Have you said anything, sir?' she answered, reverting to formality. Charles was for some reason disappointed. His short moment of intimacy with the bright nineteen-year-old was over, and could never be referred to again.

'Not a word,' he assured her. 'It's between you and me, and not another soul.'

'I'll see you tomorrow then, Mr Howard. I'll phone Stanley now and tell him I'm feeling better.'

'Fine. Goodbye.'

'Bye, sir.'

Henrietta was in the garden when Charles arrived home, wearing jeans and a sun hat, a pair of pruning shears in her gloved hands.

'What are you doing here?' she asked with surprise.

'Remember me? I live here,' he said cheerfully,

72

approaching her and kissing her on the cheek. She absently kissed the air beside his face.

'Yes, but it's only six-thirty. You've not been home this early for years. Are you ill?' she asked, almost serious.

'No. I'm perfectly well. I thought we might spend some time together, that's all.'

'Good God, Charles, this is all rather unexpected. After all this time, you want to play at being husband for a night?'

Charles looked at her with his large brown eyes, the exaggerated pout on his lips not entirely hiding the fact that the remark had stung. She was almost his height, slim, with an oval face framed with silky chestnut hair. She looked, if anything, better than she did the day he met her at Cambridge, eleven years before. On that day he had been dressed as a penguin—part of some student rag accosting passers-by—and she had been late for a lecture. He had held her by her skinny arms until she had either made a donation of at least a pound, or had promised to meet him for a drink. Having almost no money with her, she had been forced to accept the latter.

That meeting had been only two weeks after he had decided to change his name, one week after the awful scene with his father. The full implications of his decision had then yet to sink in, and he was still playing at being Charles Howard, English gentleman. Perhaps that was why he had the courage to grab her wrists in his flippers and demand a date with her, because it wasn't Charles Horowitz asking, but this new, dangerous, dashing Charles Howard. Everyone knew her, of course. The Hon Henrietta Lloyd-Williams, eldest daughter of Viscount Brandeth, one of the fastest of the 'fast set' as Charles's father used to call them, and yet with an unpretentious, easy manner and, so it was said, a good brain too.

What persuaded her to go out with this dark-eyed, persuasive penguin she did not know. His arrogance was quite unlike the self-assurance of the well-bred and wealthy young men with whom she had grown up. It was dangerous, almost bellicose. It invited challenge, so much so that for the first few months of their relationship part of the attraction was her anticipation that something, *anything*, might happen when she was with him. There was also a certain bitterness about him, but coloured by a gentle self-deprecating humour that made him appear vulnerable. It was certainly his ability to make her laugh that persuaded her to see him again, but it was the 'little boy lost' that so endeared him to her. That so big a man, both in intellect and in size (for although not tall, he was as broad as a bull), could at times look so perplexed by the universe was indeed endearing. It was on the day that his vulnerability ceased to touch her, but irritated her instead, that she realised something was wrong. But by then it was too late. They had married, without telling anyone. Two days before the ceremony he had told her that he was in fact Jewish, by birth at least, but not practising. That didn't matter to her, she'd said, as long as they could continue to eat bacon and oysters. Not practising—someone should have told her that to be Jewish doesn't require practice.

Her parents loathed him, albeit in a polite way. There was nothing wrong with Jewish furriers from the East End of London, of course, nor indeed with their clever sons. They were just so . . . *unsuitable*, as in-laws. As far as his parents were concerned, it was much simpler. Their eldest son, the clever one, the apple of their eye, had died. They said prayers and mourned him for a week, and then no one mentioned him at all. (Henrietta's family were, of course, quite grateful to them for this attitude: one Jew connected to the family was bad enough – an entire brood would have been intolerable.)

David, Charles's younger brother, was once caught reading a clipping from the *Daily Telegraph* about a case where Charles's name was mentioned. David was 22 at the time, but that didn't stop his father beating him as efficiently as his 66-year-old arms and heart condition would allow. Charles had discovered by chance that the family had moved, when he had to view a building plot nearby for one of his rare property cases. Most of their street had been demolished. Where his parents were, and whether they were both still alive, he neither knew nor cared, or so he pretended to himself.

'I thought perhaps we could go out for a meal,' said Charles.

'I'm sorry, Charles,' Henrietta replied, with sincerity, 'but I can't. I've been invited to the Robertsons' for dinner; they have some friends over from the States, and they're holding a small party for them.'

'I'm sure Helen wouldn't mind if I came too.'

'She didn't invite you because you've never once kept a mid-week dinner arrangement since we've been married,' she replied, continuing with her pruning.

'I've told you a million times: don't exaggerate.'

'Alright; maybe not "never". But you have let them down on more than one occasion. It's a bit unfair to her to ask at this stage, don't you think? It's a small party, and it's starting in two hours. You'll throw her into a tizzy if you ask to come now. If you really want me to phone, I will.'

Charles pondered, and decided against it. 'OK; forget it.'

Henrietta stood, and came towards him. 'It was a nice idea. If you do it more often, I'll get used to it.'

She put her muddy, gloved, hands on his cheeks and pulled his head towards hers. She kissed him on the mouth.

'You smell nice,' he said. 'Like fresh washing.'

'You smell nice, too.'

'What of?' he asked.

'Just Charlie,' she answered, hugging him.

'I don't suppose . . .' he suggested.

'What don't you suppose?' she replied, snuggling closer to him.

'That you might develop a dreadful headache at about ten o'clock tonight which could mysteriously clear up on your arrival home?'

'Charlie! Whatever has come over you?'

'Nothing's come over me. I was hoping to come over you.'

'You're disgusting,' she said with a grin. 'Still, I'll see what can be arranged.'

Henrietta took his arm and they walked slowly down the garden.

'Charlie?'

'Present.'

'Can we both make a special effort? I know I've been a real bitch the last few weeks. And you—'

'I've been working too hard—' he interrupted.

'You've been distant, cold and thoughtless,' she corrected.

'Hmm.'

'I was adding it up this morning. I haven't seen you for more than six hours this whole week. That's three breakfasts, one trip to the shops, and an hour on Monday night—and that was only because your bloody computer broke down and you couldn't continue working.'

He sighed. 'It's this murder. And there's the fraud next month. They're both important—'

'—I know they are, and I'm proud of you, even though I think you're wasted doing this stuff. What does Daddy call it?'

' "The Verbals".'

'Yes, that. But I sometimes wonder how high our marriage is on your list of priorities.'

'We've been through this before, honey. If you got yourself a real job instead of this part-time rubbish, you wouldn't be waiting at home with nothing—'

'Rubbish!' she exclaimed. 'I don't know how you can say that, Charles. It's important work. Anyway, I don't want a full-time job. I want a family. I'm almost 31 and I'm getting too old!' she said, her voice faltering at the end.

'I know, I know, I know,' he said, trying to calm her. 'It's just that—'. He was interrupted by Fiona calling from the french windows.

'Is Charles in yet? Oh, you *are*. There's a chap called Stanley on the phone. He says it's very urgent.'

Charles looked at Henrietta. 'I'd better take it. I'll be right back.' He ran up the lawn and into the house where

Fiona handed him the telephone. Henrietta returned to her gardening, shaking her head to herself.

'Howard speaking,' Charles said.

'Hello, sir. It's Stanley, from Chambers. I've just had a call from Tony, the clerk to Mr Rhodes Thomas. Mr Rhodes Thomas has had an accident. It's not too bad, but apparently he's broken his thigh, and he'll be out of commission, in traction, for at least six weeks.'

Chapter Ten

'Jesus Christ! How did he do it?' asked Plumber.

'He slipped down the stairs at the Old Bailey. It must have been just after I left him last night. He's in Bart's, just opposite the court. I spoke to him on the phone last night, and he'll be in hospital for as long as six weeks. Anyway, we're pretty confident that we can get the case adjourned.'

'What, for six weeks?'

'I don't know about that. It will probably be more than six weeks before he's back at work, possibly three or four months. It's a very bad break. I'm not sure the Court will allow as long as that. It may be better to get a new silk in before then.'

'You mean start the trial again?'

'We'll have to do that, whatever happens. The jury can be sent away for a couple of days, but certainly not for weeks. They'll have to be discharged.'

'And how long will it take to find another silk?'

'I don't know. The case is not difficult in terms of what's

got to be read and assimilated; it's just a question of finding someone who's free.'

'That means someone who's second-rate.'

'Not at all,' answered Charles. 'Mr Rhodes Thomas was my first choice, but there are plenty of excellent leaders.'

'Yeh, but I'm under pressure to find one quickly. I've been on remand for months. I can't go through this again, Mr Howard. I can't sleep, I can't eat, I'm at me wits' end. I don't want to put the case off at all. Why can't you do it? Don't you feel up to it?'

'It's not that. You are charged with the most serious offence, and you're entitled to leading counsel.'

'I'm entitled to counsel of my choice, right? Well, one of them's got crocked, but I've still got one left, and I've got confidence in him. I don't want the case put off or started again.'

Charles looked at Collins, who shrugged. 'You are aware,' said Charles to Plumber, 'that I have less experience than a QC would have?'

'Yeh. But, like I said, I have faith in you. I know you'll do as well as anyone.'

'Well?' asked Charles of Collins as they left the cells.

'You've had express instructions from the client, Charles. He wants you to carry on. In fact, this is about as straightforward a case of murder as one can imagine. All you have to do is discredit one witness, and you've done that hundreds of times. I think you can cope.'

R v Plumber – Transcript of Evidence – Tuesday 14th September 1982

Sands: Examination in chief

Mr Hogg:	Would you please give the Court your full name?
Witness:	Charles Reginald Sands.
Mr Hogg:	Your present address.
Witness:	Brixton Prison.
Mr Hogg:	Two days ago, you pleaded guilty to robbing the

78

Express Dairies, London North Depot, of £98,530.16 on
5th March this year.

Witness: Aye, I did.

Mr Hogg: Did you commit that robbery alone or with others?

Witness: I did it w' him.

Judge: Let the record show that the witness pointed to the
defendant, Plumber.

Mr Hogg: Where any others involved?

Witness: No.

Mr Hogg: Were any firearms used in the robbery?

Witness: Aye. We each took an imitation, at least that's what I
thought.

Mr Hogg: Would you please show the witness Exhibits 4 and 5?

Witness: They're the ones. I cannae say which was mine or
Plumber's, 'cos they were identical.

Mr Hogg: Who obtained these guns?

Witness: I did.

Mr Hogg: When you obtained them, were you anxious to obtain real
or imitation firearms?

Witness: I wouldnae have gone on the job at all had I known that
real shooters were to be used.

Mr Hogg: What was your part in the robbery?

Witness: We both went in. I stood by the door and collared the
employees as they came through; Plumber handcuffed
them to the pipes. We took two cars, well a van and a
car. Plumber was the getaway driver. The van was used
to block the alley after us.

Mr Hogg: There came a time when a member of one of the crews
returning to the Depot was reluctant to enter, did there
not?

Witness: There did.

Mr Hogg: Will you tell the jury what happened then?

Witness: The wee laddie on the door opened up, but the fella
wouldnae come in. He must have been suspicious, 'cos
he ran off, shouting something.

Mr Hogg: What happened then?

Witness: I rushed out tae grab him. He was about ten yards ahead
of me, running to his van.

Mr Hogg: Where was Plumber at this stage?

Witness:	I thought he was still inside, 'cos that was his job, right? Guarding the employees. But then I heard something behind me, and the next second there was this bang. The guard caught it right in the middle of the back. Blew him off the ground and down by the van.
Mr Hogg:	Did you see what had caused the noise?
Witness:	Not till I turned. There was Plumber wi' that in his hand and smoke coming from it.
Judge:	Let the record show that the witness indicated Exhibit 2. Have a look at it, Mr Sands, please.
Witness:	That's the one.
Mr Hogg:	Show us how Plumber was holding it, please. (Witness takes exhibit.) You are holding it at waist level with your right hand on the butt and the left supporting the barrels. Where was it pointing?
Witness:	Straight at the dead man, or at least, where he had been when he was upright.
Mr Hogg:	What happened then?
Witness:	I ran up tae Plumber. He was, eh, stunned, like.
Mr Hogg:	How do you mean?
Witness:	Well, he was, like, frozen in position. I shouted at him.
Mr Hogg:	What did you shout?
Witness:	I cannae recall that now. 'Let's go!', or something like that.
Mr Hogg:	Did he react?
Witness:	Not immediately. I had tae grab him, turn him round. We ran back inside, grabbed the money, and left. I'm sure he didnae mean tae do it. It was just the panic.
Judge:	It's for the jury to decide if he meant to do it or not, Mr Sands, not for you. Please don't make comments like that. You are here to answer questions.
Witness:	Certainly, my Lord. I just wanted, eh, tae help him out if I could.
Mr Hogg:	Wait there, Mr Sands; there will be more questions for you.

(End of examination in chief)

Sands: Cross-examination

Judge: Mr Howard?

Mr Howard: Thank you, my Lord. Mr Sands: as far as you were concerned, two imitation guns were to be taken on this robbery?

Witness: That's right.

Mr Howard: You've told us that you were responsible for obtaining them?

Witness: Aye.

Mr Howard: So you know where one can obtain such things?

Witness: Aye, I do. Lots of shops sell them.

Mr Howard: What shop did you buy them from?

Witness: Er, I didnae buy them from a shop.

Mr Howard: You got them through less orthodox channels?

Witness: You could say that.

Mr Howard: Illegally?

Witness: I don't know.

Mr Howard: You got them from a man in a launderette. That's not likely to be a lawful source, is it, Mr Sands?

Witness: No.

Mr Howard: That 'unorthodox channel' is the sort of channel that could have provided you with a real gun, had you wanted one.

Witness: I don't know. I didnae ask him.

Mr Howard: If you were only after imitation guns, which you have told us can be bought legitimately from 'lots of shops', why did you use less orthodox channels?

Witness: (Pause.) I don't know.

Mr Howard: It was not because you wanted a real gun too, and that had to be obtained illegally?

Witness: No.

Mr Howard: Why then?

Witness: I don't know. I suppose I didnae want the police asking at shops an' that.

Mr Howard: Let's move on. How did you feel about Mr Plumber's having taken a real gun with him?

Witness: I've already said. I wouldnae have gone had I known.

Mr Howard: By that, I take it that you disapprove of real firearms.

Witness: Aye, I do. They're liable to go off.

Mr Howard:	You must have been furious with Plumber then, for taking the shotgun and for using it?
Judge:	That's two questions, Mr Howard. First, Mr Sands, were you furious that he had taken the shotgun?
Witness:	If I'd known before I went, I wouldnae have been exactly furious, but not happy. I woulda told him to leave it behind.
Judge:	Were you furious that he had used it?
Witness:	I couldnae believe what he'd done. He had no need to. Once the guy had seen the imitation, he woulda stopped. They're no' armed, those men. Aye, I was furious.
Mr Howard:	Why?
Witness:	You ask me why? Jesus, the guy had been shot in the back! Robbery's one thing — murder, that's something else altogether.
Mr Howard:	Your concern then was that you might be implicated in a murder that you had no part in?
Witness:	Exactly.
Mr Howard:	Did you express that concern to Mr Plumber?
Witness:	I don't follow.
Mr Howard:	You've told us that you were unhappy that he took a real gun along with him, and furious that he used it. Did you tell Plumber that?
Witness:	Well, I gave him a right bollocking in the car, but what could I do? He'd already shot the guy by the time I knew what was going on.
Mr Howard:	So by the time you are in the car, your principal concern is to get away?
Witness:	Obviously.
Mr Howard:	You don't want to hang around where someone has been shot?
Witness:	Correct.
Mr Howard:	You don't want to be tied in any way to a murder of which you say you are innocent?
Witness:	Correct.
Mr Howard:	Where did you go immediately after the robbery?
Witness:	To my flat.
Mr Howard:	What did you go there for?
Witness:	To divvy up.

82

Mr Howard:	Did you go there directly?
Witness:	We did. Well, we changed cars once on the way, and dumped the guns and masks and that.
Mr Howard:	Where did you do that?
Witness:	We left them locked in the car, and scrapped the car.
Mr Howard:	When you say 'locked in the car', it's true, is it not, that they were left hidden under the rear seat?
Witness:	Aye.
Mr Howard:	And when you say 'scrapped', what do you mean?
Witness:	A compacter. We sold the car tae a scrap metal dealer I know, and he agreed to squash it. He didnae do it though. He got greedy.
Mr Howard:	I'm sorry?
Witness:	Well, we paid him over the odds to squash it, but he obviously took a fancy to it, 'cos it was still in the yard when the police went there.
Mr Howard:	I see. And how did you get back to your flat from the scrap dealer?
Witness:	In ma own car.
Mr Howard:	You scrapped the BMW before you went back to your flat?
Witness:	Yes. I've already said.
Mr Howard:	Within minutes of the robbery?
Witness:	Not minutes, no.
Mr Howard:	How long, then?
Witness:	Within half an hour.
Mr Howard:	That's thirty minutes.
Witness:	OK, within thirty minutes.
Mr Howard:	And the reason you did that, I assume, was because you didn't want to risk being found in possession of incriminating evidence one moment longer than necessary.
Witness:	You could say.
Mr Howard:	I *do* say, Mr Sands. What do you say?
Witness:	Well, if you like. It's just common sense. I didnae want tae be connected to any of it.
Mr Howard:	Indeed. The one item of evidence that you would have been most concerned to get away from, would have been the shotgun.
Witness:	Not necessarily.

Mr Howard:	But everything else ties you to a robbery. The shotgun ties you to a potential murder.
Witness:	Well?
Mr Howard:	So the item you would most want to get rid of is the shotgun. (Pause.) Isn't that right, Mr Sands?
Witness:	I suppose so.
Mr Howard:	We know from the police evidence that Mr Plumber gave them the name of the scrap yard, and that they recovered the car, as you say, before it was compacted.
Witness:	So?
Mr Howard:	They found the two imitation handguns, two masks, and some pairs of handcuffs, but no shotgun. What did you do with it?
Witness:	I didnae do anything wi' it. Plumber had it. I never touched the thing.
Mr Howard:	So you placed the other items under the seat?
Witness:	Aye.
Mr Howard:	And locked up?
Witness:	Aye.
Mr Howard:	But you did not put the shotgun there too?
Witness:	No.
Mr Howard:	Why not, Mr Sands?
Witness:	It wasnae mine.
Mr Howard:	But you have just told the jury that the thing you most wanted to distance yourself from was that shotgun. There you are getting rid of all the other evidence, but you keep the shotgun. Why?
Witness:	I told you, I didnae keep the shotgun. Plumber had it.
Mr Howard:	And you let him bring it into your car, driving to your flat, when you wanted it nowhere near you? You couldn't have wanted to distance yourself that much from it: you let him hang on to it, while sitting in your car!
Judge:	I think counsel's asking you a question Mr Sands, although he's not phrased it as such. Why did you permit Plumber to bring the shotgun with him in your car?
Witness:	I don't know. I just did.
Mr Howard:	What happened when you arrived at your flat?
Witness:	We divvied up the money.

Mr Howard:	That must have taken some time, counting out and dividing £98,000.
Witness:	Maybe.
Mr Howard:	How long?
Witness:	I don't know; an hour maybe.
Mr Howard:	And you let Plumber leave the shotgun in your car all that time?
Witness:	No.
Mr Howard:	In your flat then?
Witness:	(Pause.) I cannae remember what happened to it.
Mr Howard:	From when do you not remember?
Witness:	I don't know. I'm not even sure I saw it in the car at all. Maybe he did leave it at the scrap yard, but someone found it.
Judge:	Mr Sands, in answer to a question from me, not two minutes ago, you said you didn't know why you let Plumber bring the shotgun in your own car, you just did. So you must remember it at that stage.
Witness:	I must remember it then, yes.
Mr Howard:	So you remember it in your car. I suppose from what you've already told us, you would not have been happy about it being there?
Witness:	Not really, no.
Mr Howard:	Even less happy about it being brought into your flat?
Witness:	Aye, correct.
Mr Howard:	Why did you not tell Mr Plumber to get rid of it at the scrap yard?
Witness:	I didnae think to. I must have been in too much of a panic.
Mr Howard:	Yes, but your panic was *because* of the shotgun. Are you really telling this jury that, although you wanted nothing to do with the shotgun, and having had the opportunity to get rid of it, you allowed Mr Plumber to bring it into your car and maybe your flat?
Witness:	I don't know. I suppose so.
Judge:	Mr Howard, would that be a convenient point at which to break for luncheon?
Mr Howard:	It would, my Lord.
Judge:	Two o'clock, members of the jury.

Chapter Eleven

(continued)

Mr Howard:	When you were first arrested for the offence of robbery, you were interviewed under caution, were you not?
Witness:	Aye, I was.
Mr Howard:	That interview was tape-recorded.
Witness:	Aye.
Mr Howard:	And in it, you said that there was a third man on the robbery, and that it was he who took and used the shotgun.
Witness:	I said that, yes.
Mr Howard:	That was a lie, wasn't it?
Witness:	It was, but I only said it because he threatened me if I didnae.
Judge:	You pointed at the defendant. Are you saying that Plumber threatened you?
Witness:	I am. Well, ma family.
Mr Howard:	When did he make this threat?
Witness:	On the telephone, the day after the robbery.
Mr Howard:	And what, exactly, did he say?
Witness:	He said that he reckoned we might be caught, and that if we were, we should both give the same story, about the third man.
Mr Howard:	Did you agree to this plan?
Witness:	No' at first. Only after he made the threats.
Mr Howard:	What threats? What exactly did he say?
Witness:	He said that if I didnae agree, he would see to ma family.
Mr Howard:	He wasn't going to see to you personally?
Witness:	You gotta be joking. Him?
Mr Howard:	I take it that you are not personally afraid of Mr Plumber?
Witness:	Correct.
Mr Howard:	Exactly what members of your family did he refer to?
Witness:	He didnae say.
Mr Howard:	Does he know your family?

Witness:	I don't know.
Mr Howard:	Well, what family do you have?
Witness:	I've got a mother.
Mr Howard:	Is that all?
Witness:	Eh . . . I got an uncle too.
Mr Howard:	Where does your mother live?
Witness:	I don't know. I havenae kept in touch. She remarried a while back.
Mr Howard:	To whom?
Witness:	Some chap. I cannae remember his name.
Mr Howard:	Where does you uncle live?
Witness:	He used to live in a place called Helmsdale.
Mr Howard:	Where's that?
Witness:	It's on the north-east coast of Scotland, about 100 miles north of Inverness.
Mr Howard:	Have you ever introduced Mr Plumber to your mother?
Witness:	No.
Mr Howard:	To your uncle?
Witness:	No.
Mr Howard:	So, to summarise: you neither know your mother's name nor her address, and your uncle *used* to live in the wilds of north-eastern Scotland. Correct so far?
Witness:	Aye.
Mr Howard:	Mr Plumber has met neither of them, and probably didn't know that they existed.
Witness:	Maybe.
Mr Howard:	This must have been a mighty powerful threat in your mind, eh, Mr Sands? (Laughter.) Well, let's move on. In August this year, you had a visit in Brixton from Detective Inspector Wheatley.
Witness:	Yes.
Mr Howard:	You asked your solicitors to get in touch with him, and as a result, he paid you a visit?
Witness:	I don't remember.
Mr Howard:	That's his evidence. Do you disagree?
Witness:	I suppose not.
Mr Howard:	And at that visit, you told Inspector Wheatley that you

	had lied before about the third man, and that Plumber had carried the shotgun?
Witness:	Yes.
Mr Howard:	You obviously felt by then that your dear lost mother was no longer under any threat. (Laughter.)
Judge:	That's a comment, Mr Howard, not a question.
Mr Howard:	I apologise, my Lord. What I should ask you, Mr Sands, is this: did the Inspector believe you at first?
Mr Hogg:	My Lord, I object to that question. It is of no relevance to the jury whether the Inspector believed this witness or not; the question is, do the jury believe him?
Judge:	That's right, isn't it, Mr Howard?
Mr Howard:	Put thus, my Lord, yes. But the purpose of the question is not to usurp the function of the jury. I wish to ask about the motives of this witness's discussing other matters at the same time.
Judge:	You may certainly ask about other things spoken about, and Mr Sands's motives, but not about how they affected the officer's mind.
Mr Howard:	Very well. Mr Sands: in addition to telling Inspector Wheatley about what you say was Plumber's role, you gave the officer other information, did you not?
Witness:	(Pause.) Do I have to answer that question, my Lord?
Judge:	You do.
Witness:	I . . . er . . . I really don't remember now. It was a couple of months ago.
Mr Howard:	Do try and assist the jury, Mr Sands. I'm sure you'll remember if you think hard about it.
Witness:	I cannae recall what we spoke about.
Mr Howard:	Let me refresh your memory, Mr Sands. You gave the police information about other crimes, didn't you?
Witness:	I don't know.
Mr Howard:	You informed on a number of your friends.
(Disturbance in the gallery. Shouting at the witness.)	
Judge:	If this noise does not cease immediately, I shall clear the Court!
Mr Howard:	You turned grass, didn't you, Mr Sands?
Witness:	No, I never!
Mr Howard:	Do you wish me to call Inspector Wheatley to prove that

	that's a lie?
Witness:	No.
Mr Howard:	Then the truth please, Mr Sands. You informed on a number of your criminal friends, did you not?
Witness:	I did.

(Continued disturbance in gallery.)

Judge:	Master at arms, take those men out! Any further person making any noise from the gallery will be committed for contempt forthwith! Carry on, Mr Howard.
Mr Howard:	The reason you informed on your colleagues, was so the Inspector would believe that Plumber, and not you, used the shotgun, isn't that right? (Pause.) Do you intend answering that question? (Pause.) May I take it that you have no answer? (Pause.) As a result of the information you gave to the police, you have received a lighter sentence for the robbery, haven't you?
Witness:	I don't know.
Judge:	Sentence is a matter for me, Mr Howard. The jury is entitled to know that I was made aware of certain matters in deciding sentence.
Mr Howard:	Thank you, my Lord. Furthermore, Mr Sands, having been originally charged with murder in the alternative to Mr Plumber, the charge was dropped against you.
Witness:	Aye, it was.
Mr Howard:	I suggest to you, Mr Sands, that in giving evidence to this jury you are not in the slightest motivated to tell the truth.
Witness:	I am telling the truth.
Mr Howard:	I suggest that your sole motive was to escape conviction for murder yourself, and if that meant dropping Plumber and all your other mates in it, then so much the worse for them.
Witness:	No.
Mr Howard:	You were the one with the gun, Mr Sands.
Witness:	No.
Mr Howard:	*You* murdered William Wright.
Witness:	No, Plumber did it, I tell you.

(End of cross-examination)

| Mr Hogg: | I have no re-examination. Does my Lord have any questions for the witness? |

Judge:	No, thank you.
Mr Hogg:	That is the case for the Crown.
Judge:	Mr Howard?
Mr Howard:	There is a matter of law, upon which I should like to address your Lordship.
Judge:	I suspected there might be, Mr Howard. Members of the jury, counsel has a point of law for me to decide and, as questions of law are for me alone, I shall ask you to leave the jury box. I do not anticipate that this will take long. I shall send for you in about ten minutes.

Chapter Twelve

R v Plumber — Transcript of Evidence — Tuesday 14th September 1982

(continued)

Judge:	Mr Howard submits to me that Mr Plumber has no case to answer in respect of the murder charge. He concedes, as is submitted by Mr Hogg for the Crown, that in most cases the weight and credibility to be given to a witness are matters for the jury to consider. He however submits further that this is one of the borderline cases where the evidence is so tenuous, weak or inherently unreliable that no jury properly directed could convict the defendant, and that therefore I ought to stop the case. Mr Hogg agrees to the principle, but says that this is not such a borderline case.
	The foundation stone of the Crown's case is the evidence of a Charles Sands, who is conceded to be in the category of an accomplice. If that evidence in

	tenuous, weak or inherently unreliable the Crown cannot succeed. In deciding if the evidence is so tenuous or weak or inherently unreliable as to render it unsafe, I must apply my own judgment. I am therefore bound to say that in my view Mr Sands was a patently unreliable witness. His evidence is contradictory and, in my view, his motives for giving it, suspect in the extreme. I am of the view that no jury properly directed could possibly rely on his evidence with any safety, and I shall therefore direct the jury when they return to acquit Mr Plumber. Mr Hogg?
Mr Hogg:	My Lord?
Judge:	Before I ask the jury to return I feel constrained to express the view that in the light of the evidence that has been given, I am most concerned at the decision taken by the Crown to offer no evidence against Mr Sands. I am not a jury trying him, but it is my view that he has wrongly escaped conviction of murder. In the circumstances, I propose referring the matter to the DPP to see if any further action should be taken.

'If you don't let go of my hand, Mr Plumber, it will fall off!'

'I still don't know what to say, Mr Howard, it was terrific! I'll never be able to thank you enough,' said Plumber, still pumping Charles's hand.

'Take it easy now; you do have six years to serve for the robbery.'

'Yeh, but even that's a result. I'd, wasname, resigned meself to the same as Sands got, you know, nine. To get six, on top of getting off the murder, well . . .'

'You don't have anything like as bad a record as he does, don't forget,' said Collins.

'Not only that,' said Charles, grimly, 'but your six will be a doddle compared to his nine. He'll have to spend it all under rule 43—solitary.'

'That's right,' said Collins. 'As a grass his life inside is going to be hell.'

'I'd not thought about that,' replied Plumber. 'Still, serves him right. By the way, what was all that about the DPP?'

91

'In simple terms, if the Crown can find a way, by hook or by crook, to try Sands again for the murder, they'll do it.'

'Is that possible?' asked Collins.

'He's technically been acquitted once, and he can't be tried again for the same offence unless there was some technical defect, for example in the indictment. Of course, the other possibility open to the Crown would be to charge him with attempting to pervert the course of justice. That, I'm pleased to say, is not my problem.'

Charles's problem awaited him in the form of an envelope addressed to him in his pigeon-hole when he reached Chambers.

Howard
You may think you have won, but I assure you,
no filthy little Jew and his whore shall defeat
me. The disgrace you have made me suffer
will be as nothing to what I shall cause you. I
shall repay you with interest. Isn't that what
your race expects?

K-B

Charles read it, laughed, and threw it in the bin.

*SERIOUS CRIME FILE E4/1379/82 [Murder/robbery—
EXPRESS DAIRIES, LONDON NORTH DEPOT 5/3/82]*
   Memorandum for computer files:
   *Central Criminal Court Indictment No: 83/0012 (see
   linked indictment 82/1375–6)*
   *Charles Reginald SANDS (CRO E/6563/20) convicted on
   3rd February 1983 of attempting to pervert the course
   of public justice. Sentenced to 4 years imprisonment
   to run consecutive to present sentence of 9 years for
   armed robbery. No further action re: murder William
   Wright.*
   File ends.

Part Three
Six Years Later

Chapter Thirteen

Charles and Henrietta sat in icy silence for the entire journey to Chambers. Charles had turned on the car radio at one point, but Henrietta had leaned forward without a word and turned it off. When they arrived in the Temple, Henrietta got out of the car before Charles had turned off the ignition, and walked off up the stairs, leaving Charles to catch up. She arrived at the door to Chambers still ahead of him.

'Henrietta! You look wonderful!' Sebastian Campbell-Smythe opened the door to her, and the sound of the party floated downstairs to Charles.

'Thank you, Sebastian,' she said with warmth. 'How nice that there are some gentlemen who still know how to pay a compliment,' she continued, and sailed past him into the room. Sebastian looked over her head to Charles who arrived at that moment and wagged his finger at him.

'Tut tut,' he reproved Charles. 'Didn't you notice how ravishing your wife looked tonight?' he asked, making stirring motions with his right hand.

'She can kill at ten paces with that tongue of hers, Sebastian,' replied Charles, entering the room. 'When she's in that sort of mood, it's wiser not to open one's mouth, even with a compliment.'

Chambers was laid out for a party. The room usually occupied by Sir Geoffrey Duchere, the largest in Chambers, had been cleared, and now contained two large tables laden with food and drink. At the end of the corridor were the unattended instruments of a jazz trio. Two waitresses circulated among the guests with champagne and hors d'oeuvres. Most of the members of Chambers were already there with their wives. It had been the lateness of the Howards that had caused their present cold war. The guest of honour, Sir Geoffrey, soon to be His Honour Judge Sir Geoffrey Duchere, had still to arrive.

Charles wandered over to the makeshift bar and waited to be served. He looked to his left, and saw Sally.

'Hello Sally,' he said. 'You look lovely.'

'Thank you, sir,' she replied, blushing slightly at the compliment. She wore a strapless, and almost backless, evening dress in crimson, and she wore her dark hair up. Charles found himself wondering how the dress held itself up. He also found himself wondering, not for the first time, what she would look like with no dress on at all. She was certainly a beautiful girl and, until she opened her mouth, could easily have passed for one of the barristers' wives.

'Is Mrs Howard here?' she asked Charles.

For one bizarre moment, Charles thought that Sally was referring to his mother, notwithstanding that she had been Mrs Horowitz (and never Mrs Howard) for the last forty years. He smiled to himself.

'Yes she's here . . . somewhere.'

He cast his eyes around the room, not able to see Henrietta immediately. Then he caught sight of her in the far corner, deeply engrossed in conversation with Simon Ellison. Their heads were close together, as if sharing some confidence, and then they both laughed. Henrietta patted Ellison on the cheek. The gesture was affectionate, but at the same time patronising, and Ellison flushed. Then, as if she had known that he was observing her, Henrietta turned round and caught Charles's eye.

Her mouth hardened, and the smile died on her face. Charles considered for a moment if the whole scene might have been staged for his benefit. They had been invited to a dinner party only two weeks previously at which Henrietta had flirted outrageously with another of the guests, and had become progressively more furious when Charles ignored it. That evening had prompted an entire week of silence.

Ellison moved away from Henrietta and spoke quietly to Peter Finch, one of the senior members of Chambers. They had a brief whispered conversation, Finch nodded, and then stepped quietly into a side room, closing the door behind him. It looked to Charles as if there was a telephone call for him.

Laurence Corbett was already in the room, sitting at Finch's desk. 'Hello, Peter,' he said, getting up unhurriedly as the older man came in. 'Borrowed your desk for a moment.'

'What is it, Laurence?' asked Finch. He was in his middle fifties, with long grey hair swept back to conceal his bald patch. When it was windy the thin mat of hair would sometimes fall forward over his face like a silver curtain, much to the merriment of his pupil. He had watery grey eyes, and he blinked frequently.

'A few of the chaps and I have been chatting about the succession, and I have been asked to canvass your views.'

'I wouldn't have thought my views were very important,' replied Finch. 'We all know who's going to be Head of Chambers.'

'That's not a safe assumption,' said Corbett obliquely.

'What do you mean?'

'Well . . . we wondered if you would like to stand?'

'Me?' said Finch, genuinely astonished. 'I've no ambitions in that direction.'

'Liar!' said Corbett with a grin.

Finch spread his hands in admission. 'OK. I couldn't afford the rent. The Inn wouldn't have me.'

'They might, if a number of us stood as joint guarantors.'

Finch thought about that for a moment. 'You're saying that if I were to stand against Bob for the tenancy from the Inn, you and some others would support my application? Which others?'

'Enough.'

'No. I want to know exactly who. A contest for the place would be extremely divisive, and . . . well, I may have had my differences with Bob over the years, but I will not be responsible for splitting Chambers.'

'I can't tell you at the moment. Just believe me.'

Finch sat at his desk and looked up at Corbett, who leaned nonchalantly against the wall. 'And what would you want from me?' he asked shrewdly.

Corbett smiled. 'Sack the "Little Toad".'

'Oh, not again, Laurence. You've raised this half a dozen times, in Chambers meetings and outside. What *have* you got against the poor man?'

'You must be joking, Peter. Do *you* like his child molesters sitting in the waiting room? How do your banker clients like sitting next to unshaven derelicts, who smoke roll-ups and stink of cider?'

'Granted—'

'Have you noticed how long Stanley is out every afternoon checking the criminal courts lists? During the busiest time of the day? A hugely disproportionate time is given to one man's practice, at the expense of everyone else's. How many times do I have to say it? We are not set up to do crime here. He would be far better off somewhere else.'

Finch listened patiently, a small smile on his face. Then: 'You make a good, rational case, Laurence. But we all know the truth: for reasons which I don't understand, you simply loathe him. That's all it is, right? You just can't bear him.'

'Well, can you? He's an arrogant, common barrow boy, just like his clients. Anyway, that's hardly the point. There are plenty of perfectly valid grounds for sacking him, if you needed them, which you don't. The tenant of the Inn can give notice to any barrister in Chambers. We are all your licensees.'

The door suddenly opened and a couple of the junior members of Chambers entered. 'Oh, sorry,' the first apologised.

'That's alright,' said Corbett. 'Why don't you both stay?'

'Have you . . .' asked one of them of Corbett, indicating to Finch.

'Just doing it,' replied Corbett. 'Well?' he asked, returning to Finch. The door swung to silently, and the two young men leaned against the desk on the far side of the room.

'I'm not sure. I can't say it isn't attractive, but I don't think there will be enough support. I think Bob's got it all sewn up. He's very popular. You'd need at least twelve to vote against him, and I can't see . . .' His voice faltered as he saw Corbett's face. 'You've got twelve?' he asked.

'In fact we have fourteen.'

'I don't believe it.'

Finch looked towards the others, and received a nodded confirmation. Finch wavered. His little pale eyes watered at the prospect, but then he began to shake his head. Corbett took several steps towards him, and leaned over the desk menacingly.

'Why don't you face facts, Peter? Your practice is going nowhere—' Finch spluttered a half-protest but Corbett held up a finger to silence him '—I've looked in the diary: you've only had two decent court appearances in the last six weeks, and your desk's empty. Don't tell me you're doing paperwork, because I know you aren't. You're filling in. You've had it, and inside you know it. If you're going to be able to keep the twins at Buckingham for the next two years, you've got to get an appointment. And we both know that that is pretty unlikely. But as Head of Chambers, well, we all know how much difference that might make. Principles are fine, but they don't pay university fees.'

* * *

99

Charles sat on a chair near the clerks' room, nursing his drink. Henrietta had disappeared some time ago. He wasn't sure whether she had gone home, or was just in one of the other rooms, but he didn't care enough to go looking for her. Sally glanced over at him every now and then, feeling sorry for him. He looked so miserable! There were times when she could quite fancy him, even though he was a bit old.

Charles stood up, drained his glass, and made for the door. He was intercepted by his Head of Chambers. His Honour had arrived an hour late, already quite the worse for drink. He had made an impromptu and totally unintelligible speech, and had started the dancing. Thus far, Charles had managed to avoid him. Geoffrey Duchere's bonhomie was all that was required to give the evening the *coup de grâce*.

'Ah, Charlie!' he said, putting his arm around Charles's shoulder. 'I shall miss you, you and your tacky little clients.'

'Will you, Geoffrey?'

'I certainly shall. You know, I don't mind telling you now, I was against your coming in. But you came, and I don't mind admitting it: I was wrong. Thoroughly nice chap . . . and I can tell you, you know, you're going places. I admire someone who doesn't let his background hold him back.'

'Thank you, Geoffrey,' said Charles, trying in vain to extricate himself. 'That will always be a great comfort to me.'

'You know, there's this Indian chappie. Ran a corner shop near me a few years back.' He frowned, trying to concentrate. 'Worked every hour God sent. Dammit if he doesn't own the whole bloody block now! Huge supermarket!'

'It's amazing, isn't it? Sorry, Geoffrey, but I really ought to find Henrietta.' Charles wrenched himself out of the other's grip.

'Certainly, old chap. You really must bring her round some time soon. Ages since we saw you socially.'

'Never.'

'What?'

'We've never seen you socially, Geoffrey.'

'Oh, of course, no one's been to the new house—only been there a few months—'

'Not to the new house, nor the old house, nor any bloody house! For all I know, you may live above your mate's supermarket.'

'You know, I could have sworn . . .'

'Bugger off, Geoffrey, there's a good chap,' said Charles, as he walked off. Charles opened the door and stalked off down the stairs. He reached the courtyard outside, and paused. For a second he couldn't think where he had parked the car. Then he remembered, and looked over to the space. It was empty.

'Bitch!' hissed Charles, pulling his collar up and setting off for the Strand.

Chapter Fourteen

'Charles? What on earth are you doing with that old jalopy?'

Charles withdrew his head from under the bonnet with some effort. It was the night after the party, and he was still suffering.

It was Simon Ellison, walking down the steps from Chambers.

'Oh, hello Simon. Frankly, I begin to wonder. I can't get the bloody thing to start.'

'Here, let me have a look.'

'Do you know anything about these things?' asked Charles, hopefully.

'Well, not about MGs in particular, but a bit about cars,' answered Ellison, dropping his briefcase, and looking under the bonnet. He started to fiddle with the distributor. 'What's happened to the Jag?' he asked. 'This is a bit of a come-down isn't it? It's, what, fifteen years old?'

'I leave the Jag in the village. Henrietta drove it back last night,' said Charles with feeling. Ellison did not appear to hear, but was instead inspecting closely the rusting metal to which the distributor was fixed. 'Since we moved out of town I've been commuting on the train,' continued Charles. 'I tried driving in for a year, but it takes too long. So since I'm restricted to public transport, I decided I needed a runabout in town, and I bought this. This morning, in fact.'

'Your only problem is, it won't run about.'

'Quite,' said Charles.

Ellison grunted with effort, and finally shifted the distributor cap. 'I'm not surprised, Charles. This thing hasn't had a service in years, I'd guess. Look at the dirt! And the points are worn so badly they're almost useless. Look,' he said, showing them to Charles.

'I know,' replied Charles, looking over his shoulder. 'That's why it was such a good deal.'

'Are you sure you're the sort of chap to be driving an ancient and decrepit sports car? They need loving care and a great deal of attention.'

'That's why I bought it. Use this,' said Charles, handing Ellison a screwdriver. 'You'll never turn it with your fingernail.'

Ellison fiddled with the points for a minute.

'There,' said Ellison, 'let's try again.' He leaned under the bonnet once again, and began to replace the points. 'It may not get you as far as Bucks, though.'

'That's alright. It's got to get from here to the flat; that's about 150 yards.'

102

'I heard about that. You've got yourself a little London pad, now, eh? Very convenient,' he said with a wink.

'Nothing like that,' said Charles with a laugh. 'It's just for those nights when I finish too late to get back. Or can't get home for any reason. If I finish at ten, or later sometimes, there's no point waiting for half an hour for a train, and then getting home by midnight—just to get up again at six. Henrietta's in bed by then anyway, so I never see her. A flat a couple of minutes' walk from here is ideal.'

'Why move out so far then?'

'*Force majeure.* Henrietta wanted to be nearer her pals, and her parents.'

'You're near Thame, aren't you? I go riding there quite often,' said Ellison.

'You must pop in some time, then. We'd like to see you and Marjorie.'

'Just give us a date, tell us how to get there, and we'll come.'

Ellison put the points back in the distributor and, without replacing the cap, sat in the car, and turned the engine over. Charles watched the distributor as he did so.

'It's opening,' called Charles. 'Let's try starting her.'

Ellison got out again, and they both stood at the front of the car.

'Been busy?' asked Charles.

'No. Far too quiet, in fact. Keep it under your hat, but I may be leaving Chambers soon. I've applied for an appointment.'

'What, you too?'

'Yup,' said Ellison.

'Well, best of luck, your Honour,' said Charles.

'It's not certain yet, but it's looking very promising.'

'How long before you know?' asked Charles.

'Shortly. Right,' said Ellison, 'do you want to get in and try starting her?'

Charles climbed in and turned the key. The car started immediately. He revved a few times, and leaned out, the engine running.

'Well done!' he shouted. 'I owe you a pint! I'll be off, before she stalls again,' he said, and closed the door.

Ellison waved, and the MG moved off. Ellison watched its spluttering progress towards the Temple gates, looking thoughtful.

'Hello?'

'Henrietta? It's me.'

'Yes, Charles.'

Charles paused to see if she would mention the night before and her premature departure from the party. She did not.

'I'm just calling to see how you are.'

'That's very thoughtful of you, dear. I'm very well, thank you. Do I take it that you are not coming home tonight?'

'No; I'll stay at the flat.' Charles bit his tongue and managed to stop before he added 'again'.

'Very well. Shall I see you tomorrow night?'

'I expect so. I don't think I'm in court Friday, so I'll probably stay.'

'Ah. I've been meaning to mention it, Charles. I thought I might go away for the weekend.'

'Oh. I see. Where to?'

'I've been invited to Shropshire.'

'With whom?'

'With friends, Charles. I have some, you know? Anyway, I don't see why I should answer all these questions. I don't ask you what you get up to all week in London, do I?'

'I don't *get up* to anything, Henrietta. I work.'

'So you say.'

'For God's sake, Henrietta, you're always able to get me either here or at Chambers. I can hardly be up to much!'

'Charles, I don't know, and I really don't care.'

'For years you nagged at me to take on some civil work—'

'I knew somehow it would all be my fault.'

'—and it takes a lot of time. Especially when I'm in court all day. I have to work some evenings to keep up.'

There was a long pause at the other end of the line.

'Are you there, Henrietta?'

'I'm here.'

'Do you have nothing to say?'

'Not really, no. If there's nothing else, I'll get back to my scintillating evening of television and gin.'

'Oh, Etta—'

'Bye, Charles.'

The line went dead.

Charles replaced the receiver, and returned to the room that doubled as his bedroom and study, picking up his now-cold coffee as he went. The room reminded him of his student days—a bed and a desk, papers everywhere, books and coffee cups littered about the floor.

He liked the flat. Apart from the fact that it was very convenient—in New Fetter Lane, right opposite the Temple—it was his bolt-hole. He felt relaxed there, able to do as he pleased. He often imagined that it was his townie's version of a gardening shed. He knew that he used the place to hide from Henrietta, and the thorny problem of their marriage. He knew also that a decision would have to be taken sooner or later—probably sooner—about the marriage. They had both avoided the subject since the last awful attempt to discuss it. He knew finally—or at least suspected very strongly—that Henrietta was having an affair. He had decided, at least for the present, to say nothing. He continued to be surprised by his own reaction to the knowledge. Even as little as a year before, he would have expected to have felt jealousy, rage; in fact, all he did feel was relief. The fact of it, and the fact that Henrietta could have an affair, and not really care that he knew, only proved to him what he had been saying to himself for a long time: that the marriage was over, and the sensible thing would be to divorce. Then Henrietta would be free to have the children she had always wanted, and he could stop feeling guilty.

That was his almost permanent state of mind at present: guilt. Guilt that Henrietta was so unhappy, and that he seemed powerless to alter it. Guilt that he didn't try harder, had given way to guilt that he accepted the rift between them and that it no longer hurt him. Still, he rationalised, where would a Jew be without guilt? It was what he was brought up to do best.

Charles picked his way towards his desk and sat at the small computer he had bought to do his paperwork. He put in a new disc, and started work.

Chapter Fifteen

The Barristers' Clerks Association did not need to meet formally all that often. The 'Mafia,' as the clerks were sometimes affectionately known, had a number of watering holes where most nights, and many lunchtimes, groups of clerks would congregate to share gossip, discuss lists and list officers, and report on the rising young stars, the grand old men, and the fading lights of the Bar—their 'guv'nors'. The operation of this bush telegraph was informal and extremely effective. Most clerks knew long before any official announcement who was about to 'be made up'—become a judge—or who was having an affair with whom.

The term 'Mafia' was not altogether inappropriate either. Barristers' clerks—even in the new world of salaries rather than percentages of earnings—were still powerful enough to dictate the course of the careers of their guv'nors. Everyone knew of at least one story in which the clerk had ruined the practice of a barrister on the grounds of offence taken at a Chambers party, a perceived slight of the clerk's wife, or simply a personality clash.

One of the most popular watering holes was the 'City Squash and Tennis Club'. Stanley had never played squash in his life, and had last held a tennis racket at the age of fifteen, but then, despite its name, strenuous sports did not figure large in the City Squash and Tennis Club's activities. Its principal attraction, at least as far as Stanley was concerned, was its selection of four real ales of magnificent specific gravity.

On this particular evening, Stanley had only popped into the Club for a quick half before catching his train home. Rita, his beloved, wanted to do some late-night shopping, and woe betide him if he were to miss that. He chatted for a few minutes to a number of clerks he knew quite well, and downed the rest of his beer. As he was about to leave, he saw a familiar face. Peter McPhee was the clerk at a set of common law chambers in Essex Court. He and Stanley were old mates, having come into the Temple as juniors together thirty years before. He bustled up to the bar.

'Have another, Stan,' he said, somewhat out of breath. 'I've some interesting gossip.'

Stanley looked at his watch. 'I can't stay long, Peter. I've got to get the 6.50.' McPhee leaned over and peered at Stanley's wrist.

'Plenty of time,' he said. 'This won't take long. It involves one of your ex-guv'nors,' he said tantalisingly. Stanley was hooked.

'OK,' he said. 'Just a half.'

Peter obtained the drinks and the two of them moved away from the bar to a side table.

'I've just bumped into your old favourite,' said McPhee, leaning across the table confidentially. His words were almost lost in the chatter of the drinkers and the click of snooker balls from the tables behind him. Stanley looked puzzled.

'Ivor Kellett-Brown,' announced McPhee with a flourish.

'My God,' said Stanley, 'I thought he died years ago. The last I heard he was dossing in Temple Gardens.'

'So he was. I saw him myself only . . . what? Eighteen months back? He was evicted by the Inn when he couldn't pay his rent. Nutty as a fruitcake, always talking to himself, shouting at thin air, you know. One of my juniors once saw him addressing one of the statues on the Embankment as "My Lord".'

Stanley grinned, and took a mouthful of beer. He looked at his watch.

'Anyway,' continued McPhee, 'the point is, he's come into some money. Quite a lot of money from what I could tell. He's driving a new Jag—almost ran me over, actually—and dressed up like Fred Astaire, tails and all. I've never seen him look so . . . what's the word? Opulent?'

'Good heavens,' said Stanley. 'Are you sure it was him?'

'Certain. I spoke to him. He was parking in the Temple, and I had to jump out of the way. When he got out I recognised him and said hello. He remembered me as your mate, and asked how you were.'

'Is he back in practice?' asked Stanley. 'I thought he'd packed up originally because of poor health.'

'That's what I'd heard—I think it was you who told me—but he reckons he was never ill at all. I tell you, Stan,' and here McPhee leaned over even further and dropped his voice almost to a whisper, 'he's barmy. He said, straight out, that he was being blackmailed.' McPhee leaned back in satisfaction, his punchline delivered.

'Blackmailed? Who by? What for?'

McPhee shrugged and drank some beer. 'Dunno. He didn't elaborate. Just said it was someone in your Chambers, and that they had a nasty shock coming to them. He was ranting on and on—it was like lighting a firework. I'd just asked if he was recovered enough to go back into practice, and he was off like a greyhound,' said McPhee, mixing his metaphors. ' "There's nothing wrong with me!" he stormed. "There never was! I was forced out by that blackguard!".'

' "Blackguard?" Who says "blackguard" these days?'

'Ivor Kellett-Brown does. That wasn't all. "Retribution shall be mine," he shouted. Reminded me of my old vicar. He had a real wicked look in his eyes, too. He got me quite scared, I don't mind admitting. Then, without another word, he stormed off, talking to himself, and shaking his fist.'

'And you've no idea who was supposed to have been behind all this?'

'No. The only thing he said was "little toad". "Little toad of a blackguard" was the exact expression. Not exactly elegant, but I got his drift.'

Stanley pondered the phrase. It was his private opinion that at least half a dozen of his guv'nors could aptly be called 'toads', and quite a few were little. On the occasion of the annual Chambers cricket match—barristers against clerks and their mates—the clerks usually thrashed the barristers by an innings or more. Robert, the junior, had once been heard to say that the guv'nors might be 'shit-hot on the law, but when it comes to sport they're a bunch of wimps'. The question was, who best fitted both appellations?

'I can't think of anyone in particular,' Stanley concluded. 'Too many contenders.' He thought for a few seconds more, and then shrugged. He looked at his watch again. 'I've got to run,' he said, knocking back the last of his drink. 'If you pick up anything more, Pete, will you let me know?' he asked.

'Sure.'

'Right. See you.'

Stanley started for the door, but suddenly thought of something, and turned round to McPhee again. 'You don't think we ought to tell the police, do you? Is he dangerous?'

'Nah,' answered McPhee dismissively. 'The bloke's

round the twist, but he's harmless. He lives in a fantasy world, I reckon.'

'Yeh,' said Stanley, reassured. 'I 'spect you're right. Cheers!' he said, and dashed off.

A tall angular man with a hat pulled low over his eyes watched Stanley's departing back from the adjoining table. Laurence Corbett had listened with great interest to the last part of that conversation. He knew who the 'little toad' was—as it had been he who had coined the phrase. It had gained some currency in a certain coterie of Chambers members. The 'little toad' was Charles Howard.

Corbett also knocked back the last of his drink, picked up the blue cloth bag he and many other barristers used to carry their robes, and slipped out of the pub. He had him! It didn't matter now who was elected Head of Chambers: Charles Howard's days were numbered.

Chapter Sixteen

Henrietta wove her way unsteadily through the hubbub and the guests to the far side of the room, apparently oblivious to the fact that the contents of the champagne glass in her hand were slopping over the edge and down her forearm. Her face was flushed and her eyes sparkled. She wore her hair up, accentuating her lovely neck and shoulders, but a few strands of hair had escaped and fell over her eyes. She reached her destination, but then stopped suddenly, unable to see whom she had been seeking. She frowned and squinted around herself,

110

sweeping her wayward hair back over her forehead with an impatient gesture of her free hand. She eyed a group of men standing in a tight circle to her left. Most of the men at the party were in dinner jackets, and thus hard to distinguish from the rear, particularly to someone who had drunk two bottles of champagne unaided. Henrietta appeared to recognise a member of the group and turned rather unsteadily towards him. She giggled to herself. She crept up behind a tall man with a broad back and flowing blond hair, slipped her hand up the back of his jacket and pinched his bottom.

The man whirled round, jogging Henrietta's arm in the process, and causing her to lose the final drops of liquid in her glass.

'Henrietta!' he hissed severely, but with a smile on his handsome face. 'Behave yourself!'

She shrugged and laughed. 'I want to dance,' she pouted, taking hold of his arm, and tugging at him. 'Oh, come on, Laurence, you've been talking for ages.'

Henrietta beamed a smile round the group of men she had interrupted. One or two of them smiled back politely.

'For heaven's sake,' replied Laurence Corbett, turning away from the group slightly, 'can't you be even a little discreet?'

'No one minds,' she protested. 'Why do you think Polly invited us both?'

'That's no reason to make a spectacle of ourselves. Some people here know Jenny. We've still got to be careful.'

Henrietta had not been listening, but had instead been watching his lips as he spoke. She saw his even, white teeth, and the pinkness of his tongue, and thought of what they had been doing to her nipples a few hours before when they had been changing for the party.

She leaned towards him and whispered wetly in his ear. 'Take me upstairs and fuck me,' she said just loudly enough to be heard by the others in the group. Some smiled to one another; others pretended not to have heard.

'For God's sake, Henrietta, stop acting like a whore!' replied Corbett. He made no attempt to keep his voice low, indeed, he almost deliberately raised it, and a number of people outside of the immediate group turned and looked at them. 'Just go away, and please: stop drinking!'

Corbett turned his back on her and resumed talking. Henrietta looked peeved for a moment, and then shrugged. She turned and walked towards the door. An aisle of silence opened before her as she proceeded. 'You're boring, Corbett, just boring,' she said with that curious distinctness that often characterises the speech of habitual drunks. 'Would someone *please* tell me where I can get a drink?' she concluded as she left the room.

'A word, Laurence,' said one of Corbett's friends, pulling him gently to one side, as conversations restarted.

'Yes, Philip?'

'Look, I hope you won't think this out of line, but . . . well, I've known about you and Henrietta for some time, and frankly, it doesn't bother me in the least. Best of luck to you, is what I say. But she's getting a bit . . . unpredictable, isn't she? Aren't you worried about Jenny?'

Corbett looked at him worriedly. 'Does she know?'

'Not as far as I'm aware, but it's only a matter of time, isn't it? All it would take is for Henrietta to get cheesed off with you after a few drinks—and she's drinking like a fish nowadays—and she could tell Jenny. Henrietta's not like that nanny of yours, what was her name?'

'Gretchen,' answered Corbett, with a fond smile.

'That's it, Gretchen. She was a bit of fun; over for a few months, and now safe back in Sweden, or wherever it was.'

'Switzerland.'

'Wherever. But Henrietta Lloyd-Williams is a different thing altogether. You work with her husband, don't you?'

Corbett grinned. 'I do. That's half the fun.'

'Fun?' asked the other, puzzled. 'You're obviously not in love with the girl.'

'Henrietta? Good God, no! What a thought!'

'Well why do it then? It's your business, Laurence, but it strikes me as a hell of a risk.'

'You're quite right, Philip, it *is* my business, and no one else's.'

'But what if Howard finds out? She could easily tell him—just to pay back some old score. You've seen the way they row.'

'You mean he doesn't know already? Ha!'

Philip regarded his friend seriously, unable to understand his response. He shrugged. 'I don't understand you, Laurence.'

Corbett grinned, and put his arm around the other's shoulder. 'I wouldn't try,' he said. 'It's just a bit of fun, no more to it than that.'

'And that's how Henrietta sees it too: a bit of fun?' Philip shook his head with a wry smile. 'Give it up, Laurence. For your sake and for Jenny's. Get another nanny, eh?'

Corbett turned to him sharply, his good humour vanished. 'I will not give it up, and certainly not because you think I should!' he hissed, with sudden violence. Philip regarded him with surprise. 'I know you're trying to be a pal, and all that,' continued Corbett in more moderate tones, 'but just mind your own business, eh?' His eyes were wide and hot in their intensity. Philip, several inches shorter than Corbett, almost shrank back.

'Fine. Whatever you say, old chap. I'll never mention it again.'

'There's a good fellow. Now,' continued Corbett, looking about the room, 'where's that lovely hostess of ours? Ah, there she is. Excuse me, Philip, but I'm owed a dance or two.' He stalked off.

Henrietta wrapped her fur more tightly round her, and paced slowly around her car again. The country road was pitch dark and little used. She had waited in the car for 45 minutes, until her legs began to get stiff, and since then she had been standing outside. Shortly after her 'thing' with Laurence (she loathed the word 'affair'—it was so Mills & Boon) had started, she had begun to realise that the largest part of it was not, as she had thought, snatched moments of passion, candlelit dinners and romantic assignations, but just waiting. She was always waiting for him to call, waiting at a hotel, waiting in restaurants where he never showed. Now she was waiting in the lay-by where they had agreed to meet on the way back.

The entire weekend had been a disaster. It had been the first time she and Laurence had ever planned a whole weekend together, and she had looked forward to it for weeks. Two whole days together without having to look over their shoulders, give false names, or pretend they were strangers. Days of planning and lying had provided her with a credible cover in case Charles had inquired where she was going and with whom—not that he ever would. He never did, that was what was so infuriating. He didn't seem to care at all.

Then Laurence had arrived hours late. By the time he turned up, other guests were beginning to arrive, and they had managed only a snatched half-hour together before going downstairs. And his excuse? He had been held up on a case! She vowed to him that the next time she committed adultery, she'd pick a bus conductor; at least his sex life wouldn't be governed by the whim of a judge. So they'd rowed, and then made up, which had been lovely, but the atmosphere had remained. She had drunk too much, and he had been rude, although quite how rude she did not remember. She knew that she had been upset, but the latter end of the evening was rather unclear. However, she did remember quite distinctly that Laurence and some other chap, an ex-member of Chambers she thought, were planning to do something horrid to Charles, and Laurence took great delight in gloating over it with a number of the people there. And just as the house had begun to empty, and she had thought they would have a few uninterrupted hours together, some old chum of Polly's had just dropped by, and, wouldn't you believe it, she knew Laurence and Jenny. Used to play tennis with them. Henrietta had packed and departed, arranging to meet Laurence *en route*. He was an hour late.

Not for the first time, Henrietta wondered if it was all worth it. So much effort for so little return. If I put half as much effort into pleasing Charles as I do Laurence, she thought, I'd probably have a successful marriage. The thought amused her at first. Then she considered it seriously, and was no longer amused. She got back into the car, feeling miserable. 'I'll give you five more minutes, Laurence Corbett,' she said out loud, 'and then I'm going home.'

She turned the heater on, but by then the engine had got completely cold, and it blew freezing air on to her legs. It was the last straw. 'Sod him!' she cried, and turned on the ignition. She revved the engine, and was in the process of moving off, when she saw headlights in her mirror. She waited for them to pass her, and realised that they were slowing down. Corbett pulled alongside. He wound down his window.

'I was just leaving,' said Henrietta.

'Sorry. I got held up. Your place or mine?' asked Corbett with a grin, referring to their two cars. This had become 'their' lay-by since they had made love for the first time there in the back of his car. They had subsequently spent many hours on this lonely country road. She felt that hotel rooms were seedy and unspontaneous and, in any event, she experienced a particular excitement in making love only feet from complete strangers as they passed by, the black interior of the car suddenly ablaze, as headlights swept across her, straddling Corbett's thighs on the back seat. The thought of it now only irritated her further, and she shook her head quickly.

'Neither. I'm cold and tired, and pissed off,' she said. 'I'm going home.'

'Just hang on a sec—' he said, putting his car into gear to pull in in front of her.

'No, really, don't bother,' she insisted, 'I want to go home.'

'Can't we even talk?' he asked.

'I don't want to talk to you, Laurence. I'll speak to you later in the week. I want to have a think first.'

'What about?'

'Everything.'

'What are you talking about, Henrietta?'

'I don't know. I just want time to think. This is all so . . .' she searched for the right word, '. . . unsatisfactory. I mean . . . I don't know. Maybe I need a break for a while, just to think things through . . .'

'What's there to think about?'

'Everything . . . you, me, us, Charlie, Jenny.'

'What have Charles and Jenny got to do with it?'

'For heaven's sake, Laurence, we're married to them! What's more, Jenny's my friend—my best friend, for that matter.'

'Look, will you just let me pull in, and talk to you sensibly. This is ridiculous,' he said, indicating their two cars standing side by side with their engines running. 'I feel like we're about to start a race.' He smiled his most winning smile, but she was not to be budged.

'No! Stay there!' She did not want him in her car. She knew what would happen. He would start whispering in her ear, and stroking her hair; his hand would travel up her thigh under her skirt; he would nibble her earlobes and slip his hand under the leg of her panties, and she would be lost. In separate cars, with the cold night air on her face from the open window, she could be firm. He looked at her with suspicion. His face hardened.

'Are you telling me it's over?' he demanded.

'No,' she said, quite surprised, 'at least . . . I don't know. Maybe I am, but I haven't realised it yet.'

'Well, you can get that out of your head immediately,' said Corbett. 'You're not dumping me.'

Henrietta stared at him, astounded. 'What the hell do you mean by that?' she demanded. 'If I don't want to see you again, I bloody well won't!'

'You're being completely unreasonable! Everything was fine this morning, and suddenly you spring this on me—'

'I have nothing more to say, Laurence,' she said, closing her window.

'Well, I've got something to say to you,' he said, getting out of his car, 'you gin-soaked, spoilt little—'

But Henrietta did not hear the rest. She let in the clutch and her car shot forward, narrowly missing him, and swerved into the road. She put her foot down and raced off. She looked back in her mirror and could see him still on the road, staring after her. She caught sight of herself in the mirror. Her face was white and she looked frightened.

Chapter Seventeen

Sunday evening settled over the peaceful Buckinghamshire village. The Howards' garden was large. It adjoined fields to the rear and was bordered on both sides by tall shrubs. Someone clearly spent a great deal of time working on it, as the lawns were well manicured, and the flower-beds colourful and orderly. Outside the french windows of the house, on a patio that ran the width of the house, were placed a garden table and four chairs. There was also a long stripey seat with its own awning, that swung back and forth in the gentle breeze. The far end of the garden, beyond a massive hedge through which there was an archway, was half-wild. There the grass was taller, and dotted with wild flowers. There was the stump of a huge old oak, now long dead, and several apple trees, ideal for climbing. It would have been an exciting place had there been any children in the household.

Vehicles passed the front of the house infrequently, and the noise of their engines was only just discernible at the back. In the distance could be heard the voices of some children, and occasionally the sound of horses' hoofs floated over from the stables in the lane.

Beyond the hedge at the rear of the house, at the point where a stile led from the garden into a field, a man shuffled from one foot to the other. He wore a thick anorak, heavy comfortable boots and thick socks, for his work often required waiting patiently in uncomfortable situations. He was short, and had a round, jovial face, with ruddy cheeks. He looked as if, in another life, he should have been an innkeeper. He had been standing there for over two hours, and he was getting tired. He looked at his watch. He took a pad out of his jacket pocket, and made a note with a small stub of pencil. He replaced the pad, and chewed the pencil thoughtfully. The subject and the man—the watcher had decided that he was her husband, as they had hardly spoken all day—had passed the afternoon uneventfully, and it had been a dull shift. The subject had spent most of the time in the kitchen. The man had washed his car, but apart from that he had not been out of the large room overlooking the garden. He had read a newspaper, and had watched television. About half an hour ago the subject had gone in to the man and said something. She did not appear to be in a good mood. The man had followed her upstairs. The light went on in a rear upstairs room, and through the window, the watcher could see what appeared to be an argument in progress. Although he could not hear what was being said, the voices rose and fell, and at one point she shouted something at him, in a high-pitched tension-filled voice.

The man left the room and there was silence in the house. After a few minutes, the watcher heard the back door open, and he darted back into the shadows as the man emerged. He had changed from his jeans into a smart pair of trousers and a jacket. He had a briefcase with him, and a pile of heavy books held together with a strap. He closed the back door after him, and walked across the patio to the rear door of the garage that lay to the right of the house. The watcher heard a car engine start. The sound was muffled at first, but grew suddenly louder as the car moved out of the garage. Within seconds, the vehicle could no longer be heard. The watcher stayed where he was. He had never actually met the client, but he had definite orders from his employer: the woman was the subject. He wondered if it was a divorce case—it usually was, these days. Why the man wanted his wife watched, when he was there all day to do it himself, the watcher had no idea. Still, it was an easy job, and as long as he was paid, he didn't care.

The watcher focused his attention again on the upstairs room. There was a sudden shriek, unmistakably of anger, from the subject, and he saw a fast movement. A fraction of a second later there was the sound of an object smashing, a vase perhaps. The watcher grinned to himself. Temper, temper, he thought.

INTERIM REPORT NO 4 TO BS1 ON OBSERVATION AT The Cedars, Putt Green, BUCKS.

Tuesday 19th:
Surveillance recommenced 08.45 hrs. Subject seen to be up and about house. No callers, 09.34 hrs left address by bicycle. Surveillance continued with Operative B by car. Subject cycled to station and approached Jaguar motor car Regn No CLH 7. Unlocked boot and placed bicycle inside. Drove back to address arriving 10.01 hrs. Car parked in garage. Visit from female neighbour 10.45

hrs to 11.13 hrs. Subject left address in Jaguar 11.54 hrs. Followed to local shops. Returned to address 12.48 hrs. Jaguar broke down outside address. Subject enlisted two male workers from adjoining farm to push it into garage. Subject returned to house. Worked in rear garden until operative relieved. No further incident.

'May I speak to Mr Howard, please?'

'Is that Mrs Howard?'

'Yes, Stanley. How are you?'

'Not bad, thank you. A bit rushed this week as Sally's on holiday. Just putting you through. Mr Howard? Your wife for you, sir.'

'Yes, Henrietta?'

'The bloody car's broken down.'

'Oh great. Where?' asked Charles.

'Just outside the house, thank God. I'd just been out shopping, and it conked out as I was driving back into the garage. I got some of Jim's men to help push it back in, but I've tried it since and it won't start at all.'

'What do you want me to do about it?'

'It's your bloody car.'

'Then I'll bloody manage without it until the weekend, won't I?'

'What am I supposed to use in the meantime?'

'I thought you just said it was my bloody car. What you mean is, it's my bloody car, but you want to drive it.'

'Charles, you know very well how isolated it is here. There's no way I can get around without transport. Particularly if you're not proposing to come up again until Friday. I've got arrangements this week.'

'You've got a nerve, Henrietta, after your performance last night. It's funny how all you want is to be left alone until something goes wrong. I'm certainly not coming up to fix the car before Friday, so if you need it so urgently, I suggest you get it booked in with Breck and Co in the village.'

'They're Volvo dealers.'

'They repair other cars too. They're very good. You

might even persuade them to lend you a car while the Jag's in for repair. Now if it's alright with you, I have a set of papers to read before my conference arrives.'

'You're a real bastard sometimes, you know that, Charles?' She hung up.

'Is that you, Mr Howard?'

'Yes.'

'I've got nothing further to report. She stayed in all evening. No visitors. Went to bed about an hour ago.'

'Nothing else?'

'No. If she is committing adultery, Mr Howard, I've seen no evidence of it in the last week. Do you want us to continue the surveillance?'

'Yes, for the present.'

'Very well, sir. I'm calling my men off for the night. I'll report again tomorrow.'

It was 3.30 a.m., a dark and damp night. It was warm, however, and the closeness seemed to muffle the usual night-time sounds. No lights showed from any of the houses in the lane. The brook that ran parallel to the lane, on the side opposite the houses, gurgled over its rocky path under the trees towards the farm. A tall man with broad shoulders, wearing a boiler suit and a woolly hat pulled low over his ears, walked softly up the drive of the Howards' house towards the garage. He tried the main door, but found it to be locked. He skirted round the garage, keeping to the shadows, and entered by the rear door. A minute later the main doors swung silently open. He emerged, pushing the Jaguar motor car, steering it with one hand. When he reached the lane, he turned the car left, and allowed it to stop. He walked on a few paces to the tow-truck in which he had arrived, got in, and let off the handbrake so that it rolled quietly backwards to within a few feet of the front of the Jaguar. He let down a hook from the hydraulic hoist mounted on the back of the tow-truck. This made some noise, and he paused for three or four minutes before continuing. Then he crawled

121

under the front of the Jaguar, attached the hook, and operated the hydraulic hoist for a second time. The front of the Jaguar rose smoothly off the ground. The man then climbed swiftly into the cab of the truck, started up, and drove off, towing the Jaguar behind him.

Chapter Eighteen

Charles threw down his pen, stood, and paced about his room. He had been trying to draft what should have been a very simple Advice on a personal injuries matter for the last hour, and had written the first paragraph no less than four times. He just could not concentrate. In fact, when he looked at the chaos of papers and instructions lying on his desk, he realised that he had achieved almost nothing in the last two days. He knew the reason too: Henrietta. For the tenth time since arriving in Chambers that morning, he reached for the telephone, and changed his mind. He did not relish the prospect of a showdown. He had always loathed exhibitions of emotion, affectionate or otherwise. He excused it to himself on the basis that he had had a surplus in his over-demonstrative home as a child, but even he realised in his more honest moments that that was not even half the story. He had not seemed averse to emotional exhibitions before he and Henrietta were married; indeed, he remembered having taken part in quite a few himself. In any event, this particular showdown had been due, overdue, for years. It would be painful, and, judging by Sunday night's row, violent. But he knew at the same time that things could not go on as they had been. He picked up the telephone and dialled.

'Peter,' he said as he dialled.

His pupil Peter Bateman looked up from the papers on which he had been working.

'Yes?' he answered.

'Make yourself scarce for a few minutes, eh?'

'Sure,' replied the young man, and scurried off for a quick cigarette. Charles did not permit smoking in the room, and the chance for a coffee and a smoke with the other pupils in Chambers was always gratefully received.

The phone was picked up at the other end.

'Henrietta?'

'Yes?' she said, recognising his voice, and truculent.

'We've got to talk. Things are getting worse—'

'Huh!' snorted Henrietta at the understatement.

'—and I'm sure you're no happier than I am. I was thinking of coming up tonight, if you've got no plans.'

'It's your home, Charles. You pay the mortgage; I can't stop you coming up.'

'The point is, will you be there? For a chat?'

'I've got arrangements tonight.'

'Tomorrow?'

There was a pause at the other end. At first he could hear her breathing, but then the line was silent. Just as he was about to check that she was still there, he heard a sob, and realised she was crying.

'Etta, honey, don't cry. We can sort everything out, one way or another. This can't go on, for either of our sakes.'

'I'll be here tomorrow,' she sobbed. 'Come then.'

'Can you give me a lift from the station?' he asked, remembering the decrepit state of the MG, and realising that it would be unlikely to make it from London to Buckinghamshire.

123

'Course I bloody can't! Your car's not working, remember?'

'God, of course. Did you book it in?'

'Yes, but as it needs towing, they're too busy to come for a few days. You'll have to get a taxi from the station, or if there aren't any, you'll just have to walk.'

Henrietta slammed the phone down, and cried. She thought of calling her mother, but then didn't think she could stand an hour's worth of 'I told you so's'. So she dried her eyes and went out to the garden. Gardening normally calmed her down, but she couldn't concentrate on what she was doing. She decided to go for a ride to the village. She threw down her gardening gloves, and went to the garage for her bike.

At first she did not appreciate the significance of the emptiness of the garage. Then, with a shock, she realised that Charles didn't have the car in London, that it was not in the drive, and that it should have been where she and the men from the farm had pushed it the day before. She did all the foolish and illogical things one does when refusing to believe the obvious: she checked the drive and the road, and even looked over the road to the stable yard. It was not there. Eventually she acknowledged with surprise that someone really had stolen it. Why anyone should want to steal a car that didn't run was beyond her. She caught part of herself enjoying in anticipation Charles's fury when he found out, while the nicer part of herself telephoned the local police. There wasn't a police station in the village, but there was a police house with a blue lamp outside it where the local bobby lived. She rang the number, and was met with an answerphone. She felt a little idiotic telling an answerphone that her husband's defunct car had been stolen from a locked garage, but she did it, nevertheless. Then she cycled into the village, feeling unaccountably cheerful.

In fact, Henrietta need not have bothered to leave her message, as late that night, while she was asleep, the same man that had stolen the car quietly drove up

124

in it, now repaired, to the house, carefully opened the garage doors as he had before, and replaced the car in the garage. Had Henrietta looked in the garage the next day and seen the Jaguar there, she would no doubt have thought that she was going mad, or that she had been drinking too much gin. In fact, it so happened that she had no cause to go to the garage again on the following day, and she never realised the car had been returned.

INTERIM REPORT No 6 to BSI ON OBSERVATION AT The Cedars, Putt Green, BUCKS.

Surveillance recommenced 06.00 hrs. Subject rose and seen to be about house 08.15 hrs. Received telephone call 08.38 hrs and spoke animatedly for five minutes. Seen to dress in hurry, and depart house 08.59 hrs. Subject left house on foot. Followed to junction of Church Road and by-pass (A421). Waited for ten minutes. Red Mercedes Saloon, Regn No E800 HLH approached travelling east on by-pass, stopped, and subject got in. Vehicle drove into church car park where invisible from road, without direction from subject, therefore suggesting car park used for venue in past. Due to lack of cover, an approach to vehicle deemed not safe, and observation continued from corner of church at distance of 150 metres. Driver: male caucasian, late-thirties/early forties, light colouring, no facial hair. Driver attempted to kiss subject, was resisted, although parties clearly familiar with one another. Discussion in car for ten minutes. Driver continued to press himself on subject. It appeared driver attempting to persuade subject. At 09.26 hrs subject descended from car, slammed car door, and began to run out of church car park. A few feet from car, subject turned and shouted to driver. Subject's back was turned to operative, but words apppeared to be: 'And don't phone any more. I mean it, I'll tell—' and here subject used a name, possibly 'Melanie'. Subject ran back to house. Vehicle remained stationary until 09.32 hrs, then continued in easterly direction on A421.

Chapter Nineteen

Henrietta watched out of the window as Jo, the stable girl, closed the stable gates opposite the house. Jo waved goodbye to someone still in the stables, and walked off down the lane, her riding boots crunching on the gravel at the side of the road. There was no pavement on that side of the road. The tarmac disintegrated into gravel, and then there was a strip of tall grass, and the brook.

It was 6.20 p.m. and Charles might arrive at any minute. That thought caused Henrietta to pick up her gin and tonic and gulp down what remained of it. She wandered into the living room, catching sight of her reflection in the doors. For most of the last two days she had pottered about the house, determined not to get excited. It was almost as if she would tempt fate if she made too much of it. After all, Charles's coming home 'for a chat' mid-week was nothing to get excited about. But half-way through that afternoon she had had a change of heart. She had scurried through the rest of the day, preparing a meal, having a bath, and getting dressed. She had got made up, and now wore a long, quite formal dress that showed off her slim figure.

She inspected her reflection, and, deciding that she wanted a closer examination, she went upstairs to regard herself in the full-length mirror in her dressing room. She peered at her face. She looked tired. Her cheeks were red, not the healthy red of exertion after riding or playing tennis, but the red of one gin too many. She had been drinking steadily since lunchtime. For a second her nerve deserted her, and she thought of calling a taxi, and going off somewhere, maybe to her parents'. For months, years probably, she had wanted, prayed for, the opportunity to talk to him, really to talk about what they each wanted and where to go from here. She had given up believing that it would ever happen, resigned herself to it. And now, out of the blue, when Charles seemed to be prepared to listen to what she had to say, she was nervous. Excited too. She had been wavering so far as Laurence was concerned, and it had helped her to make a decision. Now she was ready; ready to own up, to wipe the slate clean, and start again. But, God, she was nervous!

She returned downstairs, poked at the meal in the kitchen, and wandered into the living room. She had tried to lighten her mood by playing some music earlier, and the hi-fi was still on, but she decided against putting on any more music. She topped up her drink, and threw herself into an armchair looking out of the window into the garden.

All of Henrietta's movements around the house had been observed by a man hiding at the rear of the garden. He was not the same man as the one who had stood in the identical position, observing the house, over the previous days. He was smaller in build, and his clothes were clearly unsuitable for sneaking around others' gardens. He wore well-pressed trousers hidden under a long mackintosh, well-polished black brogues, a hat, and he carried an umbrella. By his feet were a briefcase and a large blue bag made out of what looked like heavy curtain material, tied by a white rope drawstring. It was a typical barrister's bag, used for carrying court robes.

The man had been watching Henrietta pace from room to room for the last hour. He was obviously nervous, as he kept shifting his weight from foot to foot and looking about himself. Every now and then he pulled a crumpled piece of paper from his pocket and consulted it, stuffing it back into his raincoat when he was satisfied, only to take it out a few minutes later. When he appreciated that Henrietta had at last settled in one room, he picked up his bag and briefcase, pulled the hat lower down over his face, and picked his way carefully across the lawn towards the back door of the house. He kept to the bushes, and the lengthening shadows, but he need not have worried, as Henrietta had dozed off, suffering from the cumulative effect of gin and stress. He had just reached the corner of the garage and the house, when he was alerted to a noise from behind him, at the rear of the garden. He scurried round the side of the garage, and watched.

Charles puffed, panted and cursed his way over the stile at the back of the garden. He was hot and sweaty, and extremely irritated. He had arrived at the station to find himself in a losing battle for the one taxi waiting there. He was thus forced to carry his briefcase and coat for a mile and a half across rutted and extremely muddy fields made all the more treacherous by the recent rain. He had taken off his jacket and started to carry it just in time to slip and get his shirt and tie covered in mud and grass stains. He plodded, his shoes heavy with adherent mud, across the lawn, aware, and unconcerned, that he was leaving footprints behind him, and clattered through the back door. Henrietta, startled out of her doze, ran into the kitchen to find him swearing as he tried to hook his shoes off without touching either of them with his hands.

She looked at him, aware of the risks of laughing, but unable to suppress giggling at him.

'You look quite a sight,' she said, holding her hand to her face to hide her laughter.

'Well, don't just stand there—give me a hand, will you?' demanded Charles, finding the situation totally without mirth. Henrietta bent down and began to untie the laces of one shoe, while Charles still tried to throw off the other.

'Mind out, Charles!' shouted Henrietta. 'This is a decent dress. Be patient, and I'll do them both!'

He obeyed, and looked down at her head as she crouched in front of him. He saw the stains all over his front, the footprints on the kitchen floor, and felt the sweat running off his brow, and he too finally appreciated the humour.

'I had planned such a civilised entrance,' he said. 'I feel like John Cleese.'

'Right,' said Henrietta, standing up, having taken off the second shoe. 'I suggest you get out of those clothes immediately, and I'll put them straight into the washing machine. I'll put dinner on hold until you've had a bath.'

Charles did as he was told. Henrietta brought him a drink up to the bathroom, and they kissed. 'We need to talk about—' he started.

'Not yet,' she said, putting her finger to his lips. 'We can talk while we eat, face to face. Not while you're in the bath.'

An hour later, cleaned and refreshed, Charles sat down to eat.

'Now?' he asked, as he started his soup.

'Now.'

'I've sort of divided the subjects up into categories,' he started.

'Typical,' said Henrietta, not unkindly.

'I know, but it's the only way I can tackle this, so please bear with me. Firstly . . .' He paused, struggling. 'Etta . . .' he began again. He put down his soup spoon. 'I'm just so sorry. You've got to believe that . . . I never wanted to hurt you . . . it's just that . . . it's not that I don't care about you, it's just that we don't seem to be able to live together without fighting and hating one another.'

Charles was aware that he was miles off the civilised speech he had prepared, but he floundered on. 'I know how unhappy you've been . . . and I know that it's all my fault. Every time we have these awful discussions

129

we both promise to try harder, and God knows I do for as long as I can . . . but in the end, I start being myself, you start bitching . . . and we end up fighting.'

He looked at Henrietta for the first time since he had started speaking, and realised that she had stopped eating too. She stared silently into her soup, her arms resting either side of it on the table. He stood up, and plunged on, pacing up and down his side of the table.

'You know I've resisted the idea of . . . splitting up . . . divorce, for so long . . . and you're probably right, I was afraid of admitting defeat. Maybe you were right when you said I'd invested too much in it . . . you know . . . cutting off from my family and so on . . . to admit it was a mistake. But in the last few weeks I've realised. This is no good for either of us. I care about you, I really do. I keep wondering what happened to the sparkling, charismatic beauty I met at Cambridge, and I feel so guilty . . . because it's my fault you've changed . . .'

He looked at her again. Tears rolled down her face and splashed heavily into her tomato soup. She seemed unaware of the spots of red accumulating on the tablecloth and her dress.

'Oh, sweetheart!' he said, from the heart, and rushed over to her.

'Get away from me, you bastard!' she screamed, pushing herself back from the table so violently that she almost overbalanced in her attempt to avoid him.

'What?' said Charles, totally uncomprehending.

'You've got a bloody nerve!' shouted Henrietta, spitting at him in her fury. 'For months you ignore the problems between us, stick your head in the sand, hope it will all get better on its own. Then you swan up here, having at last found out that you can live on your own without Mummy there to hold your hand, and calmly announce that you think it's time for a divorce! Do you know how long I've waited, hoping you'd grow up enough to start taking marriage seriously!'

'I don't understand,' said Charles.

'I know you don't, you imbecile! That's the bloody

problem! You never did understand, and you still don't! I've been waiting for years for you to understand, for you to stop fiddling around. Years of doing nothing, finding solace in meaningless relationships . . . waiting for my husband, whom I loved, to grow up and realise that he was married.'

'I do realise! That's why I'm here! I know I've not treated you well, and I thought the best thing I could do was . . . let you go . . . do what you want . . '

'So rather than put it right, heal it, you'd rather end it all? What's wrong, Charlie, haven't you got the nerve to find out why it won't work? I know: you'd rather end it than go to the trouble of putting it right. You might find out that you're at fault.'

'I accept that I'm at fault—'

'And don't give me that guilt crap either! That's all you know how to do, isn't it—feel guilty? You plumb the depths of angst, give yourself excuses at every turn, and then announce that you've done everything you reasonably can, but now you want out!'

'You're not being reasonable—'

'Who the fuck cares!' she screamed. 'I don't want to be reasonable!' Henrietta raised her hands as if in supplication, but, unable to find the words, she just wailed. 'Get out, Charles! Just bloody get out!'

He did as he was asked. He picked up his coat, struggled into his muddy shoes, and left without another word. He retraced his steps down the garden, climbed over the stile, and made off towards the station.

The man in the garden, still hiding behind the garage, had heard most of the end of the discussion, as indeed had many of the neighbours. He smiled grimly, and approached the back door. Henrietta was in the kitchen, crying as she emptied the soup into the sink. She heard the back door, and assumed that it was Charles who had forgotten something. She did not turn round when she heard footsteps behind her. She was unaware of the cosh as it descended on to the back of her head. She did however move at the last moment, and it ended its downward arc by striking her cheek and then her shoulder. She cried out in pain and surprise, and turned for the first time. The man raised the cosh again, but before he could bring it down she lashed out with the heavy ironware saucepan in her hand. It struck her attacker in the eye, and he grunted with pain. He nonetheless got in his second blow, and this one landed directly on Henrietta's temple. She collapsed the instant it landed.

The man bent over the sink and washed cold water into his eye. It was already closing, and extremely painful. It was not, however, bleeding very much. He bent and retrieved the saucepan which had rolled on to the floor. He rinsed it thoroughly under the hot tap, and placed it neatly with the other utensils in the drying rack. Holding a dishcloth to his face, with his free hand he dragged Henrietta's unconscious form into the lounge. He placed her in the middle of the Persian rug, and took out of his coat pocket a cut-throat razor. Bending over her from behind, and careful to stand away from the direction of his swing, he swung the blade swiftly and efficiently down across her throat. Blood spurted out in a great leap, arcing over the coffee table and splashing in bright red washes over the wall. It continued pumping for a few seconds, and then gradually stopped, as Henrietta's life ebbed away.

The man stood, picked up a chair and threw it at the display case of vases given to Henrietta and Charles for their first wedding anniversary by her godparents. It smashed, sending shards of glass and porcelain over the room. He then turned over the other occasional table, and flung the decanters at the wall. At the same time he shouted: oaths, curses, meaningless words, a one-sided argument, concluding in a long, high-pitched shriek.

He then raced back to the kitchen where he had left the briefcase and blue cloth bag, picked them up, and entered the garage. He unlocked the main doors, but did not push them open. He ran back to the house, sprinting through it to the front door, the cloth bag and briefcase sending

132

an umbrella stand flying, and re-emerged on to the front drive. He pulled wide the garage doors, allowing them to crash back with a force against the walls. He unlocked the Jaguar, threw the case and bag inside, got in, and started the engine. He revved it loudly, and then, just to make sure, drove the car at an angle out of the garage, so that the coachwork was dragged along the concrete doorpost. The screech of tearing metal could have been heard a street away.

The Jaguar shot out of the drive, sending dust and gravel into the air, and disappeared down the lane.

Chapter Twenty

Charles gingerly opened one eye, and squinted at himself in the mirror. Light rushed in, prompting the little men inside his head to increase the tempo of their hammering. He groaned, and bent over the sink, feeling sick, but knowing that release would not be that easy. He ventured another glance and assessed the damage. His eyes were badly bloodshot, underlined by heavy bags, and he needed a shave.

He had returned to Chambers to collect some papers, remembered the bottle of whisky he kept in his bottom drawer, and had a drink. Then he had had another, and a third. By the time he had lost count and realised that he could not walk anywhere, let alone drive, he had settled down in the library to finish the bottle. He had woken, cold and stiff, in an armchair, feeling like death.

It was 9.00 a.m. and the clerks would be arriving soon. He staggered back into his room clutching his head, and fished in his drawer for the spare razor he kept in Chambers for emergencies like these. He went back to the lavatory, and began washing. He was interrupted by the sound of the outer door being opened, and two voices chattering. He peered round the door. It was Sally and Robert, the junior clerks. Sally saw him first.

'Ooh, Mr Howard, you do look a sight!' she exclaimed. Charles looked down at himself, naked to the waist, his shirt still tucked into his trousers, with a small hand-towel held to his face.

'I expect I do,' Sally,' he agreed. 'Had a rough night.'

He returned to his toilet, and left the two clerks whispering and giggling as they went into the clerks' room.

A few minutes later he emerged from the lavatory, feeling slightly better. He went into the clerks' room, where the juniors were already opening the post.

'Listen, you two,' he said. 'As you saw, I was forced to sleep over in Chambers last night. A solitary celebration, you might say, rendered it impossible for me to get home.' He winked at Robert who appeared at least to have some sympathy.

'But the flat's only a hundred yards or so, isn't it, sir?' asked Robert, with a smile.

'Yes,' said Charles, looking contrite. 'It was quite a celebration. Anyway, I should be grateful if you would keep it between us, you understand? It doesn't look too good if a barrister starts the day hung over, having slept in his clothes. Not good for public relations.'

'That's alright, sir,' said Sally. 'I'm sure we both understand. I don't suppose you'd like a cup of coffee, would you? I'm about to put the kettle on.'

'Sally, I could propose to you,' replied Charles with gratitude.

'Yes, but what, sir? Marriage, or something more interesting?' she said cheekily.

'I'm afraid it may be some days before I'm up to anything more interesting,' he replied.

He returned to his room, and stared blankly at the papers in front of him. The desk was as he had left it the previous afternoon. He had barely sat down, when there was a knock at his door. Coffee, he thought.

'Come in,' he called.

Sally entered, looking worried. 'Erm . . . sorry Mr Howard . . . there's a couple of men here to see you. They say they're policemen.'

Charles frowned. 'Better show them in,' he said.

Sally stood back, and permitted two large men to enter the room. The first of them spoke.

'Mr Charles Howard?'

'Yes?'

'I am Detective Constable Sloane, and this is Detective Constable Redaway.' The officer showed Charles his warrant card. 'We're from the Thames Valley Police.'

'Yes, officer. Do you want to take a seat?'

'Er, yes, alright, sir. You'd better sit down too, sir, as I have some bad news.'

Charles remained standing, his heart suddenly pounding. 'What is it?' he asked, aware of a slight tremor in his voice.

'Your wife, sir, Henrietta Howard. I'm afraid there's been an incident at your home in Putt Green. I am very sorry to tell you that your wife is dead.'

'Dead? She can't be. I saw her yesterday evening.' Charles did not register that his answer was being quietly recorded by the second officer. 'What sort of incident? You mean a car crash?'

'No, sir, I don't think it's that sort of incident. I've been asked to collect you, sir, if that's convenient, and take you to Putt Green now to identify the . . . your wife. I'm sure the situation will be made clearer when we get there.'

'Yes, but . . . what happened? Please, officer, you must tell me!'

'I'm sorry sir, I would if I could. But we're just chauffeurs, so to speak. We've been asked to come here and take you up to your house. I don't know any more detail than I've just told you,' he lied. 'Do you have a coat?' he asked, as he stood up.

'Er, yes, over there,' replied Charles, pointing to his coat lying over the chair where he had thrown it the night before.

The second officer picked it up, and noted that there were mud stains on the hem. 'I'll carry it for you, shall I sir? You won't need it in the car.'

'Yes . . . very well. May I just speak to the clerks? Tell them what's happening?'

'We've already had a word with them, sir. Best that we get a move on.'

The police car swung into the drive. There were already several cars there, two obvious police cars with their lights still flashing, two or three unmarked cars, and an ambulance. There was a man in a light grey raincoat and a very smart suit at the front door, speaking to several other men, all of whom wore plastic shawls and wellington boots. One had a dog on a lead. They departed, and went round to the back of the house. The man in the raincoat approached the car as it stopped, and opened the door.

'Mr Howard?' he asked.

'Yes.'

'I'm Detective Superintendent Glazer, in charge of this investigation.'

'Would you please tell me what's going on?' Charles pleaded. 'All I know is that Henrietta's supposed to be dead.'

'That's right, sir. In a moment I shall show you inside—' Charles tried to walk straight towards the house, but the Superintendent's hand was placed firmly on his chest, restraining him.

'In a moment, sir,' he insisted. 'I must warn you that

it is not a pretty sight. It appears as if your wife has been murdered.' The Superintendent watched Charles's face intently as he gave this information.

'Murdered?' asked Charles, shaking his head in disbelief. 'Who by?'

'We don't know yet, sir, do we?' replied the other. 'All I'd like you to do at the moment, sir, is to formally identify her.'

The Superintendent led the way through the front door. Two men were crouched by the umbrella stand that was lying on its side in the hallway, dusting it with powder. The Superintendent guided Charles around it and into the lounge. The scene that greeted Charles was like a scene from one of the video-nasties he had watched during an obscenity prosecution. The walls were splattered with blood; there was furniture everywhere; broken glass crunched under his feet. A blanket—the blanket he and Henrietta used to take on their country walks—was spread over a bundle in the centre of the room, as if it had been laid on a tussock of grass at some obscene picnic. From under the blanket he could see dark, almost black stains, that had seeped into the thick pile of the rug.

'Please don't touch her, sir,' said the Superintendent. He lifted a corner of the blanket, and Henrietta's face came into view. Her eyes were closed tightly, like a child's, waiting for a surprise. A wide black grin disfigured her neck.

'That's her,' said Charles, choking back tears.

'Thank you, sir.'

The Superintendent replaced the blanket, and took Charles firmly by the arm, guiding him back through the carnage to the hallway.

'I shall ask an officer to take you to Aylesbury police station where we have an incident room. We shall need to take some details from you, and it would be better to do it there. He'll be able to arrange for some tea. Sergeant?' he called.

A stocky broad man who had been doing something on the stairs bent down so he could see them. 'Sir?'

'This is Mr Howard.'

'Right, sir,' he said, coming down. He reached the foot of the stairs, and turned to Charles. 'If you're ready, sir?' he said to Charles.

Charles walked past him into the porch, in a daze. He knew it was a cliché even as he thought it to himself, but he wondered if it was all a drunken dream, and that in a moment he would wake to find himself on the floor of the Chamber library. He had the detachment to wonder also if everyone in this sort of situation took refuge in hoping it was fantasy, and decided that they probably did.

'Sergeant,' called the Superintendent quietly. The other turned, and the Superintendent beckoned to him. 'By the book, Sergeant. *Everything* by the book.'

'Understood, sir,' confirmed the Sergeant.

Charles sat in the interview room, nursing his third cup of tea, now cold. Brief details had indeed been taken from him, but that had taken ten minutes. He had been left alone with his thoughts now for almost an hour. He had been asked to await the return of the Superintendent. At that stage he had felt no compulsion about his remaining, but the longer he sat there, the more suspicious he felt. Why was he being detained? He was not officially under arrest, but there seemed to be a fine line between that and his current status.

He was about to get up and complain when the door opened and the Superintendent entered, flanked by another officer.

'I am sorry to have kept you waiting so long, Mr Howard, but there were a number of matters that I had to deal with before speaking to you. I must now officially arrest you on suspicion of the murder of your wife, Henrietta Howard. You are not obliged to say anything unless you wish to do so, but anything you say will be taken down and given in evidence.'

Chapter Twenty-one

The impression that Charles had changed roles with one of his clients grew more palpable by the minute. It was as if he were following an all too familiar script, one that he read every day of his life, but he was acting the wrong part.

He had been led out again to the custody room, his possessions collected from him, and his personal details taken down. A custody record sheet bearing his name at the top had been opened, and he had been placed in a cell. His request for a solicitor had been refused on the grounds that the presence of a solicitor would lead to a harming of the evidence connected with the offence. Charles knew that the grounds for the refusal were questionable at best, spurious at worst, but he was powerless to do anything about it. It was all very well scoring points in court; he was a long way from the armour of his wig and gown and the protection of a benevolent judge.

The temptation to do as he normally could, that is, simply knock on the door, make some quip with the gaoler, and be let out, was almost overwhelming. The question kept running through his brain. Why am I here? The answer was always the same: Because they think you murdered Henrietta. But Henrietta can't be dead, he kept saying, refusing to believe the plain evidence of his own eyes.

He paced the cell, unwilling to sit on the filthy bunk, and the even more disgusting blanket. He had no conception of time, as his watch had been taken from him with his other belongings, but he guessed from the rumbling of his stomach that he had been there some hours. He remembered how so many of his clients used to tell him that the best way of keeping track of time was the state of one's digestion.

Finally, he heard footsteps from the far end of the corridor, and his door was unlocked. 'This way, sir,' said the gaoler, and he was taken back to the interview room in which he had first sat.

Superintendent Glazer and another officer awaited him there. The Superintendent re-introduced himself for the benefit of the tape recorder, correctly cautioned Charles again, and the interview began. Charles found himself in such a familiar situation that he almost laughed. Time and time again throughout his career he had told clients: Say nothing! Even when you're innocent, say nothing! Words get twisted, displaced, muddled; then they are dissected, in minute detail, by experts, surgeons of syntax, in the cold harsh light of a courtroom, until you don't remember what you've said, or what you were trying to say. And yet, the impulse to speak, to blurt out the whole story, so they'll believe you, and the nightmare can end! For the first time ever, Charles appreciated how experienced, clever criminals, who ought to have known better, spoke out, and gave themselves away. And yet, knowing all this, he still spoke.

The Superintendent asked all the questions, the other officer making notes and watching the tape-counter.

'How was your married life, Mr Howard?'

'In what sense?'

'Were you and your wife happy?'

'Not very, no.'

'Did you live at home?'

'Er . . . yes. I have a flat in London which I use some week nights. But we live together.'

140

'Did you have arguments?'

'Yes, we argue. What couple doesn't?'

'Violent arguments?'

'I wouldn't say so, no.'

'So you would say it would be impossible for your neighbours to have overheard arguments on occasion?'

'No. It wouldn't have been impossible. But it would have been rare. I don't like to argue.'

The policeman looked at some papers in front of him, and then changed tack.

'You come from London, do you not?'

'Yes.'

'East London?'

'Yes.'

'Your parents are . . . what?'

'My father used to be a furrier.'

'And now?'

'I don't know. I'm not in touch with them.'

'You'd no doubt agree with me: there's not much money in your family?'

'I can see you from a mile away, Superintendent.'

'I've no doubt you can, Mr Howard. You're as much an expert at questioning as I, no doubt. But let's not play games. Your wife is dead, and you are under suspicion of killing her. I'm trying to arrive at the truth, so just answer the questions if you will. She was the daughter of a Marquis?'

'A Viscount, but if you're asking if she was rich, the answer is, plainly, yes. If you're asking if I killed her for her money, the answer is, definitely, no.'

'You stand to gain a fortune from her death.' It was a statement.

'That depends on what you consider to be a fortune. I have quite a lot of money in my own right. I will certainly not be poor, if she hasn't changed her will.'

'Might she have changed her will?'

'It is possible.'

'Why?'

'Because, as I said before, we were not very happy.'

'So divorce was a possibility?'

'Yes.'

'At whose instance?'

'I wanted to divorce her. I went there last night to talk about just that.'

'And what do *you* say was her attitude?'

'I resent the implication that what I am about to say is a lie. That is hardly open-minded questioning.'

'I have already told you that I suspect you murdered your wife. I am not open-minded. What was her attitude?'

'She was very upset. She cried, and shouted, and told me to get out of the house.'

'So you say that she was not happy at the prospect of a divorce?'

'It appeared that way.'

'Did you not write to her only last week, threatening her that if she divorced you, I quote,' and here he picked up a letter, ' "It'll be something that you will regret, I assure you"?'

'Let me see that!' demanded Charles.

'No. I may show you a copy later. For the present I shall read it to you.'

He did. In it Charles told Henrietta that his career depended on being perceived as a happily married man, and that he would never countenance divorce, threatening her in veiled terms if she proceeded with it.

'This, Mr Howard,' said the Superintendent, 'was written on a computer. You have such a computer, do you not?'

'I have a small word processor-cum-computer, yes. So do millions of others.'

'Are you saying you did not write this?'

'I most certainly am.'

'We executed a search warrant at your Chambers this afternoon. In your desk we found this diskette—' he held up a computer disc like those used by Charles, '—and guess what we found? This very letter had been written on that disc. Certainly, it had been wiped off but, thanks

142

to the wonders of science, we brought it back, fresh as a daisy! What do you have to say?'

'Nothing. I did not write it. I wanted a divorce. She was the one who didn't.'

'Can you think of anyone who might have the slightest motive for writing this, erasing it from the disc and putting the disc in your desk?'

'Of course I can! Someone's trying to frame me for Henrietta's murder!'

'Who? Who might have any motive for killing your wife? Who hates you so much as to kill an innocent woman, just to frame you?'

'I . . . I don't know, Superintendent. I wish I did.'

'You were seen to leave your house last night immediately after a violent row with your wife.'

'Yes, that's right. Although it wasn't violent other than in the sense that she screamed and shouted at me.'

'Well, we agree thus far. You were then seen to drive off, in such a hurry as to smash the side of your Jaguar on the garage doorpost. Your wife was found dead half an hour later.'

'Drive off? I didn't drive off. I went over the back to the station!'

'You did not, Mr Howard.'

'I swear I did!'

'Why should you do that? You had the car?'

'I didn't have the car! It had broken down and I had to use the train!'

'So you say the car isn't working?'

'I do!'

'Your car was found this morning by police officers from Snow Hill Police Station outside the Temple. It drove perfectly. It is now sitting in the yard of this police station.'

Charles looked at his interrogator in open-mouthed disbelief.

'Do you wish to make any comment?' asked the Superintendent, a victorious grimace wreathing his face.

'I . . . don't understand . . . it can't be right. You must have made a mistake.'

'Why don't you start telling us the truth, Mr Howard? Surely, a man with your training can see how hopeless it is? What did you do with the knife?'

'I didn't do anything with any knife. I never had a knife. We argued, I was told to get out. I went across the fields to the station, and got a train to London. I didn't kill her!'

'We've found your muddy shoes. I suggest you wore them when throwing the knife away in the fields behind your house before driving off.'

'No! I wore them across the fields, yes, but I never had any knife.'

'I propose ending this interview now. One last matter: we have been unable to find a copy of your wife's will. Now, I am prepared to wait until Monday when we can contact her solicitor. On the other hand, if you wish, you can assist us by telling us where it is.'

Charles thought quickly. 'I can help you,' he said, slowly, thinking as he spoke. 'It's in the safe at my flat.'

'Thank you. Will you tell us the combination?'

'I can't, I'm afraid. I only had the thing installed two weeks ago, and I wrote the combination down somewhere on a piece of paper.'

'And where's that piece of paper?'

'In the flat somewhere. I'd have to look for it.'

'We're proposing to search your flat this evening. Whereabouts shall we look?'

'I'm sorry. I can't help further. If your chaps make as much mess as they usually do, I doubt it'll be found. Best of luck.'

The Superintendent looked hard at Charles, weighing him up.

'They tell me that people in your profession value integrity more than anything else.'

'What of it?' asked Charles.

The Superintendent did not answer. 'Alright,' he said, after a moment. 'There's no time like the present. We'll go now. You'll come with us. Sergeant, get him some lunch. We don't want you saying that the interrogation was unfair, or that you were so hungry you'd have admitted to anything.'

Superintendent Glazer signed off the interview, gave Charles the form he'd seen a hundred times telling him how to obtain a copy of the tape, and sent him back to his cell.

Once there, for the first time since the day began, Charles permitted himself a small, weary, smile.

Chapter Twenty-two

Charles stepped out of the police car on to New Fetter Lane, hampered by the handcuffs on his wrist attaching him to a young detective constable. The road was thronged with people, cars parked on the pavement, vans double-parked, the usual Friday afternoon clamour. Charles had bolted the hamburger provided for his lunch, and had been pacing his cell with impatience to start on the journey back to London.

Once on the road, handcuffed to the detective in the back of a police car, his impatience had been almost intolerable. It was essential they reached London soon, while it was still busy. At last, after fifteen minutes of crawling traffic, Superintendent Glazer directed the driver to put on the siren, and they completed the rest of the journey in half an hour.

The four of them got out of the car. Charles indicated a new mansion block, and the group crossed the road. The porter at the door recognised Charles immediately and was half-way into a salute when he saw the handcuffs. His hand froze in mid-movement, leaving him looking like a signpost pointing right.

'Mr Howard?' he asked.

'Not to worry, Denis. Parking fines,' Charles replied. Denis nodded and smiled, then looked puzzled. The group entered the lobby.

'It's the fourth floor,' said Charles. 'The lift will take two.' He paused, waiting for the police to make a decision.

'You go in the lift with Howard,' said Glazer to the man to whom Charles was attached. 'We'll take the stairs. Wait at the top before going in.'

The lift was a tight fit even with only two big men in it, and Charles and his escort had to do a little dance before they could arrange themselves for the button to be pressed. They arrived on the fourth floor only just ahead of the others.

'Keys,' demanded Glazer of one the detectives. He fished in his pocket for the plastic bag in which Charles's keys had been sealed the night before, and handed the bunch to Glazer.

'Which one?' asked Glazer.

'The small gold one, and the long Chubb,' Charles replied.

The door was opened, and they filed into the small living area. Charles gasped. He barely recognised the place. It had been tidied up completely since he was last there. There were flowers in a pot that he did not own on the table. A huge pink fluffy duck sat in the corner of the couch, an inane grin on its face.

'Charming,' said Glazer, with heavy sarcasm. 'Bachelor pad, is it?'

'Looks very feminine to me, sir,' said the driver.

'Maybe the handiwork of this young lady,' said the escort, picking up a photograph from the mantel. It was of a blonde, lots of bright teeth, lots of cleavage.

' "To Charlie, with love and thanks, Melissa",' read

Glazer from the bottom of the photograph. 'It looks as though there might be an accomplice in all this, doesn't it, Howard?' said the Superintendent.

Charles shrugged. 'I don't suppose for one minute it will do any good to say that all this stuff has been planted, would it?'

'Oh, you can say it, Howard. You can *say* anything you please. Whether anyone will believe you is another matter entirely,' smirked Glazer. 'Bricker: go downstairs and have a word with the porter. See if Melissa's a figment of someone's imagination.'

'Certainly, sir. But have a look at this!' called Bricker, the driver, from the bedroom. He came out with a very skimpy nightie. 'The wardrobe is full of women's clothes. Look.' He brought out an armful.

'I suppose now you'll say you're into women's clothes, eh, Charlie?' Charles noted how the respect slipped as the evidence became overwhelming. First 'Mr Howard'; then 'Howard'; now 'Charlie'. As far as Superintendent Glazer was concerned, he was now definitely dealing with a murderer, and murderers do not require any politeness.

The final piece of evidence came to light while they looked in Charles's desk. It was a paying-in book for a Midland Bank account. It was in the names of 'C Howard and Miss M Maxwell'. Glazer turned to Charles, wagged his finger at him, and tutted slowly, shaking his head.

'Very careless, Charlie. I'm surprised at you. You should have known better than to do something official like this. Now, you see, I can go to the bank, and ask for the correspondence setting up the account—done on your little computer, I bet—and then where will you be? You'll hardly be able to deny an affair then.'

'Sir!' called a breathless Bricker, having just climbed the stairs. 'The porter's seen her come in quite often. Got her own key.'

'That's enough for me,' said Glazer with satisfaction. 'Get the Scenes of Crime chaps over. I want the whole place taken apart. Now,' he said, addressing Charles. 'Where's the safe?'

'Well, first, let me find the piece of paper with the combination on it.'

Charles pulled his escort over to the desk, and began, with obvious difficulty, to go through the papers stacked inside it. The other policemen stood watching him.

'How long is this going to take?' asked Glazer.

'Quite a while; I can barely move,' said Charles, continuing to ransack the desk.

'Unlock him,' said Glazer wearily. 'He won't get past three of us.'

The escort reached into his pocket and took out the keys to the handcuffs. He undid the part on Charles's wrist and was about to unlock himself, when Charles whipped the loose end up, spun the man around, and pulled the officer's own arm round his throat. He pulled with all his might, and the officer gagged.

'Don't come anywhere near me,' Charles screamed, 'or I'll break his neck!'

The others hesitated for a second.

'You'd better believe I can do it! I'm extremely strong, and I've had commando training,' he lied, with as much conviction as he could muster. 'I can snap his neck in a second!'

Bricker looked at Superintendent Glazer for guidance. 'Where are you going to go?' said Glazer. 'You won't even get out the building. Even if you do, then where? You're no criminal, Mr Howard; you don't know the ropes.'

'Get out of my way!' shouted Charles. 'Just back off!' He pushed the escort in front of him, keeping his grip as tight as he could. The escort's face was turning purple. The others made way for him. He got as far as the landing. The lift was there. Charles backed further away to the stairs.

'You!' he called Bricker. 'Get in that lift.' The other did as he was bid. 'Close the gates. Press the alarm button!' As the button was pressed, a bell sounded in the lower reaches of the building. Charles knew that the lift was now immobilised until the alarm was shut off from below.

He backed on to the top step of the staircase, took a deep breath, and shoved the escort forward. He then turned and raced down the stairs.

He took them two at a time, hearing footsteps almost immediately behind him. He stumbled, regained his balance, stumbled again, but he kept going throughout, his hands on the rails on each side. As he reached the first floor landing he ran headlong into Denis, on his way up to investigate the alarm bell. He bundled the porter over, leaving him gasping on the landing, hoping that his body would slow up the pursuers for another second.

Charles burst into the street and turned immediately right. He sprinted across Fleet Street, oblivious to the screech of tyres and blaring of horns, and into Serjeant's Inn. He raced down the steps and through the arch into the Temple proper. He could hear footsteps behind, but not as close as they had been. He turned sharp right, ran across the open courtyard, and turned right again by Temple Church.

He chanced a look over his shoulder, and saw Bricker about sixty yards back, half-way across the courtyard. Glazer was not far behind. The third officer, the escort, had pulled up, and was speaking into a radio. Charles raced the twenty yards across Hare Court, and bounded up the steps into number 2. He had been a pupil here, and knew that these steps led to a landing which served Chambers in Middle Temple. On the far side of the landing was another short staircase, leading out into Middle Temple Lane. This was his one advantage—he knew the Temple like the back of his hand, whereas these Thames Valley officers did not. He jumped down the steps into Middle Temple Lane, and turned left, effectively turning back on himself. He felt the beginning of a stitch in his chest, but pressed on, his breath coming in short ragged gasps. He reckoned he had about ten seconds to round the next corner. If he made it without Bricker emerging from Hare Court, the pursuers would have three alternatives to choose from. He counted as he sprinted 5 . . . 6 . . . 7. . . 8. . . made it! Hugging the wall, he ran through Fountain Court and out of the night gate, leaving the Temple, and passing 'the Dev', the Devereux Public House, where he had spent so many Friday evenings standing in the sun, chatting to other barristers. That last turn, he thought, would give them three further options.

Charles emerged, sweat streaming down his forehead, on to Essex Street, and ran straight into a taxi pointing to the Embankment, and waiting to turn right. He leapt in.

'Waterloo!' he shouted. 'I've got four minutes to make a train!'

'Right you are, guv,' replied the cabbie, and away they sailed.

He was free.

Part Four

Chapter Twenty-three

'What time do you make it, mate?' asked Charles through the screen.

'Four fifty-eight,' replied the cabbie over his shoulder. They were going over Waterloo Bridge. 'When's the train?'

'Five o'clock,' replied Charles.

'Then you've had it, haven't you? It's going to take more than that from here. There's always a jam at the other side of the bridge.'

'You're right. Tell you what: turn left at the end of the bridge, and take me to London Bridge Station. I might just catch it there.'

'Righto.'

Charles hoped that, even if a police officer had been near enough to have heard him ask for Waterloo, the change of direction would finally throw them off the scent.

They made good time to London Bridge. Charles thought furiously. He had always joked to Henrietta that he knew London by reference to the court buildings. Now he remembered the back stairs leading from London Bridge to Southwark Crown Court.

'I tell you what,' he said, 'don't turn into the station, but go right into Tooley Street. If I've missed it, we can go on to New Cross, the next stop.'

He held his breath waiting for the answer. He knew he looked hot and dishevelled, but he was still in his suit, and looked reasonably affluent and, he prayed, trustworthy.

'Fair enough,' said the cabbie eventually. 'At this rate, I might as well take you all the way home!'

The cabbie turned right, and pulled up by the steps that ran up to the station.

'Won't be a sec,' called Charles, and ran off up the stairs. For a man who prided himself on his honesty and integrity, he realised with a shock that he was lying and cheating as well as any of his clients; probably better than most of them. He didn't enjoy the fact that he had to cheat the innocent cabbie who had saved him, but he was penniless, and he couldn't afford a wrangle over the fare.

He walked swiftly on to the station concourse, crossed the front of the platforms, and left the station by the far exit that took him out on to St Thomas Street. He walked off down the road, and on to the High Street.

His first problem was money, or the total lack of it. He stopped in a doorway and went carefully through his suit pockets. He always used to lose tickets in this suit because there were so many little hidden pockets. Maybe . . . just maybe . . . Yes! He felt a coin in a tiny pocket by his waistband. He took it out. Fifty pence! He felt joy out of all proportion to the sum. Somehow it proved to him that his guardian angel hadn't completely deserted him. His mind suddenly, and illogically, flashed back to when he had been a boy. He had had an awful green school uniform, with a similar small pocket in the short trousers. One day he had found a threepenny bit in that pocket. He spent it at lunchtime on sweets, and yet, the next morning, there it was, in the same pocket. Again he spent it, this time on a comic, but, sure enough, the following day it was there again. A magic coin! Or a magic pocket, it didn't matter. As long as he didn't question it, the magic would last. And it did. It never once occurred to him that his mother or father was replenishing the supply every night. He simply believed, and never questioned, the magic. It wasn't until he was an adult that, looking back, he realised that no magic had been at work, only love. And at that moment, as he stood in the High Street SE1, bereaved, accused and hunted, he smiled, and thanked his parents.

He caught sight of a bus approaching from the south. He decided to change direction again, and he crossed the road, ran to the next stop, flagged it down, and got on. It was going towards Aldgate.

He got off at Aldgate East. He would have had to pay more to go further, and he desperately needed to stop for a while and take stock. He looked around him, and saw a familiar restaurant, Blooms. It was a kosher restaurant, and he had been there many times as a boy, when his father and grandfather went up to Petticoat Lane market on a Sunday. He looked in the window. They were closing. On a Friday afternoon? Of course, he thought, it's the beginning of Sabbath.

He pressed his nose against the window, remembering those wonderful frantic Sunday lunches, the noise, the brusque, almost rude, waiters that seemed to be a feature of the place, the deals struck over a cup of lemon tea. As he stared in, a waiter put his head round the door to shoo him away.

'What do you want? We're closed.'

'I just wanted a glass of water. I . . . I've been robbed . . . all my money taken . . . I just—' He was unable to finish.

'Robbed? Come in, come in,' said the man, and put his arm round Charles as if he were an invalid. He helped Charles through the door.

'Sophie! Come quick! This man's just been beaten up and robbed!'

He deposited Charles in a chair, and raced to get him some water. A large middle-aged woman scurried over from where she had been counting money, and two other members of staff approached too. Charles's original rescuer brought a glass of water, but Sophie brushed him aside.

'Water? Is that the best you can do? Sam, get him some brandy.'

'No, it's really alright,' said Charles. 'I've not been hurt, just jostled. If I could just sit quietly for two minutes, I'll be fine. It was a bit of a shock, that's all.'

'You want a lemon tea?' asked one of the others.

'Yes, that would be lovely, thank you.'

'Do you want me to call the police?' asked the woman.

'No—there's no point. I didn't see who did it. I passed through a crowd of kids, I was shoved by someone. I don't know where they went, nor which one did it.' His audience looked doubtful. 'Really, all I want is to sit quietly for a minute.'

His tea arrived, and he sat nursing it, as the staff continued to clear up, looking across at him every now and then. He tried to marshal his thoughts, to decide what to do next.

Firstly, he had twenty pence, no credit cards, no chequebook. He had no transport—the Jag was in police custody, and the keys to the MG were at the flat, which was certainly watched. He had nowhere to sleep, and no way of paying for a room. No one from Chambers could, or would, help. By now they would all know what had happened. There were other friends, but he couldn't trust anyone to give him shelter. His escape would be on the news by now, and the reason he had been in custody. The public would have been warned that he was dangerous, possibly armed, and that they should not tackle him. Hah! thought Charles. Dangerous? Glazer had been right. Charles hadn't the slightest idea what to do next. I don't have any criminal associates who would help me, he thought, no false passport, no stash of money, nothing.

For a moment he actually considered turning himself in, but he rejected that immediately. He knew how the police operated. They loved nothing more than an open and shut case: a quick arrest and a speedy conviction was good for the public, good for the crime statistics, and good for promotion. How many times, as a defence advocate, had he cross-examined police officers, and asked why they

156

had apparently ignored good evidence that ran counter to their case? The truth was, if they had sufficient for a conviction, that was good enough. Evidence pointing the other way—that was for the defence to investigate. So what that the defence didn't have hundreds of trained officers to look for clues? So what that they didn't have forensic laboratories? So what that, in reality, they couldn't compel people to give evidence? Whoever had set Charles up had done a very thorough job. Handing himself in to the police and expecting them to investigate his wild story of a frame—it was laughable. The only possible hope of getting himself out of the mess he was in, was to do it himself. What could he lose? He was already facing disgrace, loss of his career, not to mention lifelong imprisonment.

On reaching this happy conclusion, Charles swigged the last drop of his lemon tea and stood. He went towards the cash desk, his hand in his pocket, as if to offer to pay for his drink, but Sophie stopped him.

'Don't be silly,' she said. 'How do you feel?'

'Better,' he said.

'You look it. You want a taxi or something?'

'No, thanks, I'll be fine. Thank you for your kindness.'

'What else?' she shrugged. She came round the desk with the keys to open up for him.

Charles stepped out into the street, and waved good-bye. He wandered off, walking in no particular direction. He suddenly realised with a shock that he had run directly back to the area where he had grown up. He wondered if it had truly been chance, or whether his unconscious had prompted him to head for the part of London where he had felt safe as a child. That thought was immediately followed by the more worrying one: wasn't this exactly where the police would look first? He shrugged to himself. It was too late to worry; he was stuck there with nothing to do but walk. Part of him hoped that providence would intervene and give him some idea what to do. It did. He had been walking for about fifteen minutes when he rounded a corner and walked straight into the path of two approaching policemen. He didn't know if they had seen him, but he ducked into the nearest doorway.

Charles found himself in an art gallery. He had not known that such a thing existed in the East End. The sign above the door declared this to be the Whitechapel Art Gallery. It was surprisingly dark for an art gallery, he thought. A woman walked towards him.

'I'm sorry, sir, but we're closing,' she said.

'Oh . . .' said Charles, wondering how to end the sentence in a way that didn't leave him back on the pavement. He used to joke how those in his profession would frequently start a sentence without the faintest idea what it was to contain. It was the advocate's way of not surrendering the floor, creating time to think. Never before have I needed the skill so much, he thought wryly.

'Oh . . . that's a great pity,' he continued. 'I've passed the gallery every day for months, and for the first time I've actually had a few minutes to stop and look inside, and I find you're closing.'

'I'm really sorry, sir . . .' the woman paused, somehow disconcerted by Charles's face now that she was close enough to see it, '. . . but I'm in sole charge at present, and I have to leave early tonight as I'm . . .'

Her voice died away. Charles looked at her more carefully. She was a truly beautiful woman. Short-cut black hair, so short as to be severe, but accentuating a wonderfully gentle face, with deep brown eyes so large they drew the attention, and held it fast. She was about thirty, Charles guessed, but her body looked as if it were that of a younger woman. She looked as if she was an athlete, or a dancer perhaps.

'Charlie Horowitz,' she said softly. It was the first time anyone had used his proper name for over fifteen years.

'Who . . .?' he stammered.

The woman held out her hand, shyly, and, Charles could have sworn, with a slight blush. 'Rachel Golding,' she said. 'I knew you, once.'

Charles searched his memory. A very faint bell of

recognition rang about the name, but not about its owner. He felt sure that he would have remembered her, had he known her before.

'We were at school together, and *chaider*,' she said, referring to the synagogue Sunday school. 'Well, not *together*, in truth, because you were a few years older than me. Still are, I expect.' She still held his hand in hers, and she looked at him with a strange mixture of shyness and directness. She released him, and he felt himself wishing she had not.

'I don't blame you for not remembering,' she continued. 'I was twelve when we last met, and I've probably changed. You were eighteen, and just going off to university.' As she spoke, she turned off the remaining lights, and picked up her bag to leave.

'You must have amazing powers of recall to remember me, and all that, if we last met almost twenty years ago,' he said.

'Perhaps. But I had a dreadful crush on you then,' she said with a disarming smile. 'To you, I was a squawky little girl—if you noticed me at all. And because you were the success of the school. Cambridge, wasn't it? Barrister, and all the rest. I kept noticing your name here and there in the papers. It's "Howard" now, isn't it?'

Charles smiled. 'It is.'

She indicated the door. Charles thought quickly. 'Will you permit me to make up for the appalling rudeness of not recognising you, by taking you for a drink?'

She shook her head. 'That's very kind of you,' she said, 'but I've got some shopping to do, and I'm going out later.' She ushered him out on to the pavement. He looked quickly up and down the road, but could see no uniforms. 'But if you go past so often, please pop in some other time, and I'd be delighted to come.'

She busied herself with locking the main door. Charles still had no idea what he was going to do, but he knew that this woman, and her slender connection with his past, was all he had.

'Can't I persuade you to come for even a quick drink?

It's twenty years, after all, and it would be nice to catch up.'

'No, sorry—'

'Look—there's a pub right opposite. One drink?'

She shook her head, and was about to refuse, but then looked at him strangely, and shrugged. 'Oh, what the hell! Tesco's can wait ten minutes.'

Chapter Twenty-four

Ten minutes turned into twenty, and twenty into half an hour. Rachel looked repeatedly at the clock, at first surreptitiously, but eventually quite openly, not wanting to be rude, but hoping he would appreciate that she was late. He questioned her about her past, whether she had married (she had), whether she was still married (she was not), whether she had children (none), what she did (temporarily at the gallery, but trained as a dancer). To Rachel, it felt like a cross-examination, and she told him so. There was a sort of desperation about him that was palpable. He seemed intent on delaying her departure as long as possible. It frightened her, and at the same time intrigued her.

He had also made up some lame excuse about having left his wallet in his coat, and the coat in his car, which required her to pay for the drinks. That in itself didn't bother her, but the excuse was so obviously false. He was clearly still prosperous—look at his £300 suit and gold cufflinks—so why not pay for a round of drinks that he had pressed on her? The whole thing seemed to Rachel to be decidedly odd. Perhaps he was in trouble, she thought, but what? Why didn't he go to the police, or phone a friend, or something?

She still found him attractive. The years had treated him kindly. He looked younger than what must have been his 38 years, despite the slight thickening of his waist. There was a little grey in his dark curly hair, but he looked alright on it.

After a further five minutes, Rachel decided that, whatever the mystery, she had to leave. She rose from her seat without giving him the opportunity to object.

'I must be off, Charles. It's been very pleasant, but I'm due somewhere else. Goodbye.' She turned and made for the door.

Charles leapt up, almost knocking over the small table. He caught up with her just as she reached the pavement.

'Where are you going? I mean, I wonder if we're going in the same direction?'

She shook her head in open disbelief. 'I'm going to my parents' home for dinner, alright? What the hell's the matter with you? You've become decidedly weird in the last twenty years, Charlie Horowitz.'

He grinned awkwardly, but for a second the mask slipped. He looked lost, and frightened. She approached him, concern on her face.

'Are you OK?' she asked, looking up at him.

'I'm fine, yes . . .' he began, but no plausible explanation came to him. He shrugged, and turned away, raising his hand in farewell. 'Bye,' he called.

Rachel watched him walk away, and then called out.

'Hey!' She ran after him, took him by the wrist, and turned him to face her. 'I don't know what's going on, Charles, and I know I'm going to regret this, but here goes: would you like to come to dinner tonight? I'm sure Mum can squeeze one more in.'

'Are you sure?' he asked.

'Don't press your luck, Charlie. Just say "Yes" and come along.'

'Yes.'

'Fine,' she said, taking his arm. 'They'll be pleased to see you again after all this time.'

'Will they know me?' he asked with some surprise.

'You? The brightest boy in school and *chaider*? The one who went to Cambridge and became a barrister? You've got to be joking.'

They walked arm in arm to the bus stop. For the first time Charles began to feel slightly more optimistic. He didn't know where he was going to spend the night, and he had no idea how to go about clearing his name, but he had a meal coming up in a house where the police would never find him, and he didn't have to worry about his next move for a few hours. He also realised with satisfaction that it was a house where neither the radio nor the television would be on tonight.

He was still nervous while waiting at the bus stop, but once they were aboard the bus, Rachel watched him begin to relax. She paid both their fares without comment, Charles pretending to be interested in the scenery, silently blessing her. They chatted easily during the journey. She asked questions about his job, and, ever the showman, he began telling anecdotes and stories. After a while she was almost pleased she had asked him along. He was intelligent and funny, and she found herself liking him. The only tension arose when she asked questions about his family. He deflected any subject that touched on his marriage, where he lived, or anything personal, and she learned after a few attempts to avoid the area.

After about 25 minutes she told him that they should get off, and he followed her off the bus and stepped into a terraced street. They were somewhere in Hackney. They walked, still chatting, for another few minutes, and eventually arrived in a cul-de-sac. Rachel led him to the penultimate house on the left, and knocked on the door. Charles heard the sound of approaching footsteps, and the door was opened by a slender grey-haired man in his mid sixties.

'Hello, Ray, darling,' he said, giving her a hug. 'And what sort of time do you call this?' he chided gently.

'I got held up, Pop,' she said, standing back to introduce Charles.

'Davie?' said Mr Golding, squinting at Charles.

'No, it's not Davie. Pop, you remember Charlie Horowitz, don't you? We haven't seen him for—'

'Charlie Horowitz? Millie and Harry's eldest?'

'Yes, that's right,' replied Charles, holding out his hand. Mr Golding took it. 'Come in, my boy, and meet Betty.' He guided Charles ahead of him down the narrow hallway, and glanced quickly at Rachel. She shook her head and put her finger to her lips. Her father nodded understanding.

'Go in the lounge, Charlie,' said Mr Golding, pushing Charles gently into a room on his right. Charles found himself alone in an ill-lit room rather over-filled with heavy furniture. Mr Golding disappeared off down the corridor to another room, out of which spilled a warm soft light. The smell of the house immediately brought back Charles's childhood. He could detect freshly baked bread, chicken soup, something roasting—the best smells of his early life. Safe smells.

A minute later Mrs Golding was ushered into the room by Rachel and her father, wiping her hands on her apron.

'You remember little Charlie Horowitz, don't you, Mother?' asked Mr Golding.

'I think he prefers "Charles" now, Mummy,' said Rachel.

'Yes, of course I remember. How could I forget?' She gave Charles a kiss and a warm hug. 'I hear you bumped into Ray this afternoon.'

'That's right.'

'You'll stay for supper, yes? It's not special, just a *shabbas* meal, you understand, but you will stay all the same?' she asked.

'If there's room for me, I'd love to,' he replied.

'Mummy always makes twice as much as we can eat,' said Rachel.

'So, that's settled,' said Mr Golding.

163

'I'm sorry Charlie—Charles—but we weren't expecting guests,' said Mrs Golding, looking worried. 'Will you mind if we eat in the other room? If I'd known you were coming, we'd have eaten in the dining room, but when there's just the three of us, usually I don't bother . . .'

'Mrs Golding, it smells so good, I would eat it in the garden!'

'I told you, Mother,' said Mr Golding. 'Let's eat. I'm starved.'

They went through to the other room. It was a living room, adjoining the kitchen. In the middle of the room was a table, set for three places, laden with food. At the centre of the table were the Sabbath candles, lit as dusk fell, which explained the rebuke Rachel received for arriving late.

Another place was laid, a fourth chair obtained. Charles was shown to his place. Mr Golding put on a skull-cap.

'Do you have a *capel*?' asked Mr Golding. Charles shook his head. Mrs Golding opened a drawer and handed out another, and Charles put it on his head. Mr Golding filled a silver cup with wine, and said *kiddush*, the blessing over wine. They all said '*amen*', and the cup was passed to each in turn. Mrs Golding then said the blessing over the bread, and they sat to eat.

Charles was told to help himself to hors d'oeuvres, which he did with alacrity: bread, chopped egg and onion, salted and pickled herrings, olives. Then followed chicken soup with dumplings, and then roast chicken. Warmed by the good food, the gentle hospitality and his temporary security, Charles forgot his problems for the first time, and relaxed. No difficult subjects of conversation cropped up, but Charles was not aware of anyone being careful. He felt totally at ease, part of the family if only for that evening, and he talked. He talked about university, life at the Bar, judges, cases. They spoke about the religion school that he and Rachel had attended, the synagogue, and old times. He found out something about Rachel,

164

and her failed marriage, and he guessed by her parents' response that they still had not come to terms with a divorce in the family. In a Jewish family, divorce was still comparatively rare, and was the subject of gossip and speculation in the community, and sometimes shame.

Rachel spoke of her short-lived career as a dancer, and how she had had to give it up when she divorced because she had to support herself. Charles loved watching her speak. Her face was suffused with a warm glow, made all the more radiant by the candlelight, and those huge eyes sparkled as she spoke. When she talked of dancing her whole demeanour changed—she became excited and vibrant. Charles looked at her, and liked what he saw. Mr and Mrs Golding observed him watching her, and smiled to one another.

The evening rushed by, and before he realised how the time had gone, Rachel was standing to leave.

'I must run before I miss the last bus,' she said. She looked at Charles.

'I'll walk with you,' he said, rising too.

Mr and Mrs Golding escorted them to the door. Mrs Golding gave him another kiss. 'Nice to see you, Charlie,' she said, looking closely at him. 'Any time you're in the area, please come in. And if you need anything . . .' She left the sentence unfinished. Charles did not know what, if anything, to read into the comment, but thanked her with a hug. Mr Golding took Charles's hand, shook it, and held it in both his for a moment.

'Take care, Charlie. I'm glad we could welcome you to our family. It's good to be with one's family on *shabbas*, yes?'

Mrs Golding thumped him on the arm. 'Big mouth,' she said. 'Ignore him,' she said to Charles. 'He's . . .' she raised her hands to the heavens, unable to find the right word.

'Forget it,' said Charles. 'Thank you once again. I've had a lovely evening, and a terrific meal.'

165

Charles and Rachel walked together down the path, and the door was closed behind them. They walked in silence for a while.

'I think I can guess what that last comment was about,' said Charles.

'Don't take any notice of Pop. Tact has never been his strong suit.'

'They're still in touch with my family, right?'

Rachel spoke carefully. 'They see them at *shul*, at the High Holydays, and so on.'

'How are they?'

'I thought your family was one of the taboo subjects; like your home and your marriage.'

'How are they?' repeated Charles.

'They're both fine, as far as I know. Your mother had a heart attack a few years back, but she's lost some weight, and she's alright now.'

'And Dad?'

'Well, I think. I saw them both a few weeks ago.'

'And David?'

'He's fine. He still talks about you, you know. He's very proud of his big brother, even after all these years.'

Charles walked on, lost in thought for a while.

'It wasn't just me, you know?'

'Charles, if you don't want to talk about it, that's fine.'

'I want you to understand. I know I disappointed them, by . . . marrying out . . . changing my name . . . all of that. And at the time, I saw my background as a hindrance, it was dragging me down . . . But I would never have cut all contact. That was Dad's doing.'

They reached the bus stop and stood in silence for a while. Then Rachel rounded on him.

'OK, Charlie Horowitz, Charles Howard, or whatever it is. It's own-up time. Where are you going? Back to the car that's got your wallet in it?' she asked, with obvious sarcasm. 'The one we didn't use to get here, but left '"just around the corner" from the gallery? There isn't a car, is there? You haven't got a penny on you, have you? And I don't think you've got anywhere to go.'

Charles didn't answer.

'You've conned a free drink out of me, and a free meal out of my parents. Fair enough. But I'm not paying any more bus fares for you, and I'm not taking you anywhere until you tell me what's going on!'

She frowned at him severely with those wonderful wide eyes, her mouth set in a firm line. He wanted to tell her. By God, he wanted to tell her. Just to blurt out the whole unbelievable story, to tell her everything. He wanted her deep gentle voice to say 'There, there', and her arms to encircle him, and make it alright. But he couldn't do it.

'I'm in trouble,' he started.

'I didn't have to be Brain of Britain to work that out,' she said sourly.

'Look, I can't tell you here, on the street. You're right, I owe you an explanation, but . . . it's a long story, and I can't just tell it, like that,' and he snapped his fingers. 'You are also right when you say I haven't got any money, and I haven't anywhere to sleep. If you let me come back to your place, I'll try to explain.'

She considered him, looking into his eyes. That he was genuinely frightened and in trouble she did not doubt. Whether she would get the truth out of him here, or at her flat, remained doubtful.

'OK,' she said. 'I'll take you back, and you can explain there. But no promises. If I'm not satisfied that you're telling me . . . what is it? "The truth, the whole truth, and nothing but the truth", I'll sling you out on your ear. And probably call the police too. Is that understood?'

'Understood.'

'Right,' she said. 'Here's the bus.'

He gripped her hand in thanks, and she looked up at him and smiled.

Chapter Twenty-five

'Well?' asked Rachel.

They sat facing one another across her kitchen table, each with a mug of coffee. The flat was part of a large converted house between Islington and Dalston. It had one bedroom and a large, high-ceilinged living room, plus the tiny kitchen in which they sat. Charles wondered where to begin, and how much to tell her. He knew also that as soon as she turned on a television, or read a newspaper, she would probably find out the whole story in any event. On the other hand, that wouldn't be until the morning, and a judicious filtering of the truth might enable him to stay there overnight.

He spoke into his coffee, not trusting himself to be able to lie successfully if he made eye contact with her.

'My wife . . . died . . . yesterday . . .'

'Oh, Charles . . .' Rachel said.

'It's not exactly what you might think . . . we were more or less separated. I wanted a divorce in fact. I . . . cared about her . . . but I don't think we loved each other any more.'

'Have you no children?' asked Rachel.

'No; probably fortunate in that respect. I've seen too many matrimonial cases where the children end up the most damaged.'

Rachel thought about this information.

168

'She died yesterday? Aren't there arrangements . . .
you know . . .'

'Yes. They're being taken care of.'

'But why are you just wandering around the East End? I
can understand your not wanting to be at home, but surely
you have friends you could go to?'

'As for why I'm wandering around here . . .'

'Your parents?' she suggested.

'No. Not really, although perhaps subconsciously I was
looking for something . . . familiar.'

Rachel pushed her chair back from the table and walked
to the sink. She poured away what was left of her coffee.
She spoke with a level voice.

'There's something you're not telling me, Charles. I
believe what you've told me so far, but it's not half the
story. None of what you have said explains why you have
no money, and why you were so anxious not to let me go
this afternoon. This is your last chance. I shan't call the
police, but unless you tell me what's going on, you must
leave now.'

'I'm afraid to tell you.'

'Why?'

'Because if you don't believe me, you *will* call the police.
And I don't know how to make you believe me.'

She laughed. 'That's your line of business, isn't it?'
she said as she rinsed out her mug. 'Being an advocate?
Persuading people? So: persuade me.'

Her levity vanished when she turned and saw the
genuine anguish on his face.

'That's the whole point isn't it? The very fact that lawyers
are supposed to be professional liars means that you'll
suspect *whatever* I say. I'm hoist by my own petard.'

She brought her chair and sat beside him, her hand on
his arm.

'Try me,' she said softly.

Charles took a deep, broken, breath, and started.

'I'll tell you what the headlines will say tomorrow.
They'll say "Leading Barrister Murders Wife—Escapes
from Police".'

He heard her sharp intake of breath, and felt her hand be removed, but he forged on.

'Underneath it will explain how I viciously cut her throat; how I did it for the money; how I was having an affair with some blonde floozie; how I killed her to stop her divorcing me; how the evidence against me is overwhelming.'

There was a long silence.

'And will any of it be true?' Rachel asked in a small voice. He did not answer immediately. He knew he had to be convincing. It wasn't just a matter of telling the truth—he'd had too many clients tell the truth and still be convicted. There were times when the truth alone was not enough. It had to be coached, polished, delivered, packaged. Charles turned to her, held her shoulders at arm's length, felt her freeze with fear, and looked straight into her eyes. He measured every word carefully, pouring sincerity into each one as he spoke.

'Not a single word of it, Rachel. I swear on everything I hold dear, not a single word. They'll probably misspell my name, too.'

She returned his gaze unwaveringly, as if trying to pierce his soul.

'I believe you,' she said at last.

From somewhere inside him, a sob welled up, and his eyes filled with tears. He didn't know if it was genuine, or just part of his being convincing, but he let it happen. 'I'm so fucking frightened,' he said. She put her arms round him, and hugged him.

Rachel made him up a bed on the settee in the lounge. She wondered if he would make any comment, but he was so worn out that he didn't argue. He had wanted to talk about it further, to decide what he was going to do, but she forbade him. In the morning, she had said firmly. Within ten minutes of pulling the blanket around his ears, he was asleep.

Charles woke up suddenly, momentarily unsure of where he was. Then memory flooded back, and he almost groaned aloud. He could hear a voice—Rachel's voice?—from her bedroom. The phone! He threw back the blanket, and tiptoed to her door.

'He's here now—' he heard. He didn't wait for more. Using all his considerable weight, he charged at the door. The catch gave way and he continued into the room. Rachel was sitting on the edge of her bed, her back to the door, wearing a T-shirt. She was speaking quietly into the telephone, hunched over so as not to be heard. Charles flew at her and grabbed the handset. She screamed and backed away from him.

'You bitch!' he spat.

'It's not what you think!' she cried.

Charles paused, about to rip the phone cord from the wall.

'It's not what you think,' she repeated. 'I'm not talking to the police.'

'Who then?' he demanded.

'It's David—your brother. I didn't know what to do, so I called him. We're still friends.'

'What? I don't believe you,' Charles shouted.

'Well, speak to him then,' she said, gesturing to the phone.

Charles slowly put the handset to his ear.

'Ray? What's happening?' he heard from the other end.

'David? Is that you?'

'Charlie?'

'David . . . David . . ' He could get no more out. The dam broke, and Charles wept uncontrollably. 'Davie . . . Oh God . . .' he cried. 'I'm in trouble . . . they say I killed Henrietta, but I didn't do it, I swear . . . and . . . I don't know what to do . . . Oh, Davie . . . I've missed you!'

He could say no more. He sat on the edge of the bed, his elbows on his knees, the handset in his hand, and let the tears come. For his parents, for David, for poor Henrietta, and for himself. This time he knew what he was feeling was genuine—it hurt too much to be anything else.

Rachel gently took the handset out of Charles's hand.

'Davie? I'll ring you back, either tonight or tomorrow

171

morning. OK . . . Yes . . . OK. And if they do, just tell them that you've spoken to him, and that he's innocent. Of course I'm sure. And tell them not to worry. Alright. Bye.'

She hung up. She handed Charles a box of tissues, and he grabbed a handful. He started talking. He told her everything, between huge gulps of air, from the argument with Henrietta the night before, to the moment when he met her. She put her arms round him while she listened, and hugged him, rocking back and forth, back and forth, until the storm was over. They sat in silence for a long time, her arms still around his chest, her head on his shoulder.

'Now, I'm sure I believe you,' she said, sitting up and kissing him.

He turned to her. He put his arms round her, and let her kiss his shoulder, slowly, each kiss an inch higher than the last, until she reached his ear. Then she travelled down to the angle of his jaw, and reached his lips. This shouldn't be happening, thought Charles. He responded, softly at first, but then with greater force. She opened her mouth, and gently bit his lower lip. Her hands reached to the back of his neck, and pulled his head hard towards her.

He allowed himself to fall backwards, pulling her with him, so that they were lying side by side. His left hand caressed her thigh and moved up over her waist, and under her T-shirt to her breast. She sighed as his hand reached her nipple. Her hand ran down his back to the curve of his buttocks, and then slipped under the waist of his pants. He pulled up her T-shirt and bent to her nipple, licking it at first, and then sucking gently. She moaned gently.

'Wait,' she commanded, while she disentangled herself, and sat up. She pulled her shirt over her head, and he took the opportunity to remove his pants. They were both naked. She made to get into bed, but he stopped her.

'I've been looking at you from the moment we met, and wondering. I want to see you properly.'

She stopped, and smiled. He held her slightly

172

away from himself, and looked. She didn't betray any embarrassment at this scrutiny. She had a long slender neck and the slightly hard, muscular body of a dancer, with small high breasts, dark prominent nipples, a hard, flat stomach, and long legs. Her pubic hair was short and very dark. Her hips weren't as narrow as he had imagined, nor her bottom as boyish, which pleased him.

'Well?' she said, impatient, but smiling.

'Wow!' was his response, although it was superfluous. His excitement was obvious, and had grown as he looked at her.

'Now my turn,' she said, trying to push him further away so she could look at him.

'Oh no!' he said, grabbing her and pulling her to him. 'I know my limitations,' he protested, 'and they will not stand such scrutiny.'

She allowed herself to be pulled, and they held one another, she aware of his hotness branding her stomach. His hands swooped up and down her back from her shoulders to the hollow above her waist in wonder; her skin was so soft, yet she felt so hard underneath, like satin on steel. She licked his neck, and slowly bent her knees, so that her tongue travelled down his chest, through the curly black and grey hairs, and to his navel, leaving a cool, wet trail behind it. Now she knelt before him, and continued licking into his pubic hair, her breath hot on him. Her tongue momentarily caught in the tangle of wiry curls, and then continued along his erect penis. She stroked his bottom with both hands, and then suddenly, so that it was almost a shock to him, took him into her mouth. He put his hands under her armpits, and gently lifted her to her feet. She looked at him questioningly.

'Don't you like that?' she asked.

'Very much,' he replied, kissing her neck, 'but tonight's a double act.'

He led her to the bed, and they got in. Their legs entwined, and he felt her moistness. He leaned over her, and held her face in his hands.

173

'I can't believe this. It's been quite a day,' he said, more to himself than to her.

'It's not over yet,' she said, as she pulled him towards her. He climbed between her legs, and joined her.

Chapter Twenty-six

Charles awoke to find himself alone in the bed. He rolled over and grabbed Rachel's pillow to add to his own. It smelled of her and he smiled. He dozed contentedly for a few minutes, but began to be concerned that he could hear no noise from elsewhere in the flat. Eventually he rolled out of bed, and padded into the lounge.

'Rachel?' he called.

There was no response. He went back into the bedroom to collect his underpants from where they had lain since the night before, and returned to put on his trousers.

He went into the kitchen. There was a pot of tea already made, but it felt almost cold. He poured a cup anyway, and drank it. He went over to the large window overlooking the street, and saw Rachel just climbing the steps to the house, shopping bags in her hands.

Charles opened the flat door for her as she climbed the stairs.

'You've been busy,' he said.

'Morning, sleepy,' she said, kissing him, and going into the kitchen.

'What've you got?' he asked, closing the door behind her.

'Breakfast,' she replied. 'I'd hoped to be back before you woke up. Here,' she called, and threw a plastic bag at him. He caught it, and looked inside. 'If you're anything like me,' she said, 'you can't bear putting on dirty clothes.' It was a couple of pairs of pants and socks.

'How did you know the size?' he asked.

'I think I got the measure of you pretty well last night,' she said as she passed him on her way to the bathroom.

'Rachel?' he called after her.

'Yes?'

'Do you have to work today?'

'No,' she called back. 'And I've got a few days' holiday owing, so I'll be able to take some of next week off too. By the way, there's an envelope for you on the dresser.'

He went over and picked it up. There was £100 in it.

'What's this for?' he asked.

'Emergencies,' she called back.

She came out of the bathroom.

'No, thank you,' he said, handing the envelope back to her.

'Don't be silly, Charles. If I believe you are innocent—and I do—' she added hastily, 'then I have to do everything I can to help. You can't get around without some money. God knows what you might need it for. So I got it out of the Post Office. I can get some more on Monday if necessary. Regard it as a loan.'

He went up to her, and kissed her. 'You're lovely,' he said. 'It's strictly a loan. Even if I have to repay it out of earnings from sewing mail bags!'

They went together to the kitchen for breakfast. After they had eaten, she threw a pad and pencil at him. He looked at her questioningly.

'Let's start with the clues we have,' she said.

'Already done it,' he answered, tapping his head. 'I've got a question first though. Did you speak to David?'

'Yes. I phoned him this morning. While I was out.

175

Just being ultra-careful,' she said in response to his raised eyebrows.

'OK. And what did he say?'

'The police have already been there, looking for you. He told them that he hadn't seen or heard from you in nearly fifteen years.'

'Have they been to Mum and Dad's yet?'

'No. But David's spoken to them. They'll say exactly the same thing.'

'Do they believe me?'

'I don't know. They know that David's spoken to you, and that he's prepared to accept my judgement. Anyway, there's someone watching David's house, and probably, by now, your parents' as well, so there's nothing any of them can do.'

Charles looked depressed. 'But what the hell?' she said, trying to cheer him up. 'You've got me. Let's get down to it. What have you got?'

Charles threw the pad back to her. 'You can write them down if you like.' He stood, and paced about the room, the way he always did when considering points for a speech to a jury, or a submission to a judge.

'First, the girl. Someone, probably *not* called Melissa Maxwell, had access to my flat, and a very detailed knowledge of when I would be absent. She couldn't risk being seen by me, or the whole thing would have collapsed. I wonder if she arrived by car, or on foot. That takes us to Denis, the porter. Let's put him to one side for the moment. Next: the murderer. What do we know about him?'

'Or her,' corrected Rachel.

'No, I don't think so. Apparently the witnesses thought it was me driving away, and I'm pretty big. She'd have had to have been a very big girl. Anyway, whoever it was seems to have got Henrietta from the kitchen to the lounge, according to one of the officers I overheard at the house. So, it's a him. And he's good with cars, because the car was out of commission, and then suddenly it was working—unless, of course, it was a sporadic fault, which isn't impossible.' Charles paced up and down, ticking off items on his fingers. 'He knows about computers, as he faked that letter, and then very cleverly wiped the disc, *knowing* that it could still be traced. Now not everybody knows that once erased, a document may be found again. So he knows computers. He must have some money, to pay the girl for her services. Lastly, he must have obtained a key to the flat.'

'Does the porter have a key?'

'No. And I changed the locks when I moved in.'

'So someone obtained a copy of your key?'

'Yes. That means they must have broken into Chambers or the flat. So he's a burglar too.'

'Talented man,' commented Rachel.

Charles came round behind Rachel, and absently stroked her hair.

'That's as much as we know about him. What about suspects?'

Rachel shrugged. 'I was thinking about that while I was out. Any enemies?'

Charles frowned. 'Not really. There was a bloke called Kellett–Brown. He used to be a barrister. I needn't go into the details, but something happened, and he swore revenge. I got hate letters for a while. Very melodramatic.'

'He sounds like a possibility then?'

'Maybe, but as far as I know, he's dead, and anyway I can't see the motive for killing Henrietta.'

'Do you prosecute criminal cases?'

'Some,' Charles answered, 'but only minor stuff. I didn't do it often enough to get sent good cases. I can't see petty thieves and joy-riders being so upset by their fines, or probation orders, that they want to murder my wife and frame me for it.'

'What about unsuccessful defences? Anyone with a grudge?' asked Rachel, leaning back into his arms.

'That's a possibility. And it means I have to get into Chambers.'

'Why?'

'Because I have kept every barrister's notebook I have

ever used. I record details of every case, the evidence, the mitigation, everything. Every criminal I have ever represented or prosecuted is in there.'

'Will there be anyone in Chambers on Saturday?'

'Unlikely, but possible. The problem is not so much being discovered, as getting in. My keys are with the police. But it's only on the first floor, and it's not terribly secure.'

'What would be the best time to go?' asked Rachel.

'This evening, I would guess. At least that way we can tell if there's anyone inside by the presence or absence of lights.'

'Can you suggest anything we can do until then?' she asked. He leered comically at her. 'What a wonderful idea,' she said.

The scene outside The Cedars on Saturday morning was less frenetic than it had been the day before, but there were still purposeful-looking men working at the house. Superintendent Glazer had been joined by an older officer who had just returned from annual leave. Although he was junior in rank to the Superintendent, he had been a policeman for twice as long. Two years before he had been transferred to the force from the Met. Superintendent Glazer did not like him very much. The officer gave the impression of being a bit grubby. He wore a thin moustache that seemed to perch on his top lip, and he reminded Superintendent Glazer of a rodent. His name was Detective Inspector Ronald Henry Wheatley.

Inspector Wheatley knew that he had come across Mr Howard on cases in the past; it would have been strange had they not met professionally, having both worked with major London criminals for some years, but he had no personal recollection of the man. Indeed, having been shown a photograph, he still did not recognise him. Because Superintendent Glazer did not like him, he placed Inspector Wheatley on part of the investigation where he hoped they would meet infrequently. And with Glazer dealing with the London end of the inquiry, and heading the hunt for Howard, Inspector Wheatley was assigned the task of going through the Buckinghamshire home.

So it was that when the doorbell rang at about noon at The Cedars, he happened to be the nearest to the door, and he opened it.

There was a man in oily overalls on the doorstep. 'Where's the car, mate?' he asked cheerfully.

'What car?' asked Wheatley.

'The Jag. I was told it would be in the garage, but it ain't.'

'Who told you it would be in the garage?'

'My guv'nor.'

'I think you'd better come in. Constable Jones!' called Wheatley.

'Sir?' replied an officer who poked his head out from the understairs cupboard.

'I think we may need a statement taken here. Now, you are . . .' he asked of the mechanic.

'Roger, from Breck & Co.'

'Well, Roger from Breck and Co, who asked you to take the Jag?'

'Look,' said Roger, very patiently, because he was clearly dealing with an idiot, 'Mrs Howard rings us up on Tuesday or Wednesday, or whenever it was, and says that the Jag won't go and would we book it in for work, right?'

'Right,' said Wheatley.

'Well, we were so busy that we couldn't do it till today. My foreman asks me to come and collect the car, and leave a courtesy car, which I have. It's outside, an Escort. But the Jag isn't there.'

Inspector Wheatley had not been on this case from the beginning. He was, however, a thorough man and he had read all the statements, and the brief notes of the interview with Charles Howard. He knew that Howard claimed that the car hadn't been working, but that nonetheless it had been found after apparently being driven to London. Now it appeared that there was some independent confirmation of Howard's story.

'Jones: full statement please. Then go with Roger here,

and take one from his foreman, or whoever it was that actually spoke to Mrs Howard on the phone last week. Make sure it was she who spoke on the phone. If the person who spoke to her didn't actually know her voice from earlier occasions, the statement must say so. Understand?'

'Yes, sir.'

'Sergeant Kent?'

'Up here, sir,' came the reply from upstairs.

'Get on the blower to Aylesbury, and make sure no one touches that car. I want all prints taken from top to bottom. Pay particular attention to inside the bonnet. Got it?'

'Right you are, sir.'

'What do you think?' asked Rachel.

'It doesn't look as if anyone's there,' said Charles.

They sat in the MG in the car park in Middle Temple, looking up at the windows of 2 Chancery Court. One thing about MGs, Charles had said, was that any idiot could get into them, simply by lifting up the corner of the hood and unlocking the door. They had been sitting there for half an hour, and no one had entered or left the building.

'Alright,' said Charles. 'Here goes. Sound the horn if you see anyone coming.' He got out of the car. He walked up the steps to the main door, and grabbed hold of the drainpipe that ran down the wall immediately to the left. He tugged at it. It seemed firm. He hauled himself up, leaning out, with his knees bent and his feet as flat against the wall as possible. The pointing between the bricks was poor, so that every few inches there was a tiny ledge for his feet to grip on. He found it remarkably easy, and within only a few seconds had reached the window ledge of the first floor. I'm in the wrong job, he thought to himself. Maybe there *was* something he could do after serving a life stretch. He stood on the ledge, wondering how to move to the window. It was a sash window, but it had been locked. Charles inched along the ledge to the next: locked also. The last one was not locked. He bent and pushed the bottom sash upwards, and the window opened. He stepped into his own room.

He went straight to the cupboard where he kept the notebooks. He had totally forgotten how many there were. They were stacked in two piles, each at least three feet high. He couldn't hope to carry half of them. He decided to take the most recent half. He looked at the dates on the front of the oldest of these; they started in 1982. That would have to do. He rummaged in his drawer without putting the light on and found a length of pink ribbon, usually used for tying briefs, and made a parcel of the notebooks. He then leaned out of the window, and dropped them out. For an instant he was tempted to do what every barrister he knew did upon entering Chambers—go and see if there were any cheques for him—but, reminding himself of his predicament, he resisted the temptation.

He climbed out of the window again, and shinned down the pipe. Within a minute he was back at the car. The whole thing had taken less than seven minutes.

'Are you sure you're not a criminal, Charles? That was extremely impressive.'

'Thank you.'

'Shall we go?' asked Rachel.

Charles sighed. 'It seems such a pity about the car. I've only had it a few days, and it's not even registered in my name. I could drive it with impunity, if only I had the keys.'

'And they are . . .'

'At the flat, or at least that's where they were. The police probably have them by now.'

'Does no one know it's your car?' she asked.

'Only Simon Ellison, and he's on some case out of London. I can't see how he would ever come to mention it to anyone, and even if he did, he won't know the registration number. Dammit, I'm going to have a go!'

He leapt out of the car, and leaned in the door. He reached under the steering column.

'What on earth are you doing?' asked Rachel.

'One of my toe-rag clients was once charged with doing a dozen of these in one night, so his mates could each have a car to race,' grunted Charles. 'I asked him how he did it, and he tried to tell me. You have to join up two or three of these wires, and then touch a third one. The question is which—'

But he didn't finish the sentence. There was a flash of sparking from the wires in Charles's hand, and the engine had turned over. Charles did it again, and the car started.

'Hit the accelerator!' he commanded, but Rachel was ahead of him. She pulled the choke out, and the engine ran faster. Charles jumped back in.

'Talk about Bonnie and Clyde,' he said, and off they went.

Chapter Twenty-seven

Denis hastily hid his girlie magazine under his copy of the *Mirror*, and got to his feet. 'Can I help you?' he asked the girl.

'Yes, I think so. Superintendent Glazer asked me to come and ask you a few more questions,' she said.

'Oh, right.'

Denis was more than glad to help. He had never been the subject of so much attention before. He had been interviewed by two officers at first. Then something else had come up, and he had been asked to go to the police station at Snow Hill to give another statement. He had been taken and brought back in a police car, too. He had been racking his brains for the last two days for some other detail which might have been of help. The sergeant had said, if he remembered anything, anything at all which might be relevant, he should call. He hadn't thought of anything yet, but he was still trying. He hoped they caught

Mr Howard. If they didn't he would never get to go to court. Just think: the star witness at the Old Bailey!

Now this lady officer wanted to ask even more questions. She came into his little cubicle with him. He sat as far away from her as he could, but she was still very close to him. She certainly was a looker! He could smell her perfume, and when she sat on the edge of his desk and crossed her legs, he could see her thigh. He became rather flustered. She sat further back as she spoke, and uncovered his magazine. He became even more flustered, and blushed a deep red, but she just looked at it, and then smiled at him knowingly.

She wanted to know about how the blonde woman arrived? Yes, he had seen her arrive, and leave, on more than one occasion. She wore nice perfume too. Yes, she was in a car—a Mercedes. A big gold Mercedes. It sort of matched her, he had thought. And, yes, he did note the registration number, because it was unusual: NF 777. Thank you, too, he said. It's been a pleasure to be of assistance, he said. If there's anything else that comes to mind, he'll be certain to call as he had promised. When she had gone, he could still smell her perfume in the room. Denis was quite hot around the collar. He fancied that the woman detective had taken rather a shine to him.

'NF 777,' mused Charles.

'Yes, but what now? Knowing the number doesn't help. I don't suppose it's going to be any more use than your pile of notebooks.'

'Let me think,' said Charles.

She was certainly right about the notebooks. They had been through each one of them from end to end, and had found no likely murderers. There were a number of people who might have held grudges, either because they had been prosecuted by Charles, or because they might have been aggrieved clients, but none had a motive strong enough to murder an innocent person just to frame Charles. Still, the notebooks were useful, if only . . .

'Got it!' cried Charles. 'These,' he said excitedly

brandishing one of the books, '*do* have the answer! But to a different question. Look.' He flipped open the first page. 'The case of Murphy: car thief. Robinson and Tilley: robbers. Bennett and Lewis: tax evasion. You know what this is?' Rachel shook her head. 'It's a bloody Yellow Pages of crime! I've got the names and addresses, and *modus operandi* of hundreds of active criminals, most of whom I've defended. And if I say it myself, most of them have cause to thank me, rather than do me in.'

'Alright,' said Rachel, also becoming excited. 'Got any bent policemen who can look up car registrations?'

'Let me think,' said Charles. 'There was one, but he was acquitted, and he's back in the force. He's no use.'

He slapped his forehead. 'Hang on, hang on, hang on! When was it? It had to be 1986 or 1987 . . .' He began looking down the names of the cases on the covers.

'What name are we looking for?'

'I don't know . . . I'll know it when I see it . . . Next book, please . . . Got it! The Queen against Kharadli. He's a Lebanese car dealer, in Peckham, or Crystal Palace, somewhere like that. Bent as they come. He was clocking cars—' Charles leafed through the book, looking for his case notes.

'What's that?'

'Never mind—here he is. He had a friendly copper somewhere who would check out a car if Kharadli thought it might have been stolen. Here's his address. He lives in a flat above the showroom.'

'He *lived* in a flat above the showroom,' reminded Rachel. 'That was in 1986. He could be anywhere by now.'

'True, but it's all we have.'

'Are you going to ring him?'

'No. He's an Arab. They like doing business face to face. We'll get nothing on the phone. He may not even remember me. Let's go!'

Peter Bateman, Charles's pupil, did not relish coming into Chambers on a sunny Sunday morning when he might otherwise have been at the pub. However, a brief—any brief—was a godsend for a young man just starting at the Bar, and he was certainly not going to complain about coming in to collect it on Sunday just because it hadn't arrived in Chambers on Friday.

He opened the door to Charles's room where he usually sat waiting for the pearls of wisdom to drop from his pupil-master's lips, and started. The door to the cupboard behind Charles's seat was open, and there were notebooks all over the floor. A desk drawer was open too, and it had certainly been closed when Peter had left Chambers on Friday night. Finally, the window was wide open. There had been a burglary.

Peter looked up the police station nearest to Chambers. Snow Hill. There was no point in dialling 999 — this was no longer an emergency. He dialled Snow Hill's number.

'Hello. I'd like to report a burglary at 2 Chancery Court, Temple . . . Yes, it is a barristers' Chambers. My name is Peter Bateman. No I'm not a barrister . . . well . . . I am a barrister, but I'm still in pupillage.'

There was a long pause at the other end of the line, while some enterprising policeman put two and two together and came up with four.

'Yes, these are the Chambers of Charles Howard. Yes, it is his room that has been burgled. How on earth did you know that? Yes, I'll wait.' Peter hung up, his opinion of the average Metropolitan Police Officer immensely improved.

Two officers, in the shape of Detective Constables Sloane and Redaway, arrived 45 minutes later, and Peter showed them into the room.

'Have you touched anything?' one of them asked.

'No,' answered Peter, a trifle offended. 'But in any event, my prints will be all over the place.'

Redaway opened the cupboard door using a pen. 'What was in here?'

'More notebooks. It's only the recent ones that have gone.'

185

They poked about the room a little more. 'Anything else missing?'

'Not that I can tell. There's nothing of any value in here anyway. Only his computer, and that's at the flat, I think, at the moment.'

'His computer?' asked Sloane.

'Yes,' replied Peter. 'Sometimes he uses it here, and sometimes at the flat. It's fairly portable.'

Sloane pointed to a red cloth bag lying on the floor. 'What's that?' he asked.

'That's Charles's bag, for carrying his robes.'

'I thought he had a blue one,' said Redaway.

'No. Not since I've known him. He wouldn't carry a blue one anyway.'

'Why not?' asked Sloane, puzzled.

'The blue ones you buy yourself. The red ones are given by a leader to a junior as a gift, to mark good work done on a case. Charles is very proud of his red bag. He wouldn't use a blue one.'

Sloane looked at Redaway, and raised his eyebrows. 'Alright if we use the phone?' he asked.

'Sure,' said Peter, indicating the one on Charles's desk.

'I'd prefer another one,' said the officer.

'Of course,' said Peter. 'Fingerprints. There's one just outside in the corridor.'

Sloane dialled Aylesbury police station and asked for Superintendent Glazer.

'We're at Howard's Chambers. No . . . just some old notebooks. I'm not sure, sir, but I have a suspicion it ties in with something his pupil's told us.'

He listened to the other speak for a while, and then called Peter. 'Will you have a word direct with Superintendent Glazer? It's quicker than me explaining it.'

Peter took the phone and, in answer to Glazer's questions, explained the significance of the red bag.

'Do you know what case he got the bag for?' asked Glazer when Peter had finished.

'No, I don't, but Charles did mention that the QC who had given it to him is now a judge.'

'Called?'

'His Honour Judge Michael Rhodes Thomas.'

Glazer paused and made a note, and then continued.

'What's in the notebooks?'

'Details of the cases he's done. Notes of evidence and so on.'

'Does Mr Howard defend or prosecute mainly?'

'He mainly defends, but he does prosecute.'

'Has he had any big victories, or big defeats, recently?'

'Nothing out of the ordinary that I can remember.'

'Fine. Thank you, Mr Bateman. Would you put me back to one of the officers, please? I doubt that we'll need a statement from you, but leave your address with the officers just in case, would you?'

'Certainly. Goodbye.'

Peter handed the telephone back to Sloane.

'There's one other thing, sir,' said Sloane. 'The computer we found at the flat. It apparently travels back and forward from the flat to the Chambers. He uses it in both places.'

'Hmm. OK. I want the entire room in the Chambers gone over. Get someone from the Met over there if you can—try Snow Hill, as they've been involved already. If you have no joy, get back to me. Then go back to the flat and collect the computer, and have that looked at too.'

'Bugger!' said Charles.

He and Rachel peered out of the passenger window of the MG and looked at what they had hoped would be a second-hand car showroom, but was now a kitchen and bathroom centre.

'Bugger,' he repeated. 'Come on, then,' he said, struggling out of the car. They walked across to the door. The place was open, and they walked in.

'May I help you sir?' asked a salesman in shirt-sleeves.

'Not unless you still sell clocked cars,' said Charles.

'I beg your pardon?'

'This used to be a car showroom, didn't it?'

'I don't know sir. You'd better ask Mr Cohen: he owns it. He's just around that display,' he added, pointing to a rack of tiles.

Charles and Rachel walked round the display to find a middle-aged man sitting on the floor, arranging tiles in stacks.

'Mr Cohen?' asked Charles.

'Yes?' replied the other, looking up.

'Do you mind if I ask you what became of the car showroom that used to be on this site?'

'I bought it, two years ago.'

'I don't suppose you can remember who from? We're trying to find the old owner.'

'Hah! Not another one! I had people coming in here for six months after I moved in, wanting their money back. One even had a shotgun!' Cohen stood up and looked out of the window at the MG. 'I see what you mean,' he said.

'Do you know the chap's name?' said Charles, ignoring the slight to his motor car.

'He was an Arab . . . Kalique . . . Kourami . . . something like that.'

'Kharadli?'

'Yes, could be.'

'Do you know where he went to?'

'No idea. But I do see him around the area, so he must be living somewhere nearby. He used to live in the flat upstairs, you know, but I bought the whole block. I'll tell you where you could try. See the newsagent's over there?' He pointed across to the far side of the road. 'He still gets his papers from there. In fact, he usually goes in with his children on Sunday mornings to buy them comics and so on. You could ask there.'

'Thank you, Mr Cohen. I'm very grateful.'

They left the shop. 'What do you think?' asked Charles. 'I can't see them just giving out the addresses of their customers, even if they know them.'

'If this chap is the only one we have who can trace that car, and the car's the only lead on the girl, what choice do we have? We'll have to wait. It's only 10 o'clock. There's a very good chance he's not been in yet,' replied Rachel.

'I'll go back to Cohen and ask him if he knows what sort of time Kharadli goes in normally,' said Charles.

'And I'll go into the shop and get some papers. We might as well sit in the car and read while we wait.'

Charles made his way back into the kitchen centre. Cohen was on the telephone, and Charles inspected some of the bathroom fittings. He had been meaning to replace the bathroom suite at The Cedars for months. Suddenly, Cohen tapped urgently on the wall with his pen, and Charles turned round. Cohen was still in mid-conversation, but he pointed through the plate glass window over the road. Charles looked across. Rachel was on the far pavement, jumping up and down, and pointing into the newsagent's. Charles ran out, and dashed across the road.

'I think he's just gone in,' she said excitedly. 'Arab-looking man, with two young children. Just got out of that car,' she said, pointing.

It was an old blue Rolls-Royce. 'That's our man,' said Charles. 'Let's wait for him here.'

Two minutes later, a tall, handsome, dark-skinned man emerged on to the pavement, encumbered with several newspapers, ice creams, a child in his arms, and a toddler held by the hand.

Charles approached him. 'Mr Kharadli?'

The Arab looked at him suspiciously. 'Who asks?'

'You don't remember me? I'm Charles Howard. I represented you on a string of cases, some years ago now. Remember?'

Recognition gradually dawned, and Kharadli's face broke into a smile.

'Yes, I remember! How are you?' Suddenly, his

189

attitude changed. 'Wait one minute,' he said. 'You're in big trouble with the police, yes? You killed your wife?'

Charles moved closer to him. 'Can I talk to you, just for a minute?'

'I don't know . . .'

'Mr Kharadli, when I represented you, I knew that the police were saying you had done all sorts of things, yet I believed what you told me,' lied Charles. 'You know and I know that the police say many things which are not true.'

Kharadli thought about this. 'That is true, my friend,' he replied, brightening immediately. 'Anyway, what do I care that you kill your wife. This lady,' he pointed to Rachel, 'she is much nicer no doubt. A newer model, yes?' and he slapped Charles on the back. 'Come on.'

He showed them to his car. He put the two children in the front seat, and he opened the rear door for Charles and Rachel. They got in. He went to the driver's seat, and turned round to them.

'Welcome to my office. I sold that one,' he said, pointing over the road. 'No money in cars, always hassle, hassle, hassle. Property, that is the thing. It's got no mileage, see? Now, how can I help you?'

'I remembered that you used to have a policeman friend who could trace car registration numbers. I need one traced very urgently. It's to do with . . . well . . . you've obviously read the papers.'

'Yes, but I have not used him in over two years. Still, we shall try!'

He turned back to face the windscreen and reached for the car phone. He dialled a number, and waited.

'Is Steve Compton on duty today? Tell him it's Ahmed.' There was a short pause. 'So, it's Police Sergeant now, is it?' Kharadli gave them the thumbs up sign, and continued talking. 'Congratulations, my friend! No, no, I am still out of the business. This is a private matter. For old time's sake, eh?' He snapped his finger at Charles impatiently, and Rachel quickly scribbled the number on the corner of her newspaper and tore it off. Kharadli winked at her, and resumed talking.

'The number is NF 777.'

They sat in silence, the two children reading their comics and eating their ice creams. Suddenly Kharadli snapped his fingers again, and made writing signs, and Rachel handed over her pen to him.

'Yes,' he said, as he wrote on his newspaper. 'Yes . . . got it. Thank you, Steve, much appreciated. You must come round to the house soon . . . yes, it's been too long. Bring the children too . . . OK. Bye.'

He hung up, and handed the paper over. Charles read the scribble.

'Starline Model Agency, D'Arblay Street. Great; it's a company. That may mean any number of people drive it.'

'I am sorry,' said Kharadli, with a shrug. 'That's all I can do. Now, Mr Howard, I must get back to my breakfast.' He leaned over and opened Rachel's door for her. 'I do sincerely hope that everything works out for you, but please do not contact me again. One cannot be too careful who one is seen with.' He was completely serious.

Charles and Rachel stood on the pavement and watched Kharadli drive away.

'Charming,' said Rachel.

'I can understand him. I'm on the run from the police on a charge of murder. Even by doing what he has, he's probably committed a criminal offence.'

'What now?' asked Rachel.

'I don't know, Rachel. The model agency, or whatever it is, won't be open on a Sunday. I think that's it for today.'

Rachel looked at him. 'What is it, Charlie? You're looking worried—that is, more worried than you have been.'

'I don't know. It's been too easy until now. I've got

a . . . premonition or something. Something's about to happen.'

Chapter Twenty-eight

Rachel dropped Charles off at the bottom of Great Marlborough Street, blew him a kiss, and drove off. She had wanted to come with him, but Charles suspected from the address of the model agency that it might not be safe for her to accompany him. She was to drive round the block continually until he returned.

Charles had been right. The Starline Model Agency was located up a narrow dirty staircase on the first floor of a seedy building on D'Arblay Street, in the heart of Soho, with its entrance around the corner in a rubbish-strewn courtyard. The name of the agency was stencilled on the glass door that faced Charles as he reached the top of the steps. He knocked on the glass.

'Come in,' came a voice.

Charles entered the room. There was a desk in front of him, littered with coffee cups, ashtrays, and pieces of paper. The walls of the small room were papered with pin-ups of girls in various states of undress. In the corner was a large filing cabinet with a bottle of Scotch and two glasses on top. Behind the desk sat a stocky black man, wearing a light grey, almost white suit. He wore a heavy gold neck chain and his fingers flashed and sparkled with rings. He had his feet on the desk, and was tipping his chair back so that it touched the window sill behind him. He was reading a newspaper.

'Yeh?' he said.

Charles smiled his best smile. 'My name is Collins, Ralph Collins,' he said. 'I'm a solicitor representing a Mr Fielding, Nicholas Fielding.'

'What of it?' said the other. His tone was surely, argumentative. Charles wondered whether the approach he had rehearsed since Sunday night might have been miscalculated; this sort of man did not, as a rule, like lawyers. He pressed on, beaming his most winning beam.

'Mr Fielding is about to open a chain of stores called the 777 Stores. Perhaps you can guess now why I'm here?'

'Nope,' said the black man, in a manner which suggested that he didn't much care.

'NF 777—get it?' Nicholas Fielding 777. He wants your car number, Mr . . . Mr . . .'

'Fylde, Neville Fylde. And the answer's no. It ain't for sale.'

'At any price?'

'Listen, man, that plate is worth thousands.'

'He's prepared to pay thousands.'

'Yeh, and how many thousands would that be?' he drawled.

'That would depend,' said Charles, drawing up a chair uninvited, and sitting opposite Fylde.

'On what?'

'He's seen it being driven around town by a girl, a blonde girl. He thinks she has the perfect image for the advertising. He's prepared to offer a package for the number, the car, and the girl.'

Charles saw Fylde suddenly tense the second he mentioned the girl. He remained as apparently calm and uninterested as before, but the temperature in the room had noticeably fallen.

'I ain't interested,' he said, and picked up his newspaper again.

'If you wanted to hire out the car, as against sell it, that might be negotiable, as long as the girl was part of the package.'

'I said I ain't interested. There's the door.'

'Can you give me the girl's name, so we can approach her direct?'

Fylde lowered the paper. 'I said I ain't interested, and I've said it now three times. I ain't going to say it again. Get out of here, before I throw you out.'

Charles stood up, still smiling. He sized up Fylde. The man looked tough. Charles had no doubt that he was a pimp, that he was used to using violence, and that he probably carried a weapon.

'Very well, Mr Fylde,' he said. 'Thank you for your time. I'm sorry we couldn't do business.' He approached the desk, fiddling in his pocket. 'Let me give you my card though, just in case—'

He leapt at Fylde, grabbing at his throat with his left hand, and forcing him back further towards the window. Fylde's chair tipped back, overbalanced, and his head cracked against the glass pane. Charles brought his right fist up and straight down on the other's nose. He heard it crack, and blood started to run from both nostrils. The force of the blow caused the window to smash, and Charles heard pieces of glass tinkling down on to the pavement below. Fylde flailed out with both hands, trying to get Charles to release his grip on his throat. Charles stepped to the left, retaining his hold. Fylde was reaching inside his jacket pocket.

'Don't move!' ordered Charles. 'Before you reached it, you'd be flying backwards out of this window!' Fylde was still aiming blows at Charles's body, but he was so off-balance that he could neither aim them nor give them any force.

'I'm warning you!' shouted Charles, pushing him a few inches further back. The top of Fylde's head was now resting on the broken glass of the window, and he stopped struggling immediately.

'Now listen, Mr Fylde,' hissed Charles. 'I want some information from you, and I want it this instant. Your car has been used by that blonde on a job in New Fetter Lane recently. I want to know what the job was, and who paid you. Now, talk.'

'A geezer phones,' he said, blood bubbling from his nose as he spoke. 'Asks if we used to do defended divorces in the old days. I don't know what the man's talking about. He says, sending girls to fake adultery with the husband so the wife can get her divorce. I says no. He says he has a client what needs some of that sort of evidence. He says a motorcycle courier is on his way here, with £1,000. All I have to do is provide a classy whore to pose as a man's mistress a few times, that's all. She's got to be white, drive a flash car, speak well, and that. Just go in and out this flat a few times, you know, be noticed. He says if I take the job, there's another £2,000 at the end. So I said yes. That's all I know.'

'How did you get into the flat?'

'Another courier, next day. He brings a key and a timetable, when to go and when not to go.'

'Who was the man?'

'I don't know.'

Charles heaved the chair further back, knowing that the glass was cutting into Fylde's scalp. Fylde cried out in pain.

'I swear it, man, I don't know! I never saw the geezer. He was white, spoke like you.'

'How did you get in touch with him?' demanded Charles.

'I wasn't supposed to. In emergencies I could leave a message at some detective agency he uses.'

Charles tightened his grip. 'How did you leave messages for a man with no name? You're lying to me!' He pushed Fylde down on to the glass. He could see blood trickling down the inside of the pane.

'OK, man, OK! He says to leave messages for Mr Howard. He says it like it's a big joke, right?

Charles was satisfied. He changed tack. 'What's the girl called?'

'Sharon Lovesay.'

'Where is she?' demanded Charles.

'Benidorm. She's on holiday till Wednesday. The geezer wanted her to lie low for a while after.'

'Did she see him?'

'I don't know, man, maybe. I think so. She got a few things from the man to take to the flat. Let me up, for God's sake.'

'In a minute. When do you receive the pay-off?'

'He's calling today, to tell me the money's on its way.'

'Right. Last question: where does she live, Sharon?'

'Leytonstone . . . 214 Leytonstone Park Road.'

'Thank you.'

Charles stepped smartly away from the desk and to the door. Fylde righted his seat, and bent over the desk, nursing his nose.

'I think you broke it, man,' he complained. 'You're one hell of a strange lawyer,' he added.

'So they tell me,' said Charles, as he closed the door behind him.

Detective Constable Sloane knocked on the door of Superintendent Glazer's office, and was told to enter.

'You asked to be told as soon as we had this, sir,' he said, handing a piece of paper to the Superintendent.

'Thank you, Sloane.'

Glazer looked at the paper. It was a note from the Scenes of Crime Officer. A statement would follow, but his conclusions were as follows: there were fingerprints on the car, under the bonnet, and on the computer, which matched each other, but which did not appear to match those of Howard. The officer emphasised that it was a provisional conclusion, because no sample prints had been taken from Howard before he escaped. However, prints had been lifted from his Chambers and his flat which were so numerous as to lead to the reasonable conclusion that they were his. The prints that had been found would be run through the computer to see if they matched those of any known criminal.

The Superintendent threw the piece of paper on to his desk with some irritation. What had looked like a simple case was turning into a nightmare. Within 24 hours of the murder, he had had enough evidence to convict Howard, of that he was sure. Now he had lost his suspect, and found his case slipping through his fingers. There was another knock on the door.

'Come in,' he called. It was Sloane again. 'I thought you ought to know immediately, sir,' he said.

'Now what?'

'Two things, sir. The local bobby at Putt Green has just got back from his holidays to find an undated message from Mrs Howard on his answerphone, saying that the car had been stolen. She apparently didn't think to call the police station in the next village.'

'Stolen? When?'

'That's the problem, sir. We can't say. Judging from the position on the tape, it was probably early last week.'

'I feel like Alice in Wonderland,' said Glazer miserably. 'I'm afraid to ask, but what's the second thing?'

'Even better, sir. There's a report from West End Central of a complaint being made concerning an assault in Soho. The description of the assailant fits Howard to a 'T', even down to the posh accent. Apparently, he even told his victim he was a lawyer.'

'Jesus Christ,' said Glazer. 'I don't believe it. What's the man going to do next?'

'What do you want me to do, sir?'

'Send Inspector Wheatley to see me, would you?'

'Sir?' said Wheatley as he entered.

'Have you been brought up to date about the finger-prints?'

'Not yet, sir,' replied Wheatley.

'Look at this, then,' said Glazer, handing him the note.

'You'd better divide the team into two,' said the Superintendent when the other had finished reading. 'Take Sloane and Bricker and go to Chancery Court. Take elimination fingerprints from everyone who works there. Send Redaway and Kent to see the assault victim.'

'Assault victim?'

'Sloane will fill you in.'

'I was going to use Sergeant Kent on something else.'

'No, I want him to go to London. He knows

the patch well. He was on the Vice Squad for a while.'

'Very well.'

'In the meantime, I'll see if I can locate His Honour Judge Rhodes Thomas.'

An hour and a half later, Detective Sergeant Kent and Detective Constable Redaway climbed the smelly staircase towards the glass door marked 'Starline Model Agency'. This was not the first time Sergeant Kent had been to the premises. He had, as the Superintendent knew, spent two years as a Detective Constable working in and around Soho, and Neville Fylde was not unknown to him. Fylde had convictions for assault, perverting the course of justice and living off immoral earnings.

Sergeant Kent knocked on the door, and went straight in. Fylde looked up from a glass of whisky, looking decidedly the worse for wear. He held a bloodstained paper handkerchief to his face, and when he removed it, Kent could see that his nose was very swollen, and one of his eyes was blacker than its usual hue. He looked at Kent with surprise.

'I thought you was a country copper now,' he said. 'What're you doing down here hassling me?'

'I'm not hassling you, Neville. I thought you were the victim of an assault, weren't you?' replied Kent.

'You're not fucking joking!' said Fylde with feeling. 'Look at my face!'

'Dear, oh dear, Neville,' said Kent, with great concern, 'that looks very nasty.'

'Fucking white bastard! I'll fix him,' Fylde replied, feeling very sorry for himself.

'Well, it makes a change, doesn't it? See how the other half lives, my son. It's all part of this wonderful learning experience we call "Life",' said Kent, grinning to Redaway.

Redaway handed Kent a photograph, and Kent passed it on to Fylde. 'Is that the man?' he asked.

'That's him.'

'Now, Neville. Suppose you tell me what the fight was about?'

'I don't have any idea, man. The mad bastard comes up here for a woman, and when I tell him he's got the wrong place, and I try to direct him downstairs, he goes crazy.'

Sergeant Kent sat on the edge of Fylde's desk, and tutted, shaking his head. 'That's not the truth, is it, Neville? Try again.'

'I just told you what happened. I want to press charges. He's a mad bastard. He threatened to throw me out of the window!'

'Listen, Neville, and listen carefully. We don't have time for this crap. Do you know who this bloke is? Don't you read the papers? Listen to the news? Look!' he said, grabbing Fylde's newspaper, and shoving it under his nose. 'Recognise anyone?'

Fylde took the paper handkerchief away from his nose and looked down. 'Barrister wanted by Police in Murder Inquiry' ran the headline. Underneath was a photograph of Charles.

'Well, I'll be damned!' said Fylde.

'Quite probably,' replied Kent. 'But do you now appreciate the position you're in? This man is a murder suspect and he's on the run. And where does he turn up? In this office. What am I supposed to think, eh? With a man of your background? He is not going to wander about Soho looking for you to find him a tom, is he?'

Fylde looked glum.

'He must have come here for something, Neville, and it wasn't a good time at the hands of one of your girls. So, I'm going to give you one last chance to tell me the truth, after which I shall arrest you on suspicion of being an accomplice to murder. Do you understand?'

Fylde nodded quickly.

'Good,' said Kent. 'Get your notebook out, Bob. I think Mr Fylde wishes to make a statement.'

It was, by chance, only twenty minutes after the police had left Neville Fylde's office, that his telephone rang.

He was at first inclined to ignore it, but eventually, still clutching his sore nose, he picked up the receiver.

'Yeh,' he said.

'Good morning, Mr Fylde. You'll be happy to know that your money is on the way. You did a very thorough job and I congratulate you.'

'You can keep your money, man, I don't want it!'

'Why on earth do you not want it?'

'I don't want any part of it! You never told me that there was murder involved. That bastard, the one who's in all the papers, he's been round here, causing trouble. I had to tell him everything to stop him throwing me out the window! You'd better watch your back, man, 'cos—'

Fylde was about to warn his caller that the police had also been round asking questions, but the line had gone dead before he got any further.

Chapter Twenty-nine

Superintendent Glazer strode into the room. The other officers involved in the inquiry were already there. They all rose when he entered.

'Sit down, gentlemen, please,' he said as he went to the desk at the front of the room, and sat down himself. He opened his file, took out a notebook, and addressed the others.

'I've called this meeting to re-assess where we're going in this case. There were a number of developments yesterday. For those of you who have just got back from London, in short form, this is where we stand at present:

Howard was apparently telling the truth when he said that the Jaguar was out of commission. Insofar as it can be, that has been confirmed by the local garage. We know also that the car was taken from the house some time early in the week, and it must have been replaced there by the time it was used as a getaway car from the scene of the murder. There can only be one conclusion: it was removed by the murderer to be repaired, and then replaced.

'Thus far, there's no reason to assume it was not Howard, although if it was him, it's a pretty strange way of going about things, and we have nothing to suggest he knows how to repair cars. However, and I concede it's a small point, the man seen driving off in the Jaguar was carrying a blue cloth bag, and Howard's is red. We have checked the car for the fingerprints of the repairer, and there are prints there which match those on the computer used to write the letter to the victim. Those prints do not appear to be Howard's. Any questions so far? Fine.

'We have obtained elimination prints from almost everyone working at Chancery Court, and none of them match. We are awaiting four sets of prints from barristers who are out of town; they are . . .'

'Messrs Campbell-Smythe and Corbett who are in Lewes, a Mr Ellison who is in Oxford, and a Miss Wade who is on honeymoon in America,' said Inspector Wheatley.

'Thank you, Inspector. So far, although some of the evidence is odd, there's nothing positive to make us think Howard's not our man. Mr Howard has, however, been very busy. He has broken into his own Chambers and collected a large number of old notebooks stacked full of the names of villains. He has also done the public a service by beating up a piece of slime called Neville Fylde, whom some of you have met before. Fylde has now made a full statement. It seems that he was paid by someone to set up a girl to mislead us into thinking Howard had a mistress. The person he was working for called himself "Howard", and Fylde believed that he was being asked to provide false evidence of adultery. If it had been Howard, he would have had no reason to risk showing himself, or to beat up Fylde to obtain information he already knew. It therefore seems probable that all the apparent evidence at the flat, the bank account, the women's clothes et cetera, was planted by someone else.

'Again, this alone does not make Howard innocent of murder, but two things follow: firstly, if the letter to the bank is false, then the letter to the victim must be suspect; secondly, all of this great effort has been just to set up a motive for the murder. If that is false, the rest comes into question.

'For the present, therefore, although I am not abandoning Howard as the principal suspect, I am opening the investigations up again. If Howard is *not* our man, he may well be in danger. For the present, I'm calling off active surveillance of the house at Putt Green. We need to find him, and I don't want to frighten him off. I want full house-to-house inquiries in the village and in the vicinity of the flat in London. If someone else has been watching either of these places, I want to find out who, and why. I checked on my way to this meeting, and we still have not heard from Scotland Yard as to a fingerprint match with those on the computer and the car. If that comes up, it may solve the puzzle.

'Inspector Wheatley has your immediate orders, and I shall hand over to him.'

'Your Honour: Detective Superintendent Glazer and Inspector Wheatley.'

'Good afternoon, gentlemen, come in. May I offer you some tea?' asked Judge Rhodes Thomas.

'That's very kind of you, your Honour. Thank you for seeing us at such short notice,' replied Glazer.

'Do find a seat, gentlemen. I know it's a bit crowded in here. Judge's Chambers are not designed for police interrogations!'

The police officers laughed politely. Superintendent Glazer began. 'As I expect you have seen from the media, a barrister, Charles Howard, is suspected of murdering his wife.'

'Yes, I have read that. It's nonsense if you want my view. But then I don't expect you came here for a character reference.'

'We're investigating the offence. Now, the point is a very small one, but it's been bothering me, and my copper's intuition won't let it rest. We understand that you once worked on a case with Mr Howard.'

'I worked on several with him.'

'Was there one in particular, where you led him for the defence?'

'Not really . . .'

'Where he may have been given a bag . . . of some sort . . . for, er . . . robes . . .'

'Oh, yes. Yes, it was a murder trial, funnily enough. I fell down the stairs at the Old Bailey, and he had to take over half-way through. He did very well, too.'

'Do you remember the name of the case, by any chance?'

'It so happens that I do, because one of the defendants came up on a petty thieving charge before me only a few weeks ago. I'm surprised actually that Inspector Wheatley doesn't remember it, as he was involved then too, although, if I remember correctly, he never actually gave live evidence. Anyway, that murder involved two defendants: Derek Plumber and Charlie Sands.'

'It was a cut-throat defence,' explained Wheatley on the way back to the car. 'The Judge was right, I never actually gave evidence. That's probably why I didn't tie Howard to it, as I never met him on the case. All the evidence was admitted, except for who took the real gun as against the imitations. Sands turned Queen's evidence, and was given immunity, I think. Anyway, he wasn't believed and he got nine years, plus a bit for attempting to pervert the course of justice.'

'That's where Howard's been going wrong. His note-books won't contain any reference to Sands, will they, as he was never his client?'

'You reckon it's Sands then, sir?' asked the driver, Bricker.

'I'll lay money on it,' said Glazer. 'He's a burglar, and could have got into Chancery Court and the flat; he's good with cars—'

'And,' interrupted Wheatley, 'he had the proceeds of the Express Dairy robbery to pay Fylde. We never recovered most of it. "Cut-throat",' mused Wheatley. 'It certainly fits. Sands always was a vicious bastard, and he's bright enough.'

'All I need now are the fingerprints, or confirmation as to when Sands got out,' said Glazer. 'That'll tie it up so far as I'm concerned.'

Charles sat morosely staring out of the window as night fell over London. He and Rachel had discussed it over and over again, until they found themselves going round and round in circles and bickering. So to make up, they had made love. Rachel was still in bed, while Charles sat in the lounge. Rachel wanted him to turn himself in to the police. She believed that once they knew about Fylde, they would have to believe Charles.

Charles himself was not so optimistic. The way he analysed it, the set-up by Fylde didn't prove he hadn't murdered Henrietta, only that someone, for some reason, had faked a false motive. He knew the police too well to expect them to drop the charges. They might even say that he had invented false evidence that could be destroyed in this way so as to throw them off the trail. Even he, however, had to admit they were at a dead end. No matter how much of a profile of the murderer they could compile—and Rachel's kitchen noticeboard was full of flow charts and lists of his attributes—they had no actual suspect. More than ever Charles felt the injustice of a system where the defence have no real investigative powers. At the same time, however, something was troubling him. Like a wasp buzzing away at the back of his head, every time he tried to pin it down, it slipped out of his grasp.

Rachel came out from the bedroom, and stood behind

him in the darkening room, massaging his shoulders. He felt the warmth of her body against his cold back.

'Come back to bed, darling,' she said softly. 'Sleep on it, and decide in the morning.'

He didn't answer. He didn't want to give up, but what alternative was there? Her breasts brushed against his neck, and he felt the stirrings of renewed desire. He fought to concentrate.

'The thing that keeps bothering me is his detailed knowledge of my movements,' he said.

'We've been over it hundreds of times, Charles—'

'Yes, but I keep coming back to this. That tart, Sharon, whatever her name was, she was provided with an advance timetable of when I wouldn't be there! No one could work that out just by watching me, for however long. A barrister's life is totally unpredictable. Cases come in, go out of the List, get adjourned. And another thing: whoever it was couldn't have got the key at the flat.'

As he finally began to think clearly, Charles shrugged off Rachel, and began to pace up and down the room. Rachel reached over to the settee and picked up Charles's jacket and put it round her shoulders.

'It's on the fourth floor, and completely inaccessible from the outside. The key is only there when *I* am there, and there's been no burglary while I've been there. No signs of forced entry, no supposed tradesmen entering to do work. So the only time the key could have been taken to be copied was while it was in my jacket, or in the desk, at Chambers.'

'Chambers again,' said Rachel. 'Well, why not? We know how secure it is there. Almost anyone could break in.'

'Yes, that's true. In fact, they mightn't even have had to *break* in. A lot of people have access to Chambers: clients, for example. Almost anyone can walk in during office hours, and a solicitor telephoning with a query as to my availability can easily be told when I am in court and when I'm not. For weeks in advance if he asks.'

'So that brings us back to clients—and we've been through them all. None of them has a realistic motive for cutting your wife's throat.'

Charles slammed his hand down on the table. 'Wait!' he shouted, more to himself than Rachel. 'You idiot!' he cried, slapping his own forehead. ' "Cutting my wife's throat"! Of course! There *is* someone I hadn't thought of, and I even remember his name! It was my first solo murder, and I, even more than the prosecution, was responsible for getting him convicted.'

'Well?' asked Rachel, with intense impatience.

'Charles Reginald Sands!' called Charles as he sprinted to the bedroom where he had left the notebooks. He returned a few seconds later. 'Look!' he said, leafing through until he reached the right place, and showing Rachel his notes. 'The timing's right too. With parole he could well be out now. I never thought about him because he wasn't my client! He's only mentioned here because I had to cross-examine him!'

Rachel put her hand on his arm to still his excitement. 'But Charlie, how are we going to find him after all this time?'

'I've got an idea about that, too.' He turned back to the front of the notebook. 'I represented a chap called Plumber . . . and his address is . . . here! They won't exactly be on talking terms, but I'd be surprised if Derek Plumber doesn't know when Sands's EDR was.'

'EDR?'

'Earliest date of release. Come on,' ordered Charles. 'Get that lovely body into some clothes.'

'What, now?'

'Why not? We're more likely to find him in now than during the day.'

Charles turned off the MG's lights but left the engine running. He looked out of the window up at the fourth

206

floor of the council flats where Plumber lived. There were no lights showing.

'What now?' asked Rachel.

'I don't know. I suppose I'd better go up. Do you want to come?'

'Yes.'

Charles disconnected the wires under the steering column, and the engine died away. The street was silent. They climbed out of the car and walked over to the flats. Charles indicated a flight of steps leading upwards and they began to climb.

'Phew!' exclaimed Rachel. There was a strong smell of rubbish and urine. Every now and then they had to step over Coke cans, bits of broken furniture and prams.

They reached the fourth floor and Charles led the way along a balcony. Doors opened off to the right, and below them to the left was a courtyard filled with parked cars, most in a state of decomposition. They arrived at the last door. There was no light coming from within. Charles bent down and opened the letter box. He could feel a distinctly warm and smoky current of air from inside. Charles stood, looked at Rachel and knocked at the door. There was no response. He knocked again. Rachel raised her eyebrows.

'There's someone there,' whispered Charles.

There was a sudden noise from behind them, and light spilled out on to the balcony. A thick-set man in a vest and pyjama bottoms stood glaring at them from the adjoining doorway.

'What the fuck do you want at this time of night?' he demanded in a thick Liverpudlian accent.

Charles turned to him with a smile. 'I'm really sorry to disturb you, mate,' he said in a cockney accent so accurate that Rachel just stared at him in astonishment. 'We're lookin' for a geezer called Plumber. Used to be an old mate of mine.'

'That's his flat. But I ain't seen him all day. Keep it down, eh?' The man withdrew and the door closed.

Charles and Rachel turned back to Plumber's door. They could now see someone behind it through the glass, although there was still no light from inside.

'Is that you, Mr Plumber?' called Charles. The door opened a fraction.

'Who's asking?'

'Charles Howard,' replied Charles, as quietly as he could. There was a pause, and the door opened fully.

'Come in, quick!' said Plumber. He held the door open for Charles and Rachel, and they slipped inside. Plumber closed and locked the door. The three of them stood in the cramped hall.

'Who's this?' asked Plumber, also whispering.

'She's alright,' replied Charles. Plumber looked her up and down, and shrugged. He turned to Charles.

'I sort of expected to see you,' he said.

'Why?'

'Sands is out.'

'What's that got to do with me?'

'Weren't it your wife that was . . . wasname . . . murdered?'

'I'm supposed to have done it.'

'Yeh, well, did you? Nah, didn't think so.'

Charles took a step towards the other man. 'Do you know anything?' he demanded. 'Because if you do—'

'Save your breath, Mr Howard. I don't *know* anything, but it was just too much of a coincidence. I know Charlie Sands. And I know that I ain't safe either. I'm off tomorrow morning. All packed up.'

'Where are you going?'

Plumber smiled, and tapped the side of his nose. 'My secret. If I don't tell you, you can't tell no one else, can you?'

'Very well. Do you have any idea where he might be?'

'I wouldn't look for him if I were you, sir. He's an evil bastard.'

208

'Listen, Derek, I'm on the run, on a charge of murder. I've got no choice—I have to find him.'

Plumber looked hard at him. 'Hang on a tick,' he said, and disappeared down the hall. Rachel looked up at Charles, and held his hand. Plumber reappeared a few seconds later. 'Try there,' he said, and handed Charles a dog-eared card. 'It's a boarding house he sometimes uses when he's in London. That's all I can do. But for God's sake: watch yourself.'

Plumber opened the door for them again. 'Good luck,' he whispered. Charles and Rachel stepped back on to the balcony. Before Charles could turn and thank Plumber, the door had closed again.

They returned to the car. Once inside Charles looked at the card. 'Hillcrest Boarding House, Vicarage Crescent, E13,' he read. 'Let's go. I'll take you home first.'

'No, you bloody won't!' replied Rachel firmly. 'I'm already an accessory after the fact, or whatever you call it. If I'm good enough to be an accomplice this far, I'm good enough to be in at the end.'

'But this man's a murderer.'

'Then call the police.'

'But I've got no evidence yet. They won't believe a word of it unless I can prove it to them. I've got to have a poke around first.'

'Then I'm coming with you.'

'But that's ridiculous, Rachel. You might get hurt.'

'So might you. I'll stay in the car, OK? At least I can pick up the pieces when he's finished with you.'

'No,' said Charles, very firmly. 'I'm sorry, but this is far too dangerous. I'll just worry about you.'

Rachel looked at him and realised that he could not be persuaded.

'Very well. Take me back to the flat. But if you're gone more than an hour, I'll phone the police. OK?'

'OK.'

'What are you going to do when you get there?'

'How the hell do I know? Haven't you realised yet? I'm making this up as I go along.'

Chapter Thirty

'Well?' asked Inspector Wheatley, with intense impatience.

'It's coming through, now,' answered Sergeant Kent. The computer printer came to a halt, and Kent tore off the message.

'Sands was released on parole four months ago! Last known address, a boarding house in Plaistow.'

'Got him! Circulate his description, tell Superintendent Glazer, and get two cars!' Inspector Wheatley bustled out of the room only to be halted by a cry from behind him.

'Sir!'

Wheatley put his head back round the door. 'What?'

'You'd better have a word,' said a young officer, holding up the telephone handset to him. The Inspector crossed to him and took it. 'Wheatley,' he announced. He listened intently for a minute. Then: 'Are you sure? OK. Thank you.'

Kent and the uniformed officer both looked at the Inspector. His thin weaselly face was distorted by a deep frown, and he still held the telephone in his hand. 'We have a problem,' he said finally, handing the phone to the young officer. 'That was the fingerprint lab. The prints on the car and on the computer may match up, but they do not match Sands's.'

'Well, he's out, then? As a suspect, that is,' concluded Kent.

'No. At least, I'm not sure.'

Wheatley's frown deepened, and he pursed his lips together so that his tiny moustache almost detached itself from his face. The young officer looked across at his Sergeant, smiling, but Kent shook his head quickly. Sergeant Kent had only worked with the Inspector for a few months, and he didn't like the man. He wasn't interested in a drink with the lads, and he had no discernible sense of humour. But the Sergeant had learned to respect his judgement, and he seemed to have an uncanny instinct for the way criminals thought. He could almost see the cogs whizzing and whirring inside Wheatley's head, and he waited expectantly.

'It doesn't fit,' concluded the Inspector, 'and I'm going down to Plaistow to find out why.' He set off again, and then turned to Kent. 'Coming, Sergeant?'

'Well, Howard,' said Charles out loud to himself, 'what now?' He turned the card over in his hands and held it up to the interior light of the MG. On the back, in pencil, was the name Margaret Malone. He drew a deep breath, put the card in his breast pocket, and reached for the door handle. He got out, and then leaned back into the car and reached under the driver's seat. His hand came out with a heavy short-handled hammer, used to tighten the MG's wheel nuts. He put it in his jacket pocket and shrugged to himself.

He walked across the road towards a narrow terraced house. There was skip outside it. He looked at his watch. The time was 11.45 p.m. There was a light on in one of the ground floor rooms, and Charles could see the glow of a television through the curtains. He walked up the short garden path and peered in. There was a woman sitting in her dressing gown watching television with a cat on her lap. He tapped gently on the window pane, and then rang the doorbell quickly. He saw the woman get to her feet and come to the window. She pulled the curtain aside and looked out at him. Charles stood back and smiled. The woman frowned, but she walked away from the window to the door of the room. Charles heard her approaching the door, which was opened to him.

'Would you be Mrs Margaret Malone, by any chance?' asked Charles with a broad smile and the best Dublin accent he could command.

'That I would,' replied the woman with a tentative smile and an even stronger accent. 'And who might you be, at this time of night?'

'Well, me name's Michael, an' it so happens, it's Michael Malone. A friend of mine who knows you suggested I look you up if I was in need of a room, and I am in desperate need at the moment. Now—' said Charles, putting up his hand to stop her speaking, as she was about to do '—I know you'll say that it's very late, and no doubt you'll be quite right. But I've been looking for somewhere to rest me head all night, and you're me last hope.'

The woman considered him carefully. She was fat, middle-aged, and her hair was in curlers. 'And who would your friend be?'

'Charlie Sands.'

Her scant good humour evaporated instantaneously. 'That bastard? He's nothing but trouble, so he is, and if you're a friend of his, I don't want you!' She began to close the door.

'Mrs Malone,' said Charles hurriedly, 'don't shut the door for a second. Just tell me this: is he in?'

'Yes, he's bloody in. He came home drunk as usual, making a din and a mess. I told him: no visitors after 10 p.m.'

'He had a visitor?'

'Still has. They're both up there now.'

'Mrs Malone, you'd be doing me a powerful favour if you'd let me see him for just one moment. Just a moment, and then I'll be off, and not trouble you any further.'

She considered him hard through narrowed eyes. Probably just another trouble-maker, she thought, but then, well, he *was* called Malone, even if his accent was very peculiar . . .

'Go on, then,' she said finally, opening the door to him. 'It's at the top of the stairs.'

Charles entered the hall. There was a strong smell of cats and fish. He heard the door shut behind him, but could feel the woman's eyes on his back as he mounted the stairs. He willed her to return to her television, as he could not possibly just knock on Sands's door, but, when he reached the top, he turned to find her staring at him without embarrassment. Charles smiled, and turned back to the door. He reached inside his pocket for the handle of the hammer. He couldn't take it out while she still watched, but at the same time he knew he would never be able to get it out quickly enough once inside Sands's room.

'Well, what are you waiting for?' demanded Mrs Malone in a voice like a fog horn from the foot of the stairs. Sands could not have failed to have heard her, but Charles turned to her and, with a wink, put his finger to his lips. He raised his hand to knock on the door. Mrs Malone shrugged with impatience, and disappeared from view. Charles waited until he heard the lounge door close, and the volume of the television increase, and then took the hammer from his pocket. He pressed his ear against the door. There was no sound from within, but he could see a thin line of light underneath indicating that the light was on inside. He took a deep breath, and opened the door and stepped inside in one movement, his right arm raised. The room was empty. Charles quietly closed the door behind him.

The room was equipped as a bedsit, with a single bed on one side, a small table bearing a two-ring electric hob, and a tiny refrigerator on the other. To the side of the bed was a large window, which Charles guessed overlooked the garden. The window was open, and the dirty grey net curtains billowed in with the breeze. There was a raincoat slung over the only chair in the room. On the table was a packet of cigarettes and three cans of lager, one of which was open.

213

Where the hell is he? thought Charles. He looked out of the window. There was a lean-to shed against the wall of the house about six feet below. The thought occurred to Charles that Sands had heard his arrival and run off. He went over to the table. There was nothing on it of any assistance. His eye caught the raincoat, and he noted, almost in passing, that he had one almost identical to it. He picked it up and went through the pockets. In the left pocket was a crumpled piece of paper. Charles unravelled it, trying hard not to put his fingerprints all over it. It was a simple sketch plan of a building. It looked familiar. Then he realised: it was the ground plan of his own house. A strange flush of excitement passed through Charles's body. This was it, the piece of evidence he had been searching for, praying for, without really believing that it would come to light. For the first time, he had independent evidence to suggest that someone else had murdered Henrietta. He dropped the raincoat, took out his handkerchief, and carefully folded the paper inside without touching it.

He lifted up the raincoat again and felt in the other pocket. He drew out a photograph. It was of Henrietta. It had been taken from the back of the house and showed her in the kitchen. It was very grainy, and appeared to have been enlarged. He looked at the fuzzy face in the photograph, remembering it in motion, shouting, smiling, and felt a wave of grief roll over him. It threatened to engulf him, and he put the photograph face down on the table. He knew that he had had no time to allow his feelings to come to the surface, and that soon he would have to spend time alone to find out how he felt, but not now.

He looked around him. He wanted something more, something incontrovertible, to prove that Sands was tied up with Henrietta's murder. A map of Putt Green perhaps, railway timetables, notes of Henrietta's movements, *something*. He was not disappointed. There was a built-in wardrobe in the corner of the room. He opened the door, and someone launched himself at Charles. Charles gave a strangled shout and leapt backwards. His attacker

214

fell to the ground with a heavy thud, and lay inert. His heart thumping madly, Charles bent down.

It was Sands. He lay with his face pressed into the threadbare carpet, his light blue eyes staring. Blood trickled out of his mouth. His right eye was bruised and swollen, but the injury looked to be days old. The hilt of a knife was buried in the back of his neck, and its point just protruded below his Adam's apple. Charles gingerly reached out and felt Sands's hand. It didn't feel any colder than Charles's own. Sands had been killed only moments before. At that thought Charles jumped up and turned out the light. The killer must have climbed out of the window as Charles had arrived. He might still be in the garden.

'What's all the noise for?' came a harsh voice from downstairs.

Charles looked around himself briefly, straightened his tie, composed himself, and opened the door. 'OK, see you Tuesday!' he said to Sands, who didn't appear interested, and he left the room, closing the door behind him.

Mrs Malone awaited him with a scowl at the foot of the stairs. Charles walked straight past her and opened the front door. 'Thanks, Mrs Malone,' he said. 'It'll be all quiet now.' He set off down the garden path, but then turned. 'Oh, by the way, Charlie's other guest had gone by the time I went up. You didn't see who he was, by any chance?'

'I did not. Now bugger off and leave me in peace!'

'And a very good night to you, too.'

The door slammed as Charles walked over to the MG. He got in, reached under the dashboard for the now-familiar wires, and started the car. A few seconds after he had moved off, another car, large and dark in colour, pulled away from a space a few yards further down the road, and followed the sports car.

'What the fuck do you want? Do you know what time it is?' shrilled Mrs Malone, her head sticking out of her bedroom window into the cold night air.

'Are you Mrs Malone, madam?' asked Wheatley.

'Who's asking?'

'We're police from Thames Valley,' he said. 'Do you think you can come down for a second? You don't want the whole neighbourhood to hear, do you?'

Mrs Malone looked thoroughly unhappy. This was the third time that night that she had been disturbed, and on this occasion she had been asleep. The window slammed shut. There was some foul muttering and bustling from inside, and then the sound of footsteps on the stairs. The front door was opened.

'Well?' demanded Mrs Malone. She was bundled out of the way into the garden, and Kent, followed by three officers, entered the house at a run. The policemen thundered through the house.

'What the bloody hell do you think you're—' began Mrs Malone.

Kent called out from the top of the stairs. 'Guv! Quickly!'

Wheatley left the landlady open-mouthed by the front door and raced up. Kent pointed into Sands's open room and stood back for the Inspector to enter. Wheatley examined Sands's body briefly, and stood up. 'Sergeant, take Mrs Malone into the kitchen and get someone to stay with her. Tell Bricker to get on to the Met and tell them the score. I want a quick look around here before we hand over.'

Kent went downstairs, and Wheatley could hear him ushering the protesting Mrs Malone to the back of the house. He closed the door gently with his foot, and got on with it.

Ten minutes later he came downstairs and joined Mrs Malone in the kitchen. He had a sheaf of papers in one hand, and the photograph of Henrietta in the other.

'I'm sorry I haven't had the opportunity to introduce myself before now, Mrs Malone. I am Detective Inspector Wheatley. We are engaged on a very serious inquiry. Now, I have some questions to ask you, and I need the answers very quickly. Do you know the name of your tenant on the first floor landing?'

Inspector Wheatley looked at Mrs Malone's flat face

and pugnacious expression, and watched as truculence fought with curiosity. She reminded him of Les Dawson. Eventually she answered: 'I do.'

'And that is . . .' prompted Wheatley.

'Sands.'

'Good. Has he had any visitors recently?'

'The place has been crawling with them. You must have bumped into the last one as you came in.'

'Why? One of them's just gone?'

'Aye, that he did. Dark fella—'

'About five feet nine, late thirties, broad, dark curly hair?' interrupted Kent.

'That's the one. Said he was Irish, but I had me doubts.'

Kent turned to Wheatley excitedly. 'He's really done it now, guv! Shall I get a—'

'Don't get anything, Sergeant. Howard didn't kill him.'

'But the body's still warm.'

'The body?' asked Mrs Malone sharply.

'Just wait a sec, madam,' replied Wheatley, taking Kent by the arm out into the hall and out of earshot.

'Why,' he asked quietly, 'would Howard kill the only man who could clear him? Revenge? He wanted a divorce, remember? Listen,' he said, returning to Mrs Malone, 'and be patient. Mrs Malone: how long has Sands been staying here?'

'Since he came out. I get a lot of them on licence.'

'Has he been working?'

'Him? You've got to be joking!'

'Has he had any trouble with the police since he arrived?'

'None that I know of.'

Wheatley looked at the papers in his hand. 'Has he been to Oxford?'

Mrs Malone looked at him curiously. 'He asked me about buses to Oxford last week. Said he was going to stay with a friend for a couple of days.'

Sergeant Kent frowned at Wheatley. Wheatley handed him the papers. On the top was a summons to Oxford Magistrates' Court.

'But,' said Kent, 'it's dated three months ago.'

'Yes, yes, yes, I know,' said Wheatley with impatience. 'But where does one go after the Magistrates' Court?'

'Gaol?' offered the Sergeant.

'That's "Monopoly",' replied Wheatley without any apparent trace of humour. 'In real life, which is where we are, Sergeant Kent, you have to be convicted first. And most old lags like to be convicted by a court of twelve men good and true, rather than three village worthies.'

'The Crown Court,' said Kent sheepishly.

'Exactly,' said Wheatley with infinite patience. 'And which Crown Court is likely to try a case committed by Oxford Magistrates' Court?'

'Oxford Crown Court?'

'Well done. Now I have a phone call to make. Mrs Malone, would you mind?'

'Go ahead. You're treating the rest of the house as your own, anyway.'

Wheatley dialled Aylesbury police station, and asked to be put through to Superintendent Glazer. He was not in. He asked for another inspector.

'Frank? Look, I know this is going to sound odd, but it's bloody urgent. Can you get on to a Judge Michael Rhodes Thomas. Yes, yes, I know what time it is. Tell him it's about the Howard murder. I've got a nasty feeling Howard's in imminent danger, and I've got to have a question answered. I need to speak to the Judge, or at least someone, like his clerk maybe, who can give me information about a case he dealt with a few weeks ago. If you have to, get on to the Chief Constable—if he can't dig him up, then no one can. No . . . no, that won't do. I need to know tonight. I'll give you the number here . . . call me back, or even better, get the Judge to call me. Yes . . . no, no . . . I'll take responsibility. Thanks.'

Wheatley gave Mrs Malone's number, and hung up. 'I hope you don't mind,' he said to Mrs Malone, who had been listening, 'but I'm going to have to wait for a call back. It won't take too long.'

'Okay,' said Wheatley, turning back to the landlady. 'I

don't suppose you can tell us anything about Mr Sands's *other* visitor?'

'Not a thing. I didn't see him.'

'I guessed as much. How did you know Sands had a visitor?'

'I heard talking. Charlie must have brought him back from the pub. That, or the bloke was already waiting when Charlie came back, but I never let him in. I was over the road for a while at Mrs Riley's.'

'Is the front door left open?'

'It shouldn't be, but it often is. They forget their keys, see, and leave it on the latch.'

The telephone rang. Wheatley answered it.

'Yes?' he said. 'I'm really sorry to have interrupted your evening, your Honour, but I felt that this was a matter of some importance.'

'What is it, Inspector?' asked an obviously testy Michael Rhodes Thomas. 'Neither my wife nor I are very happy at being woken at this hour.'

'I appreciate that, your Honour, but I fear that Mr Charles Howard's life may be in danger, and I think you might be able to help.'

'I'll do what I can,' answered Rhodes Thomas, his tone softening.

'When I came to see you with Superintendent Glazer, you mentioned the case of Plumber and Sands. You told us that you had recently sentenced one of them on a minor matter. Was that Charlie Sands?'

'It was.'

'And would you mind telling me where you were sitting?'

'Not at all: it was Oxford Crown Court.'

'And what sentence was imposed?'

'Let me see . . . It wasn't a serious offence, but he had a very long list of previous offences for dishonesty. Three months, I seem to remember, but suspended for two years. Why? What's happened?'

'Sands is dead. He's been murdered.'

'I see. Is there any link with Charles's case?'

'Yes.' Wheatley paused and thought to himself.

'Is there anything else I can help you with?' asked the Judge.

'Just one matter, your Honour. Do you remember who represented Mr Sands? The barrister, that is?'

'Let me think. Adamson? No . . Ellison! That's it: Simon Ellison.'

Chapter Thirty-one

'What do you mean, "dead"?'

'I mean, "Dead", as in dodo, as in "stiff", as in "pushing up daisies". Do you want the entire Parrot Shop Sketch?'

'Levity seems particularly inappropriate at the moment, Charles,' replied Rachel severely. 'Are you telling me that it's all over?'

'No. Sands was killed by *someone*, and I can't believe it was unconnected to me and Henrietta.'

'An accomplice?'

'Maybe, but more likely his paymaster.'

'Why are you so cheerful?' she cried, her voice filled with distress. 'With Sands dead, not only have we lost the only suspect, but we've no chance of finding out who he was working with!'

'Not quite,' said Charles, producing his handkerchief with a flourish. He opened it out carefully. 'Don't touch it. It was in Sands's pocket.'

'What is it?'

'It's a plan of my house at Putt Green. He also had

a photograph of Henrietta which, like an idiot, I left behind. Apart from the fact that it shows that someone was instructing Sands, it just might have that person's fingerprints on it. Come on: get dressed. We're going out.'

Inspector Wheatley ran back to the police car. 'Come on, you two, for God's sake!' he called out as he ran. Sergeant Kent looked at Bricker and raised his eyebrows. He had never seen Wheatley so agitated. They followed him to the car and got in.

'Where to, guv?' asked Bricker.

'Have you still got the file with you?' Wheatley asked Kent.

'Yes. It's in my case in the boot. I haven't had time to—'

'Never mind that. Have you got the lifts from the computer and the car?'

'Yes.'

'Right. The Temple, Bricker, and quickly!' commanded Wheatley. 'Get on the radio, Sergeant, and see if you can get on to the Met. I want a SOCO to meet us there.'

'At this time of night? We'll be lucky.'

'Don't argue with me, just do it. What station did we get that call from . . .?'

'Do you mean Snow Hill, sir?' asked Kent.

'Yes, that's the one. Get on to them. I'll speak to the Inspector, or the duty sergeant if necessary.'

'Hang on a sec, guv. You think Ellison has something to do with this?'

'Get moving, Bricker. I'll explain as we go. We know from the photo that Sands has something to do with the murder, an accomplice maybe, possibly even the murderer. He's almost certainly dead because he knew too much. That means someone else is involved. I'll lay money that that someone else is the owner of the fingerprints on the car and on the computer. Not only can the computer be got at in Howard's Chambers, but whoever set up the murder knew a hell of a lot about Howard's day-to-day movements. It points to

221

someone with access to Chambers. And who has access to Chambers?'

'Barristers,' replied Bricker.

'Good. And from which barristers have we yet to obtain elimination prints? To save you the trouble, I'll tell you one of them: Simon Ellison. Why have we no prints from him? Because he has been defending Charlie Sands in Oxford. QED.'

Kent whistled. He was genuinely impressed. 'But if he's the man, and he's killed Sands, isn't Howard in trouble?'

'Quite possibly.'

'Well, why aren't we arresting Ellison immediately?'

'Because I value my career too highly to go charging into the house of a respected influential barrister in the middle of the night without proof. I suggest, Bricker, that you put your foot down, and that you, Kent, get on the radio. We'll need the clerk at Chancery Court, Stanley Wigglesworth. Get him to the Temple immediately.'

Stanley arrived at Chancery Court at 12.50 a.m. He had still to get over the shock of having one of his guv'nors on the run, charged with the murder of his wife. He had not dared enter any of his usual haunts for the last week because of all the gossip among the Mafia. To be called out of his bed in the middle of the night, raced to London in a speeding police car still wearing his pyjamas, and required to open up Chambers for more investigations, this time into *another* member of Chambers, was the final straw. 'I shall retire at the end of the term,' he had announced to his wife Janet as he pulled a coat on over his pyjamas.

Wheatley got out of the police car where he had been waiting, and shook hands with him.

'We've not met before, sir,' he said. 'I'm Inspector Wheatley. I think you've met these gentlemen,' he said, indicating Kent and Bricker. 'This is Mr . . .'

'Reeves,' said the last man. He carried a briefcase, and was not in uniform. 'I'm a Scenes of Crime Officer,' he

222

explained, 'and I should have been off duty four hours ago,' he said pointedly.

'Now, Mr Wigglesworth,' said Wheatley, 'can you let us in, please?'

Stanley led the four men upstairs to the first floor and opened the main door.

'Which is Mr Ellison's room?' asked the Inspector.

'That's on the other side of the landing,' replied the clerk. 'I'll show you.'

He unlocked the other door on the landing, and led the way inside to the far room. He pointed to the desk facing the door.

'That's his desk, Inspector,' he said.

'Does anyone else use it?'

'Not usually, no.'

'OK,' said Wheatley to Reeves. 'Off you go.'

'Don't touch the light switch,' ordered Reeves.

Reeves took a torch from his pocket and went over to the desk. He prowled round it, bending over, looking closely at the surfaces without touching anything.

'Hmm,' he said, turning on the desk lamp and extinguishing his torch. 'The phone might be the best place to start.' He stood upright again, and walked past the other men who were watching him to the door. He examined the door frame and then the light switch. 'And then the light switch,' he concluded. Wheatley left the room.

He went back to the desk and opened his briefcase. He took out a small pot, and unscrewed the lid to reveal a brush inserted into it, rather like those used by photographers to blow dust from their camera lenses. He lifted the telephone handset off its cradle by the cable, and placed it carefully on the desk blotter. The others in the room watched silently. Reeves brushed a tiny amount of silver dust over the inside of the handset, and looked carefully at the result.

'Lovely,' he said. 'There's a couple of quite decent ones.'

He reached down into his case and took out a roll of tape. He cut a small piece off with a pair of scissors, and pressed it firmly over the handset. He repeated the procedure twice more, and then gently lifted the prints off. He immediately attached them to pieces of plastic card obtained from his case, and initialled the cards with a pen. He then moved to the light switch, and started again.

Throughout this, Wheatley had paced impatiently up and down the hallway outside. He entered the room again.

'Well?' he asked.

'What do you want me to compare them with?' asked Reeves. Kent opened his briefcase and handed Reeves an envelope from which Reeves took a further set of plastic cards. 'Is there another room I can use?' Reeves asked Stanley.

'Next door?' suggested the clerk.

'Fine,' said Reeves. He went to the adjoining room, taking the plastic cards with him, sat at the desk, and turned on the desk-lamp. He took a magnifying glass from his breast pocket and looked closely at the fingerprints Kent had provided. Then he turned to the lifts he had just taken. The Inspector looked over his shoulder, like a vulture.

'You realise this is not supposed to be my job, don't you?' asked Reeves.

'I know. But didn't you used to be—'

'Used to be, yes. But that was almost eight years ago. Would you mind, Inspector? You're distracting me, hovering behind me like that.'

Wheatley moved away, and Reeves continued his perusal. Every now and then he would make a jotting on the pad next to him. After about ten minutes, he switched off the lamp, and sat back.

'I'm not a fingerprint expert any more, you understand, and these are hardly the best conditions to work under . . . but . . .'

'Well?' demanded Wheatley. Reeves was not to be hurried.

'This would not stand up in court, Inspector. You have to have a minimum number of identical features before—'

'I know all that!' shouted Wheatley. 'Are there any at all?'

'I can see eight or nine in the thumb print on the phone, and eleven on the forefinger by the door. Yes. If you have to have an answer, I'd say that in all probability—no higher than that, understand?—they were made by the same man.'

Wheatley turned to Stanley. 'Where does Ellison live?' he barked.

'Er . . . er . . Chelsea somewhere . . . I've got the address in my room . . .'

'I need it now, please, sir. Bricker, you stay here with Mr Wigglesworth. He's not to contact anyone till you hear from me.'

'I say—' protested Stanley.

'Sorry, sir, but I'm not taking any chances.' Wheatley whirled round to Kent. 'Has Sergeant Woods returned to Aylesbury?'

'Yes, guv. I told them they could head back.'

'OK. We'll contact the Met on the way. Let's go.'

Chapter Thirty-two

Charles looked up and down the street before he and Rachel got into the MG. He could see nothing suspicious but his sense of danger had increased appreciably.

'But where on earth are we going?' Rachel asked.

Charles did not answer. He started the car, revved the engine, and got out again.

'What are you doing?' shouted Rachel, as Charles walked around the front of the car. He opened her door. For a minute Rachel thought he was asking her to get out, and she took a deep breath to start arguing. But she had misunderstood.

'Slide over, if you can,' he commanded. 'You drive. I need to think.'

Rachel climbed over the handbrake with some difficulty, and sat in the driving seat. 'Where are we going?' she asked.

'Chelsea,' replied Charles. 'We're going to steal a photograph.' She looked at him. He had a triumphant grin wrapped from ear to ear.

The MG crawled down the quiet Chelsea terrace, Charles peering at each house in turn as they passed it.

'Don't you remember the number?'

'If I remembered the number,' replied Charles with some impatience, 'I wouldn't be going through the procedure of looking at every house, would I?'

Rachel smarted, but ignored the comment, saving her rebuke for later.

'It's an end of terrace house,' muttered Charles. 'I'm sure of it. There!' He pointed to a house on the left. It was at the end of the terrace which formed one side of a large square, with gardens in the middle. The house was a typical three-storey Chelsea townhouse, with a small paved garden containing large shrubs in pots, surrounded by a low wall.

'Turn left round the corner of the house, and pull in, would you?' asked Charles. He made to get out of the car, and Rachel put her hand on his arm.

'Tell me what you're doing?' she demanded quietly.

'I'm going to break into this house,' he replied calmly.

'Why?'

'Because there's a photograph inside it that I need.'

'A photograph?'

'Yes,' said Charles, preparing again to get out. 'It's a

photograph of my Chambers' cricket team. Every male member of Chambers is in it.'

'But why do you want it?'

'I want to show it to Sharon Whatever-her-name-was.' He saw Rachel looking puzzled. 'If the murderer's a member of Chambers, she'll be able to pick him out.'

Rachel nodded. 'But there's an alarm on the house,' she warned. 'I saw it as we went past. Charles, you're not a burglar, you're a barrister. Breaking into Chambers, which has no security whatsoever, when you know no one's there, is a completely different proposition to this.'

'I know. But I also know that there's no one here either, and I know exactly what I want and where it is. Now,' he continued, 'you can't wait here. If you wait with the engine running, it will attract attention. If you turn it off, we can't make a quick getaway because I have to fiddle with the ignition wires. So, just drive round the square slowly, and I'll find you when I come out. I shall be five minutes at most.'

He bent over and kissed her lips quickly. She put her hand on his thigh. 'How are you going to get in, Charles?'

'Don't worry,' he insisted. 'The photograph is in a study at the back of the house overlooking the garden. I'm simply going to throw a brick through the window, climb in, and climb out again. OK?'

With that he got out of the car, and walked off towards the rear garden gate. With a deep sense of foreboding, Rachel drove off round the square. As she turned the corner the dark car that had followed Charles all the way from Plaistow pulled in at the kerb opposite the house. A tall angular man got out, locked the car, and went directly to the front door of the house. He took a bunch of keys from his pocket, opened the door, and entered. He did not turn on any lights. He crouched just inside the front door, and reached in the darkness to exactly where he knew the alarm controls were, and turned the key that operated the alarm. The tiny pinpoint of red light that indicated that the alarm was activated, faded and was extinguished.

The man silently closed the front door, and sped into the first room off the hallway to his right. There was a bureau in that room, and he unlocked it, opened the lid, and took out a revolver. He returned to the hallway and waited in the shadows.

Charles was in the back garden, looking at the rear of the house. The garden was mature and full of well-ordered plants, but had an overgrown look to it, as if it was usually well-tended but had been allowed to get out of hand recently. Charles smiled with satisfaction. It meant that the lady of the house was, as he had hoped, still away.

Two rooms overlooked the garden, a kitchen and a study. The study was to the right as Charles looked at the house. Both rooms had wide sash windows, and he guessed they would have locks on them. Although on the ground floor, they were higher than he remembered, and he would need something to stand on in order to climb in. He looked about himself, and saw a garden bench to his right. He dragged it across the grass and placed it under the window of the study. He stood on it and peered in. The far wall was lined from top to bottom with books. There was a leather-topped desk directly in front of the window. Charles scanned the walls, looking for the photograph he remembered seeing there. He could make out the glinting of glass on two walls—either framed prints or photographs, he could not be sure which in the dim light.

He stepped back on to the grass, and looked around for some heavy object. He needed it to be large enough to make a substantial hole in the window: he could not afford to waste time removing pieces of broken glass before climbing in. Behind him was a terracotta plant pot with a large fern in it. He lifted it up—God, this is heavy, he thought—climbed back on to the bench, and poised himself to throw it. He decided he would have to swing it first to build sufficient momentum. He started to swing, the pot held from underneath in both hands. On the third swing he let go. The pot flew through the air and crashed through the window, taking most of the pane with it, and thundering on to the desk. It then rolled heavily on the floor and smashed. To Charles's attuned ears, the noise sounded immensely loud. He waited for the bells or sirens to go off, but nothing happened. Very careless of him, he thought. He hauled himself up, climbed head-first through the gap, careful not to catch himself or his clothing on the jagged glass, crawled across the desk top, and manoeuvred himself to the floor. Glass, pottery and soil crunched under his feet. He went straight up to the wall on his left. Two prints of boating scenes; no photograph. He turned to the other wall, his back now to the door to the room. Got it! He reached up, and lifted a photograph off its hook. He looked at it in the moonlight, and smiled. It was one of these men. All he had to do now was show it to—

'Stay where you are, Charles,' said a soft voice.

The light went on and momentarily blinded Charles. He shielded his eyes and squinted at the speaker.

'Simon?' he asked. 'Is that you?'

'Yes, it is.'

'I thought you were away on a case. I'm awfully sorry. If I'd known you were in, I'd have entered more conventionally. I know this looks incredible, but I assure you everything's alright. I had to get this photo, you see, I've realised that the murderer is—'

Charles's eyes had adjusted to the light by this time. He looked at Simon Ellison. In his hand was a gun, and it was pointed at Charles.

Rachel went round the square three times. On the fourth circuit, another car suddenly pulled away from the kerb, causing her to brake violently. She avoided the other vehicle, but the MG stalled. She got out, crouched on the ground as she had seen Charles doing, and fiddled with the wires. They sparked once, making her jump. This is too dangerous, she thought. What if I touch the wrong ones and short the fuses? She decided to push the car into the kerb, and go back to Charles.

She reached the front of the house, and was about to

go round the back, when a faint light shone out of the window above the front door, and Rachel realised that someone had put a light on at the back of the house. If Charles was inside, why was he putting on lights? If he wasn't inside, someone *was* home, and Charles would be caught. Suddenly scared, she ran round the side of the house, and through the open garden gate.

As she entered the garden, she saw immediately that the light in the study was on. There were two people in the room! He had been caught! She crept along the side of the garden, keeping clear of the arc of light that spilled from the room on to the lawn. She could see Charles. He had his back to the window. Another man, a taller man, wearing a hat, faced Charles, but most of him was obscured by Charles's body. They appeared to be talking. Rachel inched closer, hoping that the light in the room would make it more difficult to see out to the dark garden, but she was unable to hear what was being said.

Charles laughed. 'You don't need that,' he said, stepping towards Ellison, his arms open, still not understanding the significance of the gun pointing at him.

'Stay back, Charles, or shall I kill you immediately.'

'Kill me? What on earth for? I know I've broken in, but you don't understand—'

'I understand everything, Charles. It is *you* who don't understand. I couldn't believe my luck when you came here! I've been following you since you left Plaistow, trying to think of a way of getting at you. I'd almost finished on your brakes, but you left the flat just too early. See?' he said, holding up his hands. They were covered in dirt and grease. 'But this is much better. It's magnificent!' he said, his eyes shining with excitement.

'It was you,' said Charles quietly, eyes wide with surprise.

'Don't play games, Charles,' the other chided, his voice sounding disappointed. 'I knew it,' said Ellison, clearly angry with himself. 'I knew he wasn't dead. Much tougher than I thought, that Scot. What I don't understand is, why

230

you came here? That really was stupid.' Ellison spoke quickly, excitedly, the words tumbling from his lips.

'If you mean Sands, he *was* dead.'

'You're lying! If he was dead, how did you know it was me? I don't know what you're playing at, Charles, but it won't work.'

'I'm not playing at anything, Simon. Sands was dead when I arrived. I had no idea you were mixed up in this.'

'Then what are you doing here?' challenged Ellison.

'I realised that it had to be a member of Chambers. Only a member of Chambers would have known exactly what my court commitments would have been. Only a member of Chambers would have had easy access to my keys—at any time—while they were in my jacket, or lying on the desk.'

'Yes, that's all understood. Full marks and all that, but why break into *my* house?'

'Simple. You're the captain of the cricket team; you've got a photograph of us all. I needed to show it to . . . that girl you hired, to pick out the murderer.'

Ellison paused, considered the answer open-mouthed, threw back his head and laughed. 'Then you didn't know! Wonderful! It was all just chance!'

Charles looked around for some weapon, some way of escape. His eyes lighted on, and were suddenly riveted to, a small table beside the desk which he hadn't until then noticed. On it, was a small computer. It was exactly the same as his.

'Yes. Don't you remember, Charles? It was you, who, three years ago, so extolled the virtues of your little word processor, that I was persuaded to buy one myself. They're invaluable, are they not?'

Rachel was by now only a few feet from the smashed window. Charles had moved slightly to his right, and was looking away from the other man. He seemed transfixed by something. And then Rachel's heart seemd to miss a beat. The other man had a gun!

She considered calling the police, but realised that that would take too much time. What if she rang the front door

231

bell? No, he could simply ignore it. She decided she had to create a distraction, something to give Charles a chance. She looked around her for some projectile.

'What now?' asked Charles.

'Now? Well, now, my dear colleague, I'm going to shoot you dead. From the moment you traced Fylde, I thought it might come to this, but I had no idea how. You've just given me the perfect excuse.'

'What, for burglary?' asked Charles, stalling for time.

'No, of course not. But here am I, your wife's lover—oh,' he interrupted himself, seeing Charles's expression, '—didn't you know that? Yes, I was her lover, till that bastard Corbett took her. Didn't you know that either? Oh yes, she's been half-way round Chambers. Anyway, I catch you, a wanted murderer breaking into my house. You've already killed your wife. I'm the lover—at least, one of them. What am I to think? You've come to kill me, too. I can't imagine anyone would convict me, even of manslaughter.'

'But, why, Simon? Why get Sands to kill her?'

'You're well rid of her, you know that?' Ellison spread his hands, as if expecting Charles to agree. Charles tensed as he realised that the gun was pointing away from him for a second, but Ellison saw the movement, and almost casually brought the weapon back to its original position.

'Bloody whore!' His mood veered again, his face distorting with hatred. 'She gave me up, for that muscular buffoon! I mean, I ask you.' He shrugged, suddenly calm. 'It's not as if he cared about her, you know? He was toying with her, a game, another conquest. Getting his own back on you, I expect. Whereas I . . .' Ellison shrugged again, smiled, and shook his head, as if to say 'I'll never understand women'.

'I loved her, you know. I tried to persuade her to come back. I begged her. You know what? She laughed at me. Just laughed, as if I'd said something funny.' The pitch of his voice rose suddenly again. 'Told me not to be silly . . . not to bother her any more, or she'd tell Marjorie. She treated me as if I was . . .' he paused and spat the word with fury: 'dirt! A nothing! A no one, as if I didn't matter! And I *do* matter! Said she was going back to you, *you* of all people! I hated her then . . .' His voice tailed off and his eyes looked vacant.

'After that,' he continued almost conversationally, 'I really had no choice. It was just a joke to her—she didn't care. But where would my judicial post be if I was suddenly involved in a messy divorce, with the co-respondent the wife of a member of Chambers? You've already ruined my career, yes, yes, no need to looked so pained; you've been stealing my practice for years, and you know it. And now, not only does your pathetic wife throw me over, but you want to take my seat on the Bench from me. In a way I'm almost sorry about this, Charles,' he said, indicating the gun. 'It would have been so nice for you to have been convicted of Henrietta's murder, so neat. I had it all planned. You see, even if they didn't make me a judge, I could have just stepped straight into your practice. My practice, really. Still . . .'

Ellison smiled. He raised the gun calmly and pointed it at Charles's face.

There was a sudden splintering crash as a terracotta pot, the sister to the one lying on the floor of the study, sailed through the kitchen window. Ellison's attention flickered for a second, and Charles leapt at him, trying to swerve away from the muzzle of the revolver. The gun exploded, and Charles felt as if a sack of potatoes had landed on his right shoulder. His momentum nevertheless carried him forward and he collided with Ellison, both of them falling to the ground. The gun was trapped between their bodies, and Charles hugged Ellison as hard as he could to stop him getting it out for a second shot. There was no pain in his shoulder, although he was aware that he couldn't use his right arm.

Ellison pounded at Charles's back with his left hand, the right one still trapped. Charles brought his knee up as hard as he could into Ellison's groin, and the other grunted loudly with pain. Charles repeated the blow, and Ellison's left hand stopped beating him. Charles took a chance, whipped his left hand out from between their bodies, and stabbed Ellison with his forefinger and thumb directly into the eyes. Ellison screamed with pain, raised both hands to his face, dropping the gun. Charles heaved himself up, knelt on Ellison's body and grabbed the revolver.

Slowly, he raised himself to his feet, and stood over the prostrate barrister. He was aware that his shoulder was hanging awkwardly. Ellison was whimpering. 'I'm blind! You've blinded me, you bastard!'

The front door bell sounded. Charles stuffed the gun into his pocket, and grabbed Ellison by the scruff of his neck. He dragged him along the hall to the front door, and opened it.

There was Rachel. She rushed in. 'Oh, God!' she said as she saw Charles's wound. She was followed by Inspector Wheatley and several other officers. Charles knew they were talking to him, but he could not make out what was being said. He suddenly felt very tired. His knees slowly buckled, and he toppled outwards towards the street. Arms caught him, and he was lowered gently to the ground. Charles remembered seeing the stars above his head, and then they began to fade, one by one, until the blackness took over.

Chapter Thirty-three

Charles levered himself up with his left hand behind him, and tried to sit up.

'Wait, wait!' ordered Rachel, dropping her magazine, and running to his bedside. She helped him upright and pushed another pillow behind his back.

'Better?' she asked.

'Yes, thank you,' he replied.

She returned to her seat, and picked up the magazine. 'I'll be leaving in a bit,' she said.

'Why? Mum and Dad will be here soon.'

'Exactly. I think you should be on your own with them. I'll come back towards the end of visiting time.'

'I don't want to be on my own with them. I want you to be here.' He pouted, and looked like a six-year-old. Rachel grinned.

There was a knock on the door. 'Come in!' called Charles.

Inspector Wheatley and Sergeant Kent appeared in the door.

'Here comes the cavalry again!' joked Charles.

'Alright if we come in, sir?' asked Wheatley.

'Yes, come in, pull up a chair, have some grapes. Everyone else does,' said Charles. 'Another statement?'

'No, sir, thank you,' answered Sergeant Kent. 'Just returning your property to you.'

'What news of Ellison?' asked Rachel.

'Hah!' snorted Kent. 'He applied for bail this morning. Made the application himself, too.'

'And?' asked Charles.

'Refused. On the basis that as he's committed one conspiracy to murder, one actual murder and one attempted murder all in the course of seven days, there's a risk of further offences and of him absconding if he's released.'

'Very right and proper too,' said Charles.

Kent handed Charles a pad of forms with all his

235

belongings listed on the top one. 'Just sign at the bottom, please, Mr Howard.' Charles did so. Kent handed him a plastic bag containing all that had been taken from him when he was arrested.

'Thank you,' said Charles. 'You'll have to open the plastic bag for me, Sergeant,' indicating his right arm, still swathed in bandages.

The officer did so, handing Charles's watch to Rachel, who put it on Charles's left wrist for him.

'I think that's all, thank you, sir,' said Wheatley. 'We'll be off now.'

'Do you mind if I ask a question, Mr Howard?' asked Kent.

'Under caution?'

'No, sir. What are you going to do now? I don't suppose you can go back to Chambers, can you? I mean, everyone knows you didn't do it . . . you know . . . but she was still the daughter of the ex-Head of Chambers, wasn't she? It must be a bit tricky?'

Charles smiled, and took Rachel's hand. 'It's a good question, Sergeant. I thought I might turn to crime. You know, burglary, assault, that sort of thing.'

'Don't joke about that, sir,' said Wheatley. 'I've always said that barristers would make the best criminals. They think things through, work logically; they can assess evidence, and know how to avoid all the things that get their clients caught. You proved me right.'

'Well, it's one option,' grinned Charles. 'I might join other Chambers. Of course, the other option is to become a private detective.'

The two policemen looked at him carefully, unable to decide if he was serious or not.

'What sort of job is that for a nice Jewish boy?' asked Rachel.

'Well, you never know,' said Charles. 'You just never know.'